LIES AND ALIBIS

Booklocker.com, Inc.
2009

LIES AND ALIBIS

Michael Schutt

CHAPTER ONE

Maura Ferguson didn't look like a killer. When she first walked in, her hands were cuffed in front of her, and there was an old black man in a security suit guiding her by the elbow toward the defense table. The orange prison jumper hanging loosely on her smallish frame battled with the red in her hair, but not in a bad way. She certainly didn't have the swagger of a killer, nor the menacing stare, and I didn't sense any chill spreading through the courtroom when she entered. Looks, they say, can deceive, though I didn't think so in her case.

Standing next to her, the guy she was paying to defend her looked like he had spent the retainer mostly on hair products. His mane was immaculate, his hands professionally manicured, and his smile perfectly calculating. He wore a navy blue suit—the expensive designer kind—with a lighter shade blue shirt and tie. And, it appeared, a very large stick up his ass.

This was the arraignment hearing for Maura Ferguson, accused of murdering her husband, his lover, and the family dog, all with little more than a sharp object and an arm to swing it.

It was the dog that seemed to fascinate the press and infuriate the masses. People desensitized to the murder of their own seemed to find a cause to care about in the murder of the floppy-eared black pooch.

Joe had been a three-year old mutt, saved from the gas chamber at the pound. He had, according to the news, tried to intervene in the foul play, only to become a part of it. Maura Ferguson, it was alleged, had two arms covered with incriminating teeth and claw marks. Right now those arms were hidden beneath the long orange sleeves.

Kill a pet and you've got real trouble. Animal rights activists had weighed in, as they always do. Did we really need to be told that taking a knife to the family pet wasn't an ethical form of treatment? They had gone so far as to organize peaceful demonstrations outside the courtroom with every cat-lady and dog-lover within a hundred miles there to carry a placard telling us Joe had died needlessly. *No kidding?*

The blowhards on talk radio wouldn't let it go either. They figured the killer had a cruel streak to have sliced up poor old Joe. I guess they missed the point that all killers tend more toward the brutality side of the ledger.

At least they were on the side of sensibility. They couldn't believe people were more concerned about a dog than two humans. The local columnists seemed to have lost their sanity on the issue. The two human victims got three columns in *The Times*, below the fold on the front page. Joe was the top of the page, and he got a picture, too.

By killing her husband, Maura Ferguson had taken the father away from her two-year old daughter. Now the state was trying to orphan the kid. The conviction, it was said, was a foregone conclusion.

Ms. Ferguson would be getting that same gas from which she had once saved Joe. This is only true in a poetic sense. We don't gas humans here, only pets no one wants. Humans get a needle full of poison. Just the same, dead is dead.

The account of the murder as presented in the local press was mostly guesswork. Sam Ferguson and Shannon Powell were found in the master bedroom of the Ferguson home, in bed. There was a bloody mess from the multiple stab wounds, but no weapon. Maura was arrested because she had no good alibi, she had access, and her husband was not being faithful. Obviously.

Oh, and she stood to inherit something just north of twenty-five million dollars.

Shannon Powell worked for Sam Ferguson. Or, more accurately, she was on his payroll. Sam Ferguson owned the Fergie's theatre chain, fourteen multiplex movie houses in the metro area alone. I know, because I counted them in the morning paper. Shannon Powell was his assistant; Regional Manager was her bogus title. She was, at least from the look of the crime scene, allowed to work naked. Maybe it was casual day at the office.

Sam Ferguson had inherited the theatre chain from his dad, Charles Ferguson, the original Fergie, upon dad's early death. Sam's mother had been gone for years, a victim of a drunk driver. Sam had been in charge for a little more than three years before he met the business end of a knife.

Where Charles had been all class, Sam had tried to go bottom line. He had discontinued several popular discounts on concessions for regular moviegoers, and had stopped bringing in much of the less mainstream fair, opting instead for the biggest potential blockbusters available. He had alienated many of the loyal patrons with these tactics. Fergie's Theaters still made plenty of money, but they were no longer number one in town.

Maura Ferguson met Sam in college. He had gone to get some business education. Maura, it was being written, had gone for her Mrs. degree. They were married upon graduation, moved into a big house north of town, and bought Joe, the poor, dead mutt. That had been almost three years ago, just after Sam's ascension to the Fergie throne.

Maura got pregnant almost immediately, since that was her primary job. The cynics out there would argue the child was her primary goal in marrying Sam, but the nuances of love are many and one can never say for sure. Nine months later, as they tend to do, their baby came. And now the little thing stood poised to toddle away with twenty five million dollars.

I'm what you could call a courtroom regular. I don't work, nor do I need to. The Fergusons aren't the only rich people in town. While their fortune was made through overpriced popcorn, my money came from a one- dollar lottery ticket. A physicist would call mine the path of least resistance. It was really just dumb luck.

So here I was in court. It was my hobby, you could say. My ex-girlfriend calls it morbid and sick. I don't see it that way, which is one reason she decided to become my ex. I was here for no good reason other than curiosity. And we know what that did to the cat.

My name is John Jacobs, but most everyone calls me Jake. I used to work as a janitor at an office building downtown. I worked nights, which I kind of liked. It didn't pay well, but the perks of janitorial service are many.

For example, you can eat anything you find. I'm not talking about the half-eaten Snickers bar you find on some junior executive's desk, though those can make a nice morsel as long as you're careful to trim away the offending edge. I don't want to give away too many secrets of the trade, but you can imagine what might be left lying about. Some nights I felt like Santa Claus on Christmas Eve, a snack left for me at each stop.

You can play the radio as loud as you like, too. No one would tolerate Billy Joel cranked all the way up, were they in a cubicle next to mine. But with no one around, no one could really complain, could they. Many were the night I had the Piano Man sing me a song.

And I probably don't need to tell you what a janitor and his girlfriend can find to do in a deserted office building in the middle of the night. A love life can't go stale with that never-ending supply of forbidden lovemaking.

No job is perfect, but mine held a certain level of enjoyment I hadn't experienced before. Without the sweet intervention of fate I may have done it for forty years before retiring to my Social Security check.

I bought a lottery ticket every Wednesday and every Saturday, along with a candy bar and a bottle of soda, on my way up to work. There was a little market tucked below the building, right next to the entrance to the underground garage. It was a holdover that wouldn't sell and get out to the suburbs. The place was called Jimmy's, and the current owner was actually the fifth in a string of Jimmys, all stubborn Irish sorts. He wasn't going anywhere.

One of those Wednesdays, when the jackpot had grown to two hundred million, I got a winner. And no one else did. After taxes I get around five million dollars a year, for the next twenty years. God bless America.

I still buy the lottery ticket every Wednesday and every Saturday, at the same little market owned by the fifth generation Jimmy, tucked into the office building I no longer work at. Sure I have two hundred million dollars, but it never hurts to have that second income, just in case the kids start to come along.

I always laughed at those lottery winners, lucky bastards like me, who said they would keep their jobs even though they were now filthy rich. Goodness, gracious, why? Unless your job is to sponge bathe supermodels, why would you want to keep it? Get a hobby. I did.

And here I was, practicing my pastime. It's a fact that most trials are boring, full of detailed testimony from uptight experts, and painfully short on drama. The defendant is almost always guilty and everyone knows it, including the defense attorney and the jury. What about innocent until proven guilty? Yeah, right.

All of which begs the question, "Why?"

Most people just don't get it I guess, but most people would never find the sublime happiness I had as a janitor, either. My ex had asked me that very question at every opportunity. Actually she would say, "What the hell, Jake?"

There isn't one good answer, though I usually told her, "Why not?" The courtroom is cooled in the summer, heated in the winter. There are numerous places to get a good lunch nearby. It's easy to check the morning box scores in the sports section, as long as your seat is in the back. And boring though it could be, it still beat staying home to watch talk shows.

The real reason, though, was the chance at something exciting. I'd sat through two murder trials, hoping for judicial fireworks. Unfortunately they produced almost no drama, one ending with an early dismissal, and the other a plea.

The highlight came in a domestic violence case. The abused, a Latino woman with seven children, took the stand against her husband. She testified he had beaten her and the kids. He never tried the "rule of thumb" defense. In old England, with laws that are no longer in place, it was okay to beat your wife. You just couldn't use anything wider than your thumb. They must not have had the same rule in whatever backwater jungle he had crawled out of.

One rainy Tuesday she had somehow managed to sneak a handgun past security, and when she said she could no longer stand her husband's abuse, she stood, pulled out that piece, and fired two shots over the wife beater's head. They hit nothing but wall, thankfully, and she was quickly arrested herself.

You don't get gems like that every day.

Both parents, by the way, are now housed in the finest correctional facilities our state can offer. The kids are in the care of a relative, one who neither beats them nor shoots at them.

I'd been pursuing leisure in this fashion for about ten months now, which would mean I'd been single for four. Leslie Watson, the aforementioned ex-girlfriend, gave me time to settle down and re-focus, as she called it, after winning the cash.

Sitting on my rear in the back of a courtroom wasn't what she had in mind. Maybe she missed the nights at the office building. When I neither settled down nor found what she considered a new, useful purpose in life she re-focused herself, at someone named Lance.

We had been together just short of two years, and they were mostly good times. She's a morning anchor for one of the local news shows, and therefore a local celebrity. Because of her, her program kicks the competition's butt. It's not even close.

I haven't been in love too many times in my life, but I loved her.

Leslie Watson helped me pick out the house I bought when I became rich. She even decorated the damn thing. And then she left because she didn't understand my interest in the poetry of the judicial process. That house sits two blocks south and three blocks east of the Ferguson place. All us rich folk live up there.

Leslie never asked for any of my money. I respected her for that. She has a good job that pays quite well, so she doesn't need it. She never realized I bought the winner with a five I borrowed from her purse. I paid it back, and even bought her a new car. And, I thought, a house.

Our neighborhood—I still talk about myself in the plural, like Leslie never left—sits in a small valley surrounded by several little hills. It's surprisingly green for being so close in to a city, and surprisingly clean. Money can buy a lot of things.

All the money in the metro area lives in that same valley, more or less. Three professional athletes, two very successful novelists, an actor/actress couple from the movies, and too many computer winners and stock market studs to count all called my little section of town home. And Maura and Sam Ferguson lived just a few blocks away from one John Jacobs.

This was the first case I'd been to where I actually knew the defendant. I guess that's a positive comment on the kind of company I keep. When I say she didn't look like a killer, it may be because I knew her. No one wants to think people they know could kill, not even if the victim were someone like Sam Ferguson.

Sam was a lout, a shit, and an all around arrogant sonofabitch. He drank too much, talked too loud, and his golf swing produced a wicked slice. Like his kind usually is, he was blissfully unaware of any personality shortcomings, which just served to make him that much more loathsome. There probably weren't many tears shed in our little valley neighborhood upon his demise.

Shannon Powell was with Sam at least as much as Maura was. His mistake, if you ask me. The Shannon Powell type appeals to a certain kind of man, and I'm not it. Her appeal, I should tell you, was of the 38DD variety. The best that money could buy.

Could Maura have finally done the deed? Did I just want it to not be her? Was the world a better place without Sam and Shannon? Did Shannon buy her boobs for Sam? Would the theaters survive?

I was just settling in to contemplate these questions in more depth when the bailiff broke into my thoughts.

"All rise," he said, "This court is now in session. The Honorable Gerald Houston presiding."

This was most certainly not a good sign for Maura Ferguson. "Gerry the Merry" they called him, and it was one of those ironic nicknames, like calling a bald guy Curly. He was anything but merry. And he looked especially annoyed walking to the bench.

11

Gerald Houston barely listened to pleas from the lawyers, rarely set a low bail, and always demanded a quick trial. If he gave the defense a month to prepare their case they were thankful. And he took shit from no one. Ever. Everyone present always knew he was in charge.

He sat down, slamming a file folder on his desk.

Ten minutes later he had already heard enough from the lawyers. The case against Maura Ferguson was pretty solid. The state didn't try to dress it up, and they didn't need to. There wasn't much for her attorney to do, but the guy tried, if nothing else.

Maura Ferguson's lawyer, dapper in all blue, said, "Your Honor, I'd like to make a motion to dismiss the case. The state has nothing but circumstantial evidence, and even that's on the weak side."

The judge sneered at him and said, "Motion denied. Anything else, Counselors?"

They said, almost as one, "No, your Honor."

Gerry the Merry said, "Trial begins two weeks from Monday. Bail will be set at one million per lost soul. Two million dollars."

The district attorney jumped to his feet and said, "What about the dog? Shouldn't Joe's soul count for something?"

"No," Gerry said, "It shouldn't. He's a dog, counselor."

The D.A. said, "The state feels Mrs. Ferguson should be held without bail, since the accused has nothing to stay in town for."

Maura's attorney said, "She does have a daughter, your Honor. She's no flight risk."

Judge Houston agreed with the defense. He said to the D.A., "Counselor, would you prefer I set Mrs. Ferguson free without bail? Because if you keep up this asinine line of reasoning, that's exactly what I'm going to do." The Judge glared at the prosecutor's table, daring them to say more.

No one said a word, so Gerry the Merry said, "Two million dollars."

He pounded his gavel a couple times and asked what was next. The uptight lawyer in the blue suit led Maura Ferguson back through the door as the next case was called.

Maura Ferguson was a wealthy woman, and if she were found innocent she'd become a whole lot wealthier, twenty-five million dollars wealthier. Unfortunately she was unable to access any of that money now. They had frozen her money, except for reasonable living expenses. I think it was a Writ of No More Allowance for the Accused, or something. In any case, she was not able to bail herself out.

Funny thing about bail money—if the bad guy disappears, the sap that paid the bail is out the cash. I didn't think Maura Ferguson was going to go anywhere, so I filled out the paperwork and wrote a check. I called my bank so it could be cleared right away. The entire process took an hour, maybe a little bit more.

And I still don't know why I did it.

CHAPTER TWO

I was sitting on a bench outside the jail, waiting. There isn't any rule that says I had to stay. Maura Ferguson was bailed out, and if I had so asked, she wouldn't have known by whom. But I didn't ask, and she already knew.

It took half an hour of patience, but she finally walked out. Her lawyer was with her, trying to find out if she knew John Jacobs.

"She only knows me as Jake," I lied to the blue suit. I stood and shook his hand.

Maura was wearing jeans and a red pullover sweater. She looked tired. I already told you what the lawyer was wearing. He looked offended.

He said, "Not to be ungrateful, but why did you post Ms. Ferguson's bail? Do you even know her?"

"Only in passing. I've seen her at some social functions," I lied again. "I'm the new guy in her part of town."

"Then why?" he asked.

"Let's call it curiosity," I offered. "I'm a student of the law, and I wanted to learn more about how this whole bail thing works. And I've got the money."

"You understand that you've put yourself in the middle of a murder trial, don't you?" he asked. "It's serious business."

"I understand," I promised.

"Can I buy you lunch, Mr. Jacobs?" Maura Ferguson asked, stepping away from the blue suit.

"Maura, I don't think that's a good idea. You barely know Mr. Jacobs, plus you've only got two and a half weeks until trial. We need to get back to the office and start working on your defense."

"I don't think I caught your name," I said to him, hoping he would stop talking.

"Grant Spencer." He said it like I shouldn't have had to ask.

Maura said, "Grant, I'm tired. I haven't eaten since breakfast yesterday. I wish to take this nice man to lunch to thank him for getting me temporarily out of jail. I think I pay you enough money to get back to the office, round up your little suck-up assistants, and get started on my defense without me so that I won't have to return to jail. I'll get some lunch and come by later this afternoon."

"I just think there's no time to waste. That's all."

"Then you best get going," she said.

We were on the sidewalk in front of the courthouse, with a cab pulled up next to us. Maura Ferguson opened the door and waved her lawyer toward the back seat. He climbed in behind his briefcase. He rolled down his window, probably to say something, but the driver took off with a squeal, sparing us.

"Pizza, Jake?" she asked, like we ate together all the time.

Another cab had pulled up and she pushed me into this one. She followed me in and told the driver to go to Guilianos, an Italian place in the business district.

"Thanks, Jake," she said once we were on our way. "And don't let Grant bug you. He's a good lawyer."

I had never seen him in action myself, but his name did carry a certain amount of respect. He may not have been in a class by himself, but it didn't take long to call the roll. He was younger than I would have guessed.

"Isn't he the guy that got McAlister off?" I asked.

Theo McAlister, former professor at the University, was tried in the brutal murder of four very attractive coeds over a two-year period. All four had him as an instructor, one each semester. Each died during the break immediately following the semester in which he was their teacher. Each was found in a hotel room, stabbed a whole lot of times. There were witnesses who testified in his defense who looked, give or take, just like the victims. It was the kind of case I would normally attend, but it finished up before I became the idle rich.

"Yes, he got McAlister off. But this isn't the same," she said.

15

Part of the case against McAlister involved evidence of sex on the bodies of each victim. More specifically, it had been sex with McAlister. There was no sign of rape on any of the victims. The theory was that he boinked each victim right before killing them, sending each out with a bang, so to speak.

"Why isn't it the same? It's a murder case. There's sex involved. It's pretty high profile. What's the difference?"

"I'm innocent," she said in a way that sounded like she didn't think he was.

"Should be a piece of cake for Mr. Spencer then," I said.

"Will he be able to do it without my alibi?" she asked.

"Sure, McAlister didn't have much of one, did he?"

"Said he was with one of his teaching assistants, I think. Maybe she hadn't slept with him yet, so he had no reason to kill her."

"Will you let me live if I testify for you?" I asked.

You see I was Maura Ferguson's alibi and this wasn't our first lunch together. She hadn't told anyone, and neither had I. Sam and Shannon had been killed sometime between two and six in the afternoon on Monday. Maura and I were at a movie, beginning at half past two. There was just one little problem. Maura dropped me off at my new mansion at about five, maybe just after. She only lives five blocks away. It wasn't a great alibi, but it was the only one Maura had.

And what about that extra hour? Well, Maura was arrested the next morning and I never had a chance to ask her about that hour. And though I had just signed over two hundred thousand dollars to spring her from jail, I felt awkward asking her about it. I was hoping she would tell me when she was ready.

Our city sits in between a series of rolling hills, covered with towering trees. Few streets are straight, so the going can be a little slow. Tourists come from everywhere to see this place, especially in the fall. The trees were just starting to turn, and I could see why they came. I stared out the window and enjoyed the beautiful view; glad it wasn't me on trial for murder.

I asked, "Maura, how'd you ever hook up with a loser like Sam in the first place? He doesn't seem like your type."

"Turns out he wasn't," she said. "In the beginning, though, you couldn't have convinced me of that. He had a girlfriend when I started seeing him. He just said she was from the wrong side of town and it would never work. He broke it off with her right away, so I never really asked about it."

"And he thought you were from the right side of town?" I asked.

"I'm not even from this town, so it didn't matter, I guess."

"And when did you realize Sam was a womanizing piece of crap?" I asked.

"When he was hitting on the maternity nurses the night Brittney was born. I spent the night in the hospital. I think he may have taken one of them home to our house."

"Did you call him on it?"

"He denied it. He told me it was postpartum bullshit and that I imagined intentions that weren't there."

"But they were there?" I asked.

"He hired Shannon a couple weeks later. I told him she wasn't the right choice for the job, but he insisted. Lately I was pretty sure they were having an affair."

"Why didn't you leave?"

"Because of Brittney. A divorce is very damaging to a child, especially at her age." I wondered if a murder trial was any easier for the kid, especially when mom was supposed to have stabbed dad, but I didn't ask.

The cab pulled up outside Guilianos. Maura paid the fare and we went inside. The big buildings down in that part of town do most of the city's important business. Guilianos is just one in a string of high-end restaurants lined up downtown, just like the fast food joints are out by the freeway.

Guilianos is the Italian restaurant to go to, if you're anyone important. Maura Ferguson was certainly a socialite in this town. I was a lottery winner, but the genuine rich kids let me eat with them from time to time.

Come to think of it, Maura wasn't from money either. She had been raised in a typical middle class American home, just like me.

Then she married well. I guess that's as important a skill as many others.

If the smooth operator working the front desk knew Maura was on the hook for a double murder, he didn't act like it when we walked in. He greeted her by name and sat us immediately at a table with a view. I slipped him a twenty and ordered a bottle of wine.

Maura Ferguson sat across from me looking at a menu. I didn't bother. I'd been to lunch with her before and knew she would pick something out for me, and that it wasn't worth my time to argue with her. Besides, she had said something about pizza before we got in the cab.

"Jake, I can't go home tonight," she said without looking up.

"Too hard on you?"

"No. I mean I can't go home. The police won't let me. It's a crime scene. I'm not allowed in there yet. They didn't think it would matter. They said my cell would be just fine. I'd get used to it, they said."

"Little did they know that you had a rich friend with too much time on his hands and nowhere to spend his money."

"Can I stay with you?" she asked. She still hadn't looked up from that damn menu. How many topping choices could there be?

"I'm not sure that's a good idea, Maura," I said.

"Sam isn't going to find out about us now," she said. Now she was looking at me. Was there an "us" to find out about?

"No, but everyone else is," I said.

"And that's a problem why?"

"I thought we agreed we would continue to appear as strangers as much as possible until this was over. Lunch today is okay, probably even a good idea. You should be thankful I bailed you out. But I wouldn't think most people would view spending the night together as an appropriate method of showing gratitude."

She was staring right at me, but didn't speak. I doubted that my argument had convinced her. She was more likely just too tired to battle me.

"We'll find you a hotel room. Someone else can change your sheets and clean your toilet. My janitorial days are over," I added.

With my job I never had to clean any sheets. There aren't too many beds in an office building. There are, however, plenty of toilets. There is nothing worse in this world than cleaning toilets in a public restroom. I generally left that to the day crew.

The waiter stopped by with our wine and poured us each a glass. Maura tasted it, nodded her approval. She ordered something. I think it was pizza, but I wasn't sure until it showed up at our table twenty minutes later.

We barely talked through the meal. Maura ate more than her half, but I didn't complain. She had spent some time in jail. I hear it can give you a mighty big appetite.

Had she been treated well in jail? Did she have her own cell? Were the guards all lesbians like in the movies? Were they men? Had she eaten? Why do they wear orange jumpsuits? Was I still hungry?

We finished and she asked, "Are you having dessert?"

"Well, it's about five now, and I have to be home by six. I'm not sure I've got time for dessert." Actually it was one o'clock.

"Okay, Jake, I get it. You want to know what I did after I dropped you off."

"If it's not too much trouble," I said.

She took a moment to order two slices of cheesecake. I think one was supposed to be for me.

"Okay, I was there," she said.

Fortunately I didn't have a mouthful of anything to spit out. I said, "You were there? At your house? You killed them?"

"No, I didn't kill them. And no, I wasn't actually in the house. Sam's car was in the garage when I got home. He doesn't usually get home before seven most nights. I glanced in the passenger side window as I walked past it. *Her* jacket was in there. I knew *she* was inside. I turned around, got in my car, and left."

"You never went inside?"

"No."

"You might be very lucky you didn't."

"I thought of that, too," she said.

The cheesecake came and I did get a slice. It was a mountainous piece covered with a chocolate shell. I guess Maura wasn't watching her girlish figure this meal.

"Can you explain the scratches on your arms, then," I asked.

"I'd rather not right now, if that's okay with you."

"You didn't have them at the movie, Maura. And you never saw the dog alive after you dropped me off. It sounds a little fishy."

"The scratches aren't from a dog. They're from a man. Actually more of a boy."

We weren't dating, Maura and I, which is why there wasn't really an "us" for people to find out about. We had bumped into one another a couple times at neighborhood social get-togethers and so on. One night I was at the video store, and so was she. We talked ourselves into being friends. Since then we'd gone to a few movies and lunches, while Sam was at work with Shannon. We hadn't even kissed each other yet. I had no reason to be jealous, really. But I was.

"A man?" I asked.

"I jumped in my car, drove to Hud's Saloon. I saw a young kid shooting pool, so I bet him I could beat him. If he won, I'd go home with him. I let him win."

"And he scratched your arms?"

"It was what you could call angry sex, Jake. I'm pretty sure his back looks worse than my arms."

"Why isn't he your alibi?" I asked.

"I never got his name. I didn't think I'd need it. Grant's going to have to find him," she said.

The check came and she paid for it. I let her, since I had already spent my daily allowance. In the cab on the way to Grant's office she thanked me again. We agreed to stay in touch with e-mail. She said she'd have to rent a laptop to use from the hotel. Us rich people can do that sort of thing. She said her screen name would be MadSex. I told her mine would be Down200K.

As she climbed out of the cab in front of Grant Spencer's law offices she threw three twenties at the driver and told him to take me wherever I wanted to go. I watched her all the way through the doors.

The driver asked, "Where to?"
I said, "Last Friday, if you don't mind."

CHAPTER THREE

I didn't pick last Friday for any symbolic reason. It has no special meaning in any of this. It was, however, three days before Sam Ferguson and Shannon Powell were sliced and diced on a king size bed in the master suite at Palace Ferguson. It was also last Friday that Maura Ferguson and I picked the movie we would go to on that fateful Monday.

Why Monday for the movie? Good question. And there isn't a good answer, other than we almost always went to movies on Monday afternoons. I never asked him, but I think even Sam Ferguson was aware of it. Maura told him I was harmless, which I think I am. The jury is still out on her, however.

My first conversation with Maura took place about three months before the murders. It was at a Fourth of July cookout in the neighborhood. Rich people do that, too. Of course, we had our own fireworks after the bratwurst were all gone. Oh, and our own musical entertainment, since they live in our sub-division.

I knew who she was before we spoke. When Leslie was still with me we went to a similar shindig for Memorial Day. Leslie talks to people better than I do, at least in that setting. She never talked to Maura, but she did talk to Helen Roth. Helen is the town gossip, though it's not an official title. Helen told Leslie little tidbits about most everyone at the party, and Leslie passed some of it along to me. For instance, Helen told Leslie about Sam Ferguson's affair with Shannon Powell, and that Maura was unaware of any hanky-panky.

At the Independence Day party as I was bent over a huge grill in search of the perfect piece of meat, Maura Ferguson touched me from behind, on my left elbow. Our conversation went something like this.

She said, "Hi, Jake."

I said, "How did you know my name, Maura?"

"Helen Roth told me. We always talk about the new men at these things. And how did you know my name?"

"Helen told me, too. What else did she tell you?" I was curious, since Helen's information had probably come from Leslie, and it wasn't too long after the last party that Leslie had left me.

"Helen told me you were engaged to a very attractive blonde. There aren't any of those here, so you must have her tied up in your basement."

I laughed because I really did tie Leslie up in the basement once. The house had just been finished and we had just moved in. We were in the process of having sex in each and every room. It's a big house with lots of rooms, so by the time we got to the basement we were starting to get creative. There were ropes and blindfolds and various other paraphernalia I'm not particularly comfortable talking about.

I said, "She wasn't ever quite my fiancé, and she left me for some guy named Lance right after the last of these parties."

"So you've been lanced? I'm sorry," she said, though her tone said she wasn't.

"Don't be. The mourning period officially ended last week."

"So you're here all by yourself?" she asked.

"Unless that sounds too pathetic."

I had two brats in one hand and a ketchup bottle in the other. The bottle was closed, which was making it hard to get the ketchup onto the brats.

"Need some help?" she asked.

Before I could answer she took the ketchup bottle from me and shot a stream into each bun. She did the same with some mustard, then spooned on some pickle relish and a few onions. I don't like relish and onions on my grilled lunches, and I tried to tell her as much.

I held the two dogs out to her and said, "Here you go."

"No, no. Those are for you."

"I don't like relish and onions on my bratwurst, Maura. I should have told you."

"Of course you do. Eat them."

And without another word she turned and walked away. I stood and watched her disappear into the crowd. Then I ate my two bratwursts like she told me to.

Anyway, the cab driver didn't take me back to last Friday, obviously. He did take me to Hud's Saloon. Why I chose to go there, I'm not sure. I've never been particularly inclined toward putting myself in the middle of things, but here I was.

Hud's was smoky when I walked in even though it was essentially empty. I wondered if it ever cleared up, thought probably not. The guy behind the bar was puffing away, and so was the waitress standing across from him. Lung cancer must be one of those off-the-contract perks of being a bar employee.

The waitress was wearing jeans and a Hud's t-shirt. She probably wasn't any older than thirty, but she wasn't holding her age very well. The bartender was a college kid, if I had to guess. There was no hair anywhere on his head, except for his goatee. He had the sports page spread across the bar. There was a big plate of nachos in between them that they were both picking at in between drags on their smokes.

"Getcha something?" the kid asked as I walked up.

"Were you working Monday?" I asked after ordering a beer.

The goatee said, "Sure. Why?"

"Was there a woman in here, mid-twenties, nice body, reddish-brown hair?"

"I'm not sure," he said.

The older-than-she-looked waitress said, "Come on, Matt, you remember her. There's still drool on the counter back there from you. She was shooting pool, wearing those tight jeans and that low-cut sweater."

"Matt," I said, "that sounds like my friend. Was she here?"

"She your girl?" he asked.

"No, just a friend in a jam. Was she here?"

24

"She was shooting pool in the back with one of the guys that come in here all the time. She drank about three shots in less than an hour and then she left with him."

"Who's the guy, if you don't mind," I said.

"I don't know his name. There's a whole group of those guys. They go to the University. They come in here a lot, after classes are over I guess. They can't do too well in school; they're here all the time."

"Might he be back there now?"

"Too early. They come in when happy hour starts, at five."

I looked at my watch; saw that it wasn't even three yet. What's a guy going to do when he's got a couple hours to kill?

I said, "Matt, where do the hookers hang out around here?"

When he didn't look surprised by my question I got a little worried. I told him I was just kidding before he could pull the appointment book from below the bar. I thanked Matt and his weathered co-worker and went to sit in the corner.

It was at the video store, two days after the Fourth of July party, that I next saw Maura Ferguson. Again she came up behind me, touched me on the elbow.

"Hi again, Jake," she said.

"Maura, I never had a chance to thank you for my delicious lunch the other day."

She pointed to the movie I was holding in my hand. She said, "You got the last one. That's what I came here for, too. I hear it's good."

"You take it," I said, pushing it toward her.

"Nonsense." She picked another movie off the rack and took the one out of my hand. "I'll just come over to your place and we'll watch it together. And this other one, too." I'm pretty sure I didn't have a choice, not that I was putting up much of a fight.

That was a Monday, which is where our Monday movie date started. I fixed us each a club sandwich, poured two ginger ales, and fired up the big screen. We talked a little, but mostly watched the movies. When the second one ended she suggested we do it again sometime, then left.

Two days later there was a message on my machine from her. She said her daughter was with her sister-in-law every Monday, just because. She told me she wanted to see a movie with me again, but at the theater. Monday was best for her. She said I should e-mail her at MoviePal, and that I should use the name NoRelish.

At about fifteen minutes before five o'clock, the crowd at Hud's Saloon began to grow. It was an odd mix of people: students, construction workers, car salesman, and so on. I couldn't see the pool tables from my perch in the corner, which wasn't very smart I guess. What can I say? I'm new at this.

My friend, Matt the Bartender, came by at five past the hour and said, "He's back there with his pals, wearing a Green Bay Packers' jersey."

"Really? What number?"

"Nitschke. Sixty-six. He's gotta be old school."

"He can't be all bad then, can he?"

Matt agreed with that, so I slipped him a twenty for his trouble. He thanked me then went to put more bad black stuff into his lungs.

Leslie Watson, who now lived with a guy named Lance, is a huge fan of the Green Bay Packers. She's a girl from rural Wisconsin, and she bleeds green and yellow. Sunday's with her always meant watching her team.

The Nitschke at the pool table didn't look anything like the real thing. This guy was fresh-faced with short black hair, and he was, well, pretty. He was shooting against a monster of a man, three hundred pounds if he was ten. I saw two twenties sitting on the edge of the table, which I guessed was the wager. Nitschke didn't want to go home with this opponent, just his money.

The man-mountain beat number sixty-six, which I was grateful for. That meant I needed to wait no more. He headed toward the buffet line, so I jumped in behind him.

"Ray Nitschke," I said, "How you doing?"

He didn't look up. He didn't even act like he heard me. Maybe, I guessed, he didn't know who Ray Nitschke was. There was no name on the jersey, just the number. This did not make me very happy when I thought about it, and I knew it would infuriate Leslie if she were here.

"Hey, number six-six. Don't you know whose jersey that is?" I asked.

"It's my jersey. You got a problem or something?"

I thought maybe he was going to hit me, because he took one very forceful step toward me. I was bigger than him, but he had four friends less than twenty feet away. Courage comes in many colors.

I pressed on, "Ray Nitschke played middle linebacker for the Green Bay Packers during their glory days of the sixties. That's his jersey."

"Whatever," he said, "The Green Bay fudge packers, you ask me."

"You are why people think this country's going to hell. Kids like you. Why can't you just carry on a friendly conversation with another person at a bar? What is so damn hard about that? And you have no respect for your country's heritage. The Packers of that era are the very fabric of this nation."

Had I gone too far? Fabric of the nation? Would Leslie have gone this far? Farther? Did he even know he was wearing a football jersey?

"Fuck you, buddy," he said, putting his face about six inches from mine, his plate of food lodged between us.

I considered beating his snotty little face into twelve different shades of purple. It would have been fun and I could have pulled it off. I'm sure Nitschke's ghost would have approved. But violence is not my most useful weapon. Money is.

I said, "I'll give you five hundred bucks to take a cab ride with me."

"You a homo?" he laughed.

"No, I'm not. It's not about sex. At least not for me."

"What do you mean?" he asked. He backed up a little, maybe because he thought I was gay, or maybe because his interest was piqued.

"Monday afternoon was good for you, wasn't it?"

"Sure was, dog. Redhead wants some more of big Donnie, huh? What, are you her pimp? Doesn't the ho usually get paid, not the other way around?"

"I'll give you five hundred bucks if you're interested enough in seeing her again to hop in the next cab with me."

"Damn straight," he said. "Let's see the green."

I peeled five hundreds from my clip, handed him one. I said, "You get the other four when she says you do."

"You get the cab fare," he said, and off we went to Grant Spencer's office.

.

CHAPTER FOUR

"You ever hear of Vince Lombardi?" I asked the kid once we were in the cab.

"Lombardi? He work for Dominic's crew, over on the east side?"

"Not the one I'm talking about."

Nitschke turned out to be Donnie Silvestri. I tried not to concern myself with the knowledge that Frank Silvestri was the biggest mob boss in town. If Dominic's crew had the east side, Frank Silvestri had the other three. More likely, Dominic's crew worked for Frank Silvestri too. It could be coincidence, of course, that Donnie had the same last name. That's the thought I used to comfort myself.

Donnie Silvestri told me he was indeed a student at the University. It was his fifth year there, but he didn't expect to graduate for another two. He said he didn't see any reason to hurry the process. His major, he said, was chemistry, which I guess was better than body disposal. I wondered what use a chemist would be to a mob family and rationalized that he must not be from *that* Silvestri family.

Speaking of dead bodies and the disposal of them, here's a great way to spend a weekend. Contact the janitor in the building where you work—every building has at least one—and ask him when the mouse roundup is. You'll thank me later.

"So you're the redhead's agent, or what?" Donnie asked. ·

"Something like that. I'm her friend."

"That bitch fucks hard, no offense. I've never been so sore. My back was bleeding, my leg has a big-ass bruise on it, and I was just worn out. It's like we were trying to win some fucking contest or something."

29

"You were, she just didn't tell you."

"Did we?" he asked.

"You won, Donnie. That's for sure."

The cab stopped in front of the shiny building which housed the law offices of Grant Spencer. It turns out that the entire building is not his, just the fourteenth floor. A fairly attractive woman sitting behind an enormous reception desk greeted us. Her nameplate said Wanda Gaines. Seeing her, Donnie said something like, "Whoa."

Wanda Gaines ignored Donnie, proving she was smart as well as good looking, and said to me, "Can I help you?"

"I'm here to see Grant Spencer, if it's not too much trouble," I said.

"Did you have an appointment? I thought I had cancelled all of today's meetings."

"No, I don't have an appointment. Can I see him?"

"He's very busy. He's going to be tied up for weeks with a case, so he isn't taking anyone new on right now. I can refer you to someone, if you'd like. What sort of legal help do you need?" She pulled out her Rolodex and got ready to flip through, one long, painted nail locked onto the first card.

"He'll want to see me. Tell him John Jacobs is here, and that it's important."

"I'll see what I can do Mr. Jacobs, but I can't promise anything." She rose from her chair and retreated to a back room somewhere, high heels clicking on the tile floor.

Watching her, Donnie said, "There is nothing so fine as a good looking woman with an attitude. Nothing."

"Do you think she feels the same about Italian pretty boys, Donnie?" I asked.

"If she's half as smart as she is hot she does," he said, finishing just as she came back into view.

"Right this way, Mr. Jacobs," she said.

Donnie and I fell in behind Wanda Gaines as we were escorted into Grant Spencer's inner lair. I probably just imagined it, but it seemed like the air actually got colder with each step we took.

She opened the door into a large conference room. There was a long table surrounded by eight or ten leather chairs. One end of the room was a projection screen, the other a white board, with notes written in blue, red, and green. One long side had a countertop, set up with coffee and donuts; the other was floor to ceiling windows. It was a gorgeous view. Again, Donnie said something like, "Whoa."

There were books and yellow legal pads spread all across the big table, and six of the chairs were occupied. Grant had one, the other five were minor variations on the same person, all doing Grant's work.

Wanda introduced us as just Mr. Jacobs. Donnie was too busy watching her walk back down the hall to notice. Grant Spencer didn't bother to get up, and barely lifted his eyes in my direction.

"Change your mind about the bail money, Mr. Jacobs?" he asked.

"No, I ran into a friend of Maura's. Is she here?"

"I thought she was with you at lunch. I haven't seen her."

This meant, of course, that Maura must have walked in the front door on the street, waited for me to leave, then walked back out. I didn't want to consider why she might have done that, but it did cross my mind that I would never see my money again.

"I dropped her off here, about four hours ago. You do know that lunchtime is long past, don't you?"

He glanced down at his watch, which was at the end of a folded-back blue sleeve. He set down his pen, closed the book in front of him. To the five assistants he said, "Dinner break. You're all back here by eight." It took them less than twenty seconds to vacate the room. Grant waved us toward two of the leather seats, so we sat.

"She didn't show up here," he said. "I'm not sure what that means. It can't be good, though."

"My guess is she's trying to clear her head. She's had a rough couple days."

Donnie, other than his observations regarding the picturesque surroundings, had been silent up until now. He had fingered two donuts from the counter and was halfway through the first one.

Grant asked, "Who is this?" as he glanced toward Donnie.

"He is going to be Maura's alibi," I said. This, finally, woke the young Italian up.

"I'm what? What did that bitch do?" Donnie asked.

We both ignored him. I said to Grant, "This is Donnie Silvestri. He was with Maura on Monday. He's her alibi."

Grant considered this for a long moment as he scratched his nose, then he wrote something on his pad. He picked up his phone and punched a button and said, "Could you come in here, please," then hung up.

When Wanda Gaines opened the door after thirty silent seconds, it was a welcome relief. Grant said, "Mr. Silvestri, Ms. Gaines is going to take you out front, get your information, and give you cab fare home. I will call you when I need to see you again. Okay?"

All Donnie needed to know was that he got to leave with Wanda Gaines. He left, just like he was told. When we were alone, Grant spoke again.

"What the hell are you doing?"

"Trying to help," I said.

"Don't. This is not a game. We are talking about a woman's life. Stay out of it. I thought you said you understood."

"She was with him, Mr. Spencer. She was with him Monday afternoon, evening, and night. She said so, and he didn't deny it."

"She was talking to you about the case? At lunch?"

"She mentioned it, yes."

"Do you know who that is, Mr. Jacobs?" he asked.

"Donnie Silvestri. I'm the one who told you."

"Donnie Silvestri is Frank Silvestri's son. Frank Silvestri is one bad person. He's the mob. I am pretty sure that Frank would not want his boy involved in a murder trial on any level. Are you sure about the kid?"

"Maura told me she saw her husband's car in their garage, with his mistress' jacket inside. She knew they were inside, she got pissed, and she went to get some revenge of the sexual variety. The lucky bastard she picked was pretty boy Donnie. She didn't even know his name. I had to find that out myself."

"So you're a private eye now? What do you do, Mr. Jacobs? Do you work?"

"Not anymore. I'm a retired janitor. And I'm sure you already know that. I would bet that one of those legal pads is full of notes about me."

I must have been right, because he didn't press the issue.

"Frank Fucking Silvestri," he said. "We couldn't have picked a worse situation."

"I'm not sure I see the problem. So Donnie had a one-night stand. It probably wasn't his first or last. These things happen. And he did do pretty well. Even Frank Silvestri would notice that."

"Listen, this is not about what he did with my client." He emphasized *my* to let me know where I stood. "And it isn't about whether or not he had a good time doing it."

I was pretty sure he did. I said, "What is it about, then? Maybe you could educate me, since I'm here."

"I'll tell you what, Mr. Jacobs; why don't I have Frank Silvestri give you a call, just as soon as I hear from him. And I will hear from him. Donnie's stupid, but not too stupid to tell his old man. Would you like that?"

"At least I'm not afraid of him," I said. This was a lie, and it bothered me only slightly that the dishonest side of my ledger was sneaking ahead for the day. Frank Silvestri scared the shit out of me, but I wasn't about to let Grant Spencer know that.

"He should scare you," Grant said. "If he doesn't, you're as dumb as Donnie."

Was Donnie dumb? Or was he just slightly below average? Don't a lot of kids take seven years to get through college? Was it possible that he wasn't looking forward to joining the family business?

I asked, "Does Donnie work for his dad? Is he on a crew, or whatever those people call their little workgroups?"

"As far as I know Donnie is not yet working for the family. He's Frank's youngest out of four. The others all went through college first, then started working. Donnie's sister is actually the heir apparent. She's the oldest."

"His sister?"

"A bold move in the underworld for sure, but Frank's never been a real conventional mob guy. He does things his own way. His wife, if I remember, isn't even an Italian. She's from somewhere in Central America I believe. The word on the street is that having the girl as his second in command is the right move; she's already the brains behind most of what they do, or so I hear."

"Does the sister have a name?" I asked.

"Annabella," he said, sipping what must have been a very stale cup of coffee.

"Married?"

"No. She was engaged to a regular citizen, a schoolteacher. He died in a plane crash, and it was a little suspicious."

"Suspicious how?" I asked, freshening his cup from the pot on the counter.

"He was a weekend pilot, flew a little two seat Cessna. He and Annabella were supposed to fly up to the Pointe Lakes area to look over some vacation places. She told the police she had been caught in traffic and had called him, telling him to go ahead without her. He did, and the plane exploded over a lake. There wasn't much evidence the police could use. They couldn't prove it wasn't mechanical, or that it was. That's how it was suspicious. These things happen all the time around these family guys."

"It could be a coincidence," I said.

"Sure, it could be."

"How long ago was that?"

"I don't know, a couple years maybe. Why?"

"Just wondering if she's found a new victim yet. I mean boyfriend."

"I know what you're thinking, Mr. Jacobs, and you should stop thinking it. You're out of your league with these people. And I think they already have a janitor."

Didn't I tell him I was retired? Some people refuse to listen. I said, "Maybe I am out of their league, Mr. Spencer. But maybe I'm not. No one knows who I am. I might be kind of a valuable man on the inside."

"Nonsense. Don't get involved with her. You'll regret it. If you live, that is."

Could she really be that bad? Was I really that naïve? Was she smarter than her brother, Donnie? Was she as pretty? Was Grant right, the smug little bastard?

I said, "You're right, or course. I won't get involved."

Though I didn't know it at the time, this too was one more point for dishonesty.

CHAPTER FIVE

It was still gnawing at the back of my mind that Maura might have left town, which would mean I was out a big chunk of change. It wasn't going to break me, but I'd still rather have it than not. But still, I wasn't convinced she had left. Maybe she just didn't want to see Grant Spencer. Maybe she went to a movie. Maybe she was somewhere having mad sex. Maybe, maybe, maybe.

The hell with that noise.

I thumbed through the phone book, but couldn't find what I was looking for. I didn't really think I would. Women like Helen Roth aren't listed in the white pages with the common folks. If she wanted to talk to you, she would either call or give you her number ahead of time.

I dug through every closet, box, and drawer in my house in the hopes that Leslie had left it somewhere. I found a lot of dust, but no digits.

As a last resort, I dialed Leslie's number. It was stuck behind a magnet on my refrigerator where I had managed to not use it for four months. It was ten o'clock so I figured she would be home.

"Leslie's not here," said Lance. I could almost picture him looking down his nose at me. I considered whether he could help me, thought probably not, and then went ahead and asked him anyway.

I said, "Maybe you could help me, Lance. Leslie had a woman friend in the neighborhood that I need to get a hold of. I can't seem to find her number."

"She was Leslie's friend?" he asked, sure we couldn't have shared one.

"She was our friend, Lance. It's my night to bring snacks to the bridge game. I'm supposed to pick our friend up on my way over to the game. But see, I forgot about the snacks and now I'm running late and I need to call her and tell her that. I just can't put my finger on the number."

"You play bridge at this hour?"

"Sure, we're night owls. None of us work. Besides, if we played during the day we couldn't watch our soaps, and we absolutely cannot miss those."

"Who's the friend?" he asked. I don't think he wanted to help me, but he did want to be rid of me without being rude. It probably is written somewhere in the handbook of etiquette for stealing another man's woman.

"Helen Roth," I said, "Abe's wife."

He gave me the number and I thanked him. He hung up without a good-bye or a good luck.

Helen answered on the third ring. When she spoke I could tell she was well past her third drink. I heard a high-pitched dog bark and guessed it was her Yorkie. The thing more closely resembles an oversized rat than anything else, but Helen sure loved it.

"Jake, darling. What a nice surprise," she said, a little slurred.

You see there is no bridge game, regular or otherwise. I don't even know how to play and don't know if Helen does. Score one more point for deceit.

"How's Abe?" I asked just to be polite.

"Who cares?" she said. "You didn't call me to talk about my husband. And if you did, I'll hang up on you."

She then proceeded to tell me more than I wanted to know about her husband and his health problems. Apparently Abe's hemorrhoids weren't clearing up and surgery was being mentioned. And don't get her started on all that.

Finally she said to me, "So Jake, why did you call me?"

"I thought you might be able to help me with something, Helen."

"I can't say yes or no until you ask, Darling. Ask, ask, ask."

"I want to throw a little party, Helen. I thought of you, of course, because no party would be complete without you. And I thought maybe you would be willing to help me with the plans."

"Sounds perfect, Jake. Of course I'll help you out. Tomorrow at one o'clock, back by my pool. Okay, Jake?"

"Tomorrow at one," I said, and it was a date.

With no cards to shuffle or snacks to buy, I settled into my easy chair. The guy who installed my home theater—that's what the store insisted on calling my living room—told me my seat sits perfectly centered between the four surround sound speakers. He must have been right because the thing sounded damn good.

I flipped through the channels like a thirteen-year old after two double cappuccinos. With the lights off and channels flying by I got a nice strobe-like effect. I stopped only occasionally, if something caught my eye. I watched thirty seconds of an old sit-com, a minute of the news, fifteen seconds of a music video, a couple minutes of a talk show featuring racist, lesbian midgets, and so on. An overdose of culture wasn't going to happen.

When one talking head began his answer to another guy who looked like his brother with, "What I find completely fascinating . . ." I turned it off. Whenever a statement begins with those words it always means the same thing—it will be fascinating to no one but the speaker.

Sitting alone in that dark room was not a new experience for me. More often than not lately I would wake up there to see that the sun had once again risen. Why not? It's my house.

I was settling in to contemplate the pros and cons of a walk to my bedroom when a voice from one dark corner said, "You should have stopped on that threesome in the sauna back on Cinemax."

Leslie Watson stepped from the dark into a shadow. A glow from the kitchen provided good backlighting. With her there was no other kind.

I said, "I couldn't watch that. My last girlfriend would get hot whenever we saw something like that together. It invariably led to sex, and I wasn't up for a solo flight tonight."

"Had you stopped to watch, you may have had a passenger on board."

What was with the kinky sex talk? How long had she been in the house? Did she see me tearing the place apart searching for Helen's number? Did she hear me talking to her boyfriend? How about my conversation with Helen—had she heard that? Was she stalking me? Did she have to look so damn good after all this time?

I said, "It's good to see you, Leslie."

This point went to the side of honesty. She was wearing a knee-length skirt and a button down blouse. The blouse was loose enough so the kitchen light provided a nice show. And it was, well, not completely buttoned. It was undone too far for business, not enough for sin, but pleasingly between the two.

"I fell asleep out on the deck, on the chaise. The television woke me up, so I came back in. Is it okay that I'm here?"

"Sure, Leslie," I said.

She never had given me back her key, is what I thought. She just let herself in like she had never left, is what I guessed had happened.

"I considered waiting upstairs, but I wasn't sure you'd be alone, and it seemed sort of pretentious of me." *Sort of?* "It's a good thing I didn't go up there I guess. It doesn't appear as though you were going to make it off that chair."

"I was actually just considering whether or not I should bother, since I do live alone now." *Since you left.*

Leslie took a seat on the ottoman in front of me. She tucked her knees to her chest, bare feet rising off the floor.

"How long have you been out there, Les?" Her eyes looked a little sleepy still and her hair was just a bit mussed.

"Couple hours, I guess. It's a nice night to be out." We both smiled when she said it. She had used that very phrase when we were just about done with our carnal christening of my house. The only place left was the hot tub, which is on the very deck she had just awakened on. Last time she said those words she was naked and standing in the back doorway. We didn't need a movie for motivation then, even if it was the middle of the afternoon and not night at all.

"Is the pump running?" I asked with a nod toward the deck.

"It was, but I turned it off. I thought about waiting for you out there, too, but I never got in. I would have been pretty wrinkled by now."

"Is there trouble in Lance-land?" I asked, figuring we might as well cut to the chase. She wasn't exactly being subtle with her intentions. I hadn't seen her since she carried away the last of her boxes. And now, out of the blue, she's back? It didn't make sense, unless there had been a coup in the land of Lance. Had he been overthrown?

She didn't say no. She did say, "I miss you, Jake."

"I got that much. I just don't think Lance would see this as an appropriate form of expressing those feelings."

Again she didn't respond to what I said. Instead she said, "I want a drink. You want one."

"I only have beer."

She said that was fine, rose, stretched her body from blonde head to painted toe, and padded off to the kitchen. I, being a man, followed her. I came up behind her as she popped the caps off two bottles. I was crowding her personal space, but she didn't step back. She just handed me a bottle.

She said, "Lance is cheating on me, Jake."

"I'm sorry, Les."

"You don't need to be. I'm not entirely sure it's that new. He may have been with her before me. I'm just an idiot."

"That's a little strong."

"Is it? You never did anything but treat me great. The grass wasn't really any greener over there."

"You're not the first person to think it would be."

"I guess I'm assuming an awful lot by being here. I told myself you would want to see me, but why would you? I assumed too much."

"It's not that I don't want to see you," I said.

"But you're still hurt. I understand. Really, I do." She lifted herself up, sat on the counter. I stood next to her, leaning against the sink. Her naked left foot was slowly swinging back and forth, grazing my right leg with each little arc.

I said, "I won't deny that you hurt me, but I'm over it. Time heals all wounds, you know. Why don't you tell me why you're really here?"

"I saw you today, downtown," she said. Our eyes met in a comfortable gaze. "I'm worried about you, Jake."

"You're worried about me because you saw me downtown? People go there every day. There wouldn't be a downtown if they didn't. I'm down there most days."

"Jake, what have you done?"

"Nothing that I can think of. I wasn't talking to a lawyer because of anything I've done, if that's what you think."

"When I saw you, I didn't really think you had done anything. You had someone with you, and you're the kind of guy who helps his friends. I figured you were steering a friend to a good lawyer. Grant Spencer is certainly that. So I didn't really think much about it at the time."

Looking in her eyes I could see that she really was concerned about me. I said, "You don't need to worry about me, really. I'm not in any trouble or anything."

"I want that to be true, Jake. I do so much."

"But you can't believe it. Why not?"

"Well, Jake, if you haven't done anything maybe you could tell me why I got a call today, about you, that inferred you were in some sort of spot."

"A call? From whom?"

"Annabella Silvestri."

CHAPTER SIX

I learned long ago that trying to unravel the many mysteries in the spider web of a woman's acquaintances could be dangerous work. I don't use the metaphor of a web lightly. It's the brave man—or is he ignorant—who flies into that intricate piece of engineering. Few come out unharmed.

I had no idea that my Leslie Watson, in the former sense of course, knew Annabella Silvestri of the Silvestri mobsters. She had never mentioned a friend of that name to me, and she had mentioned many friends. Annabella Silvestri could have been a friend of a friend of a friend or something, I suppose.

Instead of asking her how she knew the mob queen, I said, "I don't know anyone named Annabella Silvestri."

This was not, technically speaking, a lie. I had never met the woman, and before my visit with Grant Spencer, had never even heard of her.

"We went to school together, Jake. We were both in the journalism program."

"Whom does she write for?" I asked.

"Fake ignorance has never worked for you. Please, give it up. I know you know who this woman is. I know you know she is part of the biggest mafia family in town. And I know you know she never wrote for anyone."

She drained the last of her beer and set the bottle on the counter next to her. I reached across her and pulled two more from the refrigerator, popped the tops, and gave her one. She kept her eyes locked on me as I did.

"I've never met her, Leslie. I wouldn't know her if she knocked on the door to say hello."

"Trust me, if she knocks on your door it won't be to say hello. Would you please just tell me why she's so suddenly interested in you?"

"What did she say about me?" I asked.

"She asked if it was true that I was engaged to John Jacobs. I told her no, we were never engaged, though we had lived together for a time. She wanted to know what you do with your time, if you work, that sort of thing."

"And you told her?"

"I told her that you no longer work, that it is somehow beneath you. I told her you like to hang out at the courthouse and watch the justice process in person. I told her you were a regular citizen who hit it big and that you were a threat to no one."

"And?"

"And nothing. If someone like Annabella is looking for information on you it isn't because she's looking for a date. You've somehow done something to bring yourself to her attention and the attention of her family. And that is not a good thing. And you know that, Jake. You fucking know that."

She jabbed a finger into my arm as she spoke. She was seriously concerned, and now so was I. Leslie isn't the sort given to hyperbole.

"I ran into her brother, Donnie, today. He's the guy you saw me with at Grant Spencer's law office."

"These people have their own lawyers, like Robert Duvall in *The Godfather*. Donnie Silvestri doesn't need Grant Spencer."

"True enough, but Grant Spencer needs Donnie. Or more to the point, one of his clients needs Donnie. He is the alibi for Maura Ferguson. They were screwing when the police say she was murdering. She couldn't have been doing both."

"Maura Ferguson? How'd you get involved with her?"

"Well, after you left me I sort of stumbled into a thing with her. I wouldn't say we date exactly. In fact, I'd say unconditionally it's not dating. We go to movies, maybe lunch, once a week. Her husband knew about it and didn't seem to care."

"That's because he was having an affair of his own, Jake. It probably took away some of the guilt for him."

"Look, Maura and I weren't having an affair. I've never even kissed the woman. We go to movies and lunch once a week. That's it."

"And she was with Donnie Silvestri at the time of the murders?"

"Yes, I think she was."

"And you took Donnie down to see Maura's lawyer?"

"Yes," I said.

"Damn, Jake, that wasn't a good move," she said, shaking her head. "Not a good move at all."

"In retrospect, you're probably right. But I didn't know who he was when I took him into Grant's office. He was just Donnie to me, another kid struggling through college. I honestly had no idea he was from a mob family."

"Jake, Jake, Jake," she said, her head still shaking.

"How did you ever hook up with the daughter of a mob boss?" I asked.

"I had no idea who she was when I met her, and she wasn't into talking about it. I was this naïve little country girl from northern Wisconsin. To me at that time, the big city was Green Bay. We went down every weekend the Packers were playing at home. Milwaukee was only a couple more hours down the road, but it might as well have been in another country. We never went there. I've told you all this before, haven't I? Anyway, you can imagine the culture shock I went through when I ended up in Boston for college. Coming from where I did, there was no reason for me to know about the Silvestri family. Annabella was just the pretty dark-haired girl who lived two doors down from me and who was in most of my classes."

"Was it love at first sight?" I asked.

"Not the way you think, but kind of. I felt an instant connection to her that I really can't explain. She's very charismatic. She was maybe my best friend while I was there. I never met her father, and it probably wouldn't have registered with me who he was anyway."

"Leslie, you've never said one word about her to me. Why?"

"When we graduated, Annabella just went home. Home for her, as you know, is here. We wrote to each other a little, but it got less and less over time. Then one day, out of nowhere, I get a call from her. She says she might have a line on a job for me at *The Times*. I flew out here from Boston and she put me up at her townhouse.

"That place was gorgeous. And she wasn't working, as far as I knew. I asked her how she could afford it. She said her daddy took care of it, like I should have known that. She had a driver take me to the interview, which was a set-up I think. The guy who talked to me actually looked afraid of me. He knew Annabella Silvestri had sent me and he must have assumed I was working for her."

"And you still had no clue?" I asked.

"The sun was slowly breaking through the clouds, let's just say that. I told Annabella how scared the guy looked. She told me it was because of her dad. I asked her what she meant by that. She said he was an intimidating man when it came to business."

"That would be an understatement."

"I did some research when I got back to Boston. I called people there and people here, pretending I was writing an article on Frank Silvestri. They didn't want to say too much, but I could put together enough to get the general idea."

"He's a baaad mother," I said.

"Very bad."

"You never worked for *The Times*, did you?"

"No. I was offered the job, but turned it down. She called me a couple days later to ask why. I told her I didn't want to be in her debt. She said she understood and promised that would be the end of it."

"And has it been?"

"Until today. She called asking about you. She didn't say it was business, but it was. She's changed, I think. She's deeper in."

"Grant says she's the heir apparent to Frank. She's the brains of the business."

"She always was smart, pretty level headed."

"And now she's looking for me," I said.

"I can't leave you alone for a minute without your getting into trouble, can I."

It had been more than a minute. It had actually been about 180,000 minutes, but who was counting? The breakup, as you may have guessed, was not my idea. I think it was Lance's. We'd been at it now for four months, but by the looks of Leslie, it didn't take. And I was in a forgiving mood.

I said, "What are you going to do about Lance?"

"Leave him. I'll go over there and clean out my stuff tomorrow while he's at work. He probably won't even notice I'm gone, so I better leave a note."

"Do you have somewhere to stay?" I asked

Did she want to stay in a room in my house? I have plenty, don't I? What about that half of the bed she vacated four months ago? Did she want to slide back in? It would be nice to have her around again, wouldn't it?

She said, "Yes, Jake. I've got someplace to stay."

She called a cab and pointed it to The Plaza. She said she'd pay for it with Lance's credit card, sort of a farewell gift. I didn't ask for my key back, and she didn't offer.

I flipped open my laptop computer, logged on to the information superhighway. My first stop was a bookstore and a couple presents for my new friend Donnie. I asked them to overnight the books to him, and they promised they would.

Next I went to The Plaza web page, quickly made a reservation in Leslie's name, paid for it, and asked them to put two dozen roses in the room before she arrived. I ordered an outfit from their shop and asked them to put that in her closet. Again, they were more than happy to oblige.

I was just about to sign off when a box popped up on the screen. It said I had an instant message from MadSex.

Maura Ferguson.

She wrote, "Jake, where have you been? I've been cruising the chat rooms all night looking for you. I've had a dozen offers for cybersex."

I typed, "I would think so with that screen name. I just got home. Where are you?"

"The Plaza."

Interesting. Would they be in adjoining rooms? Would they recognize each other? Had she taken any of the offers to cyber? Was she alone?

I typed, "Grant must have missed you this afternoon. He told me he hadn't seen you. He was worried."

"I never went up there."

No kidding.

"You should. Your life is in his hands."

"That's a little dramatic, don't you think? I was tired. I slept. I'll see him tomorrow. My life might be in his hands, but it is my life."

I typed, "Do you know who Frank Silvestri is?"

The problem with chatting through your computer is there is no sense of non-verbal communication. Body language, voice inflections, and pauses are all absent. Yes, there has developed a shorthand of cute little abbreviations and symbols to get around this problem, but Maura wasn't using it.

She typed, "No."

I answered, "You slept with his son."

CHAPTER SEVEN

Helen and Abe Roth live in a six thousand square foot home that sits halfway up a hill on the northern edge of our wealthy little neighborhood. It's an elegant place, fitting for a man like Abe and his wife. Abe's fortune came from selling cars. He started with a little used car place forty years ago and had built it to seven dealerships spread all around the city.

He dealt in several different makes, and that was evident in his driveway. Sitting next to a black Lincoln was a red Mercedes convertible, and beyond that a white Jaguar.

Big trees lined the driveway, and they were just starting to turn for the fall. A Mexican man was trimming the hedges in front of the entryway, and his partner was on a riding lawnmower. Two teenaged boys were busy washing the Jag, or were they just admiring it?

Helen Roth didn't work. She never had. She married Abe three weeks after they both graduated from high school. Two years later Abe saved enough money from his job to buy his first car lot. The guy he bought it from was being run out of town, something about a sixteen year old girl and the back of a Chevy, and he sold to Abe real cheap.

Helen and Abe never had children. I don't think they cared. Some people are like that. Abe's kids were his car lots. Helen busied herself with the daily goings-on of everyone else in town. She knew everyone, or so it seemed.

I found her where she said she would be, beside her enormous pool. Her dog was curled up at her feet, and he was quiet for a change. There was a pitcher of lemonade on a small round table next to Helen, and an empty deck chair next to her.

There was steam rising from the hot tub at the end of the pool, and a twentysomething woman cleaning it. Another woman, a little older, was vacuuming the floor of the pool. I waved at the first, nodded at the second. I still acknowledge my janitorial brothers and sisters. Someone has to.

It was autumn and a little cool, so I wasn't sure what use there would be for a pool. Helen, I'm sure, felt it better safe than sorry. A good appearance is an important thing, she would probably say.

There was a floppy green hat covering most of her gray hair, and she was wearing a jumpsuit ensemble that was vaguely the same color as the hat. Her wrinkled feet were bare and her toenails unpainted.

"Jake, darling," she said when she saw me. "Come have a glass of lemonade with an old woman. It'll do us both some good."

She was around sixty years old I guess, but looked at least seventy. She had probably spent too many summers by the pool, and too many evenings with her Scotch.

I bent and kissed her lightly on the cheek and said, "Thanks for having me over, Helen. I didn't know where to begin."

"And you thought of me. How sweet. And how cunning. How can I help, exactly?"

"I'm not sure. This is a first time thing for me. I've been to parties; I've just never thrown one myself. I have decided to step back and let the experts take over."

"I am that, Jake. I know more about throwing a party than anyone around here, that's for sure. Do you have a theme? Is there some special reason for the party?"

"No, nothing special. Maybe a costume party, for Halloween."

"That could be fun. When and where were you thinking of having it, darling?"

"Saturday night." She didn't bat an eye. These are the kind of challenges a woman like Helen Roth lives for. "And could we have it here?"

She said, "Forty-eight hours to plan it. No problem. You came to the right place, Jake, and of course we'll have the party here."

She pulled a notebook from the bag next to her and began to scribble some notes. She asked me a couple questions, but I got the feeling my input was no longer necessary. She told me she'd take care of things, have the bills sent to me. She handed me her proposed guest list, asked me to check it over.

It contained the usual crowd of wealthy people, and I noticed two or three couples who weren't so rich, but were well known about town. There were some names missing, too.

"Do you need to add anyone, darling?" she asked as I handed it back to her.

"Well, how about Leslie Watson?"

Twenty-four hours earlier and those words would not have crossed my lips. But there they were. Leslie, I thought, could be useful at this party. And she would need an opportunity to wear the dress she must have found in her closet at The Plaza.

"Leslie? Okay, I'll add her. What's her boyfriend's name? Lance something, isn't it? Do you want him here, too?"

"No, and neither will she. She's staying at The Plaza."

I knew this was a morsel Helen would love. The coupling and uncoupling of men and women was her stock and trade. And even if Leslie had had a change of heart overnight, it still made for good gossip.

"But she'll want to come?" Helen asked, getting into the spirit of things.

"Yes, she'll want to come," I guessed.

"Anyone else?" she asked.

"Maura Ferguson."

"Oh, Jake. Are you sure? She's a murderer, darling. She might bring the mood down just a bit."

"Alleged murderer, Helen, and out on bail. Think of all the talk there'll be with her here? Could be interesting." This, I knew, would get her.

She said, "Maura Ferguson," and scribbled her name on the list.

"She's at The Plaza as well," I said.

"Interesting. Anyone else?"

"Annabella Silvestri," I said.

Helen wrote down the name without any editorial comment. She had to know who Annabella Silvestri is, but she didn't say one way or the other.

"It sounds like a delightful party, Jake. Give me this afternoon to make the arrangements, get out the invites. And do get yourself a grand costume. It's your party."

Wanda Gaines was wearing a red skirt and white blouse when she greeted me from behind her desk. She remembered my name, which I took note of. After checking with someone on the other end of the phone, she escorted me to Grant Spencer's office.

This was not the same workroom I found him in the day before. This was an office worthy of a hotshot attorney. Maura Ferguson was sitting in a leather chair, facing the man's desk. The desk was big enough to make me think he was trying to compensate for something he lacked, like the forty year-old father who trades in the mini-van for a Harley.

Maura rose and gave me a hug when I walked in. She even planted a soft kiss on my cheek. She looked rested. Grant was nowhere to be seen. *Too bad.*

I said, "How's The Plaza?"

"Five stars, Jake. It's the best place to stay when your home is a crime scene."

"They let you in your house for clothes?" I asked.

She had traded her jeans and sweater for well, a different pair of jeans and a different sweater. It was her ensemble of choice more often than not.

"No. I had to shop."

"I thought they only gave you a small living allowance," I said.

"It's a pretty generous allowance actually. Grant convinced the judge that I had become accustomed to a certain level of living, and there's no reason I shouldn't get to maintain that. It's not enough to run away on, but it's enough to buy some clothes and a computer and a couple other things I need to get by. If they're not going to let me in my house, they have to let me buy supplies, don't they?"

"Sure they do," I said. "Are you doing okay, Maura? You don't lose your husband every day."

"Honestly, today's the first day it's really hit me. I came home Tuesday morning and they were waiting for me at my house. I was arrested, booked, and arraigned so quickly. I haven't had a chance to think about it until today."

"And what do you think? How do you feel, now that you've thought about it?"

"Shitty, Jake. Sam wasn't the best husband around, but I surely didn't want him dead. I can't understand it, really. Why would someone want Sam dead?"

"I have no idea. His golf game sucked?" I offered.

"Please don't joke about this."

"Sorry. It's my defense mechanism."

"I usually like it. It's kind of cute most of the time. Just don't do it when we talk about this, okay?"

"I promise," I said, holding up my hand in a Boy Scout salute.

I had joined Maura in a leather seat that matched hers, facing Grant's desk, waiting for him to arrive. Where was he? I figured he was a busier man than me and I could be bothered to wait. At least, I figured, my money wasn't yet lost. Maura was in the chair beside mine.

And speaking of Maura, had she run into Leslie at her hotel? Did they talk? Did they talk about me? Did Maura ask her how I am in bed? Would Maura really care? Would Leslie tell? Did Leslie really care anymore?

These were pressing questions, all of them. Okay, some of them. My take is that even if Maura were interested in my talents with the lights off, she wouldn't ask Leslie about it. Maura would do her own research into the subject. And Leslie, I figured, wouldn't tell her anyway. Her answer would have run toward the "mind your own fucking business" end of the spectrum. Besides, she did seem to have her own spark of interest rekindled.

Grant Spencer walked in from a side door, not the one Wanda Gaines had let me through. She was with him, a notebook and pen in her hand. He had traded his all blue look for an all gray one. He sat behind his security blanket of a desk and opened a file folder. Wanda took a seat off to the side, opened her notebook, and got ready to record whatever we were about to talk about. It was odd that they didn't use a tape recorder, but maybe they did, and Wanda was the backup.

Grant didn't bother with a greeting. He was in full attack shark mode.

"Mr. Jacobs, where were you Monday afternoon, between two and six?"

"Why?" I asked.

"You posted bail for Ms. Ferguson. You went to lunch with her. You seem interested in helping her. And yet, you seem to have no reason to care. Do you, Mr. Jacobs, have a reason to care?"

"Let's say I want to see justice served. I don't think Maura killed anyone."

"And that's enough? That's all it takes to get you running around town chasing her alibis? I find that hard to believe."

"I've got the time, Mr. Spencer."

"So I hear. Are you going to answer my original question?" he asked.

"Which was what again?"

"Where were you Monday afternoon, between two and six?"

"Oh right, you think I did it. If that's true, and I'm not saying it is, why would I be trying to get Maura off? It looks like she killed them to almost everyone you ask. If I killed them and she didn't, then why would I be trying to help her out?"

"Look, the question might come up, and not from me. If you react this way when it does, you'll be in trouble yourself. Can you afford me?"

"You know I can, Mr. Spencer."

He had a point, the smooth bastard.

I said, "I was at the movies Monday afternoon. I got home about five. I watched the local news, then bought a movie on my pay-per-view."

"What movie? What theater? What showing?"

Lucky for me I was wearing the same pants as Monday, and I hadn't washed them yet. Maura and I never went to movies at her husband's theaters. She didn't want to be recognized, and it was her small way of telling him to go blow. I had paid Monday, so inside the left front pocket of my pants were two ticket stubs, which I now produced for Grant Spencer. He eyed them quickly, wrote some notes on his pad of paper, and then handed them back to me.

"I would hang on to those, if I were you. Why are there two?"

"It's called a date. Maybe you should go on one sometime."

"Her name?"

"I'd rather not say if I don't have to."

"That figures. Can't find any single women your age to date? I guess we can let it go for now. And we'll hope you can keep your little secret to yourself. What movie did you buy on pay-per-view?"

"I don't remember the name exactly, but it was some kind of sex thing."

"Sex thing?" he asked.

"My date didn't put out. She said she had to get home to her husband. I needed another outlet."

To this Maura Ferguson let out a giggle. She knew she had been my date, and that putting out hadn't really been an issue. She probably wasn't sure if I was telling the truth about the movie or yanking Grant's chain, but she laughed just the same.

"Records will verify this?" he asked.

"I don't keep records of which dates put out, Mr. Spencer. That's more of a mental log."

Again Maura giggled quietly. Wanda Gaines was trying to hide a smile of her own. Grant was not a happy fellow.

"When does the bill come, Mr. Jacobs?"

"There's no bill. I don't have to pay my dates for sex," I said.

"The bill for the pay-per-view movie," he said, nearing the boiling point.

"I don't know. Just call the satellite company and ask. They'll let you know. Or subpoena them. Isn't that what you guys do?"

"You're a very entertaining man, Mr. Jacobs. It's a wonder you've remained single all these years."

Maura broke in, before it got too ugly, saying, "Grant, why is Mr. Jacobs here? I thanked him with lunch yesterday. Why is he still here today?"

Grant said, "Mr. Jacobs took it upon himself to track down the young man you said you were with Monday afternoon."

"And evening and night too, according to him," I said.

"Donnie Silvestri," Grant said.

"So that's his name," Maura said with a faraway nod.

"Of the Silvestri crime family," I said.

"He's Frank Silvestri's son, Maura," Grant added. "He's the son of a mafia don."

"A mafia don? Well that kind of sucks, doesn't it?" she said. "He just looked like any other kid in that place."

"What did you expect?" Grant asked. "Marlon Brando?"

"Marlon Brando was the father, Grant, not the son. The son was Al Pacino. I don't know who I expected the kid to be, but certainly not the mafia."

"It's okay," I said, "They look just like you and me, only with darker hair and names that end in vowels."

"So now what?" she asked.

"Now," he said, "we look for another alibi."

"Mr. Spencer, I still don't know what the problem is with Donnie," I said.

I didn't really want Grant snooping around too much in search of my movie date and Maura's alibi. He would, eventually, put them together. I wasn't worried about it, since I knew I hadn't killed anyone, but I didn't want anyone thinking I had, just the same.

He said, "Mr. Jacobs, the mafia does not like to be involved in judicial matters. They tend to settle things in their own courtroom, and it isn't always fair or just. Frank probably has twenty guys lined up waiting to say they spent the day with Donnie, just so we don't feel tempted to actually put him on the stand. These family guys don't want any kind of attention at all. Forget about Donnie."

Wanda Gaines caught my eye and held it too long. At least I think she did. Did I imagine her nodding toward the lobby? I wasn't sure, but I didn't want to sit in on any more of this meeting anyway. I decided to take my chances with Wanda out front.

"I've got to get groceries, go to the gym, pick up some beer," I said. "Are you finished with me?"

Grant nodded and said, "Would you see him out, Wanda?"

I lingered in front of Wanda's desk to see if she was trying to catch my eye. Did she want a date? A quickie? Did she have a suggestion on how to kill her boss that I might be able to assist with? Did she want to help me out? Maybe she just had something in her eye, like a hair or something.

"Mr. Jacobs," she said just as I gave up and turned toward the elevators.

"My friends call me Jake," I said.

"Mr. Spencer knows what he's doing," she said. "He's an excellent attorney. His instincts are almost always right on."

She slid a piece of paper across her desk toward me, folded neatly in half. Again, she caught my eye. She didn't want me to read it here, but she most certainly did want me to read it.

"I know he's a great lawyer, Ms. Gaines," I began.

"My friends call me Wanda, Jake," she said with a smile.

"Ms. Ferguson is my friend is all, and I just want to be sure he's doing his best work for her."

"I assure you he is," she said, quietly waving me toward the open elevator.

I stepped in, punched the ground floor button, and looked at her note. It said, "Seven o'clock, Juan's Salsa Barn, come alone and ask for me at the front desk."

Juan's Salsa Barn is a run down shack on the south edge of town, almost beyond—the kind of neighborhood that begged you to ride in with an armored car. I would have tossed the note and forgot about her were it not for the last line.

It said, "I can help."

CHAPTER EIGHT

Wanda Gaines wanted to help me? Did I need help? Was I that involved? And if I was that involved, should I be? In the grand scheme of life, what had Maura Ferguson really ever done for me that I now felt strangely compelled to be her Private Eye? And why did Wanda Gaines want to help me? Was it my smile? My wardrobe? Was it a shared dislike for her boss? Did she harbor some strange sense of right and wrong and justice being done? Or was she just looking for a little fun?

I had a couple hours before my date at the Mexican restaurant voted most likely to kill you with its food. A wise man would have bought some kind of antacid and inhaled it, as a preventive measure. Not me. I went to the library.

I looked up every magazine and newspaper article I could find on the Silvestri family. I told the research librarian that I was doing a term paper on the mafia. His look said he didn't believe me, but he helped me just the same.

I bet he didn't know he worked at a building widely known as one of the biggest engineering screw-ups of the twentieth century. The library is sinking, and not because of any problem with the ground it sits on. It falls about an inch closer to hell every year because the engineers failed to consider the weight of the books when they designed the building. Then again, he was the research librarian, so maybe he did know.

Frank Silvestri was born in the Bronx and came here after high school. He knocked around several odd jobs before catching on as a cabbie. He moved up the ranks quickly and by the time he was twenty years old he was on the management ladder, just a couple rungs from the top. By 1965 he owned the business.

The information on how he came to be able to buy it is sketchy at best. There were suggestions of crimes, both monetary and physical, but no charges were ever filed. He had a partner at the beginning that died after two years with Frank. Again, no charges were filed though suspicions were raised.

Frank had been arrested several times, but had never been convicted of anything. His rise to the top of the crime world had been quick. His former partner was the second cousin of Sal "Horse Face" Santini, he of the enormous overbite.

When the cousin/partner showed up dead, and Frank looked like the guy who did it, Horse Face sent in three of his best men to take out Frank. Legend has it that Frank instead took all three of the horsemen out, and without a weapon of any kind. When the bodies were found there was a horse's bridle on each head. Horse Face, it can be assumed, was not amused.

Two weeks later he too was dead, and the west side of the city belonged to Frank Silvestri. Whether or not that was his plan in the beginning is unclear, but he took to his new position like a politician does to lying.

In the summer of 1969, while the rest of the country was watching men walk on the moon for the first time, Frank Silvestri was systematically wiping out the rest of the competition. And he didn't limit himself to other Italians. Through the years he had fought off many who challenged his reign, including most notably the Mexicans and Chinese. And now he stood alone on top.

Currently his fingerprint could be found on several different business ventures in town, including the horse track and casino, a minor league baseball stadium, and a rather large real estate development company that was eating up land at an alarming rate.

There were rumors through the last couple of years that he was pulling out, trying to go clean. These, like most things about Frank Silvestri, were stories lacking detail. As near as I could tell from what I read, he was still very much a bad, bad boy.

I found a couple articles on his daughter, Annabella, in the society section. Her face seemed to be a regular one at charity fundraisers, political dinners, and anything else a known mobster probably wouldn't want to be seen at. Frank sent his firstborn.

She was alone in some of the pictures and with a date in others. There was an engagement announcement, followed some months later by an article about the mysterious death of her fiancé.

And that's about it. I now had a face to put with the name, but not much more. And in just over forty-eight hours she would be at my party, I hoped.

Wanda Gaines was seated with her back to the wall in a corner booth that wasn't very clean. Nothing in the place was, except for Wanda Gaines. She had changed out of her corporate secretary look and into a more casual get-up of jeans and a sweatshirt. There was a plate of nachos in the middle of the table and a pitcher of margaritas in front of her. She saw me come in but didn't wave. She just watched me tiptoe my way through the grime and crud.

"Do you want a wet cloth to wipe off your seat before you sit down, Jake?" she asked as I reached her table.

"I'd ask for one, but those are probably dirty too," I said. "This place aggravates every piece of janitorial pride I ever had. It's a mess. Maybe I could put them in touch with a good service, maybe get this place cleaned up."

"This must not be your part of town," she said.

"Is it yours?"

"Not anymore. I grew up down on this end, but it's gone to hell the last few years. This is actually one of the nicer places in the neighborhood. When I moved out it was because my boyfriend didn't like me living here. Then he dumped me anyway, the jerk. I guess it worked out okay though. I live a couple blocks from the office now. I've got an apartment with a view."

I poured myself a margarita and hoped for the best. I ordered an enchilada and rice and said a quick prayer for its safety. The nachos looked harmless, but I held off. One can never be too sure.

Wanda noticed my hesitation and said, "They have health inspections, you know. Even here. They pass every time. Get over it."

"You're probably right. All this dirt is probably just part of the atmosphere."

"I want to help you, Jake," she said between sips of her drink.

"Help me what?" I asked, playing dumb.

"Look, I know what you're up to."

"I'm glad one of us does," I said.

"You and Maura Ferguson are friends. You didn't bail her out on some whim. She's your friend. You told me as much this afternoon, though you have said no such thing to my boss. He's under the impression that you think she's got a nice ass or something and you're hoping this gesture might lead to some romance. He sees what he wants to see, I guess. I think that's why he took on this case in the first place. He likes her ass, too."

"Grant wasn't Maura's lawyer before this?" I asked.

"No. The Fergusons have a lawyer in the family somewhere that they've always used. Mrs. Ferguson felt using a relative of the victim to defend her made no sense. Grant knew her husband, Sam. They golfed together and saw each other socially now and then, that sort of thing. Sam Ferguson called the office from time to time, so they definitely were acquainted. I can only assume Maura knew Grant as well. He dropped everything when she called."

"And he wants to get in her pants?"

"I'm just guessing," she said.

"And he's treating me like shit because he thinks I'm the competition?"

"Again, I'm just guessing. And because he treats most people like shit. At least he pays well."

"I'm not in the market for Maura Ferguson. I like her, but I'm not after her. Why don't you tell Grant that so he'll lighten up?"

"I'm not an idiot, Jake," she said.

"I never thought you were," I said, "Quite the contrary, actually."

"The reason you keep pressing the issue of Donnie Silvestri is because you are the other alibi. Am I right?"

I didn't answer. I may have been too stunned. Had Maura said something to her? Had Donnie? Had she put this together on her own? *Damn.*

Wanda said, "There is a four hour window that Maura Ferguson needs to get closed. She was only with Donnie Silvestri for, at best, one of those hours. He told me so on his way out yesterday. She was your date at the movie, wasn't she?"

"Yes," I said.

"But you're not interested in her romantically?"

"She was married until three days ago. I never really thought about it."

"Why don't you just tell Grant and the police that you were with her? Wouldn't that be the simple solution to this mess? It certainly would be for you. It might not solve all of her problems, but it would minimize them for sure."

Think about this. You *can* buy a movie ticket and not go into the movie. If you're the kind of person who has plenty of disposable cash, it's not that big of deal. Let's say you're also the kind of person who wants to kill her husband and his mistress, and you think your boyfriend would be the ideal person to help. You could kill the husband, get the cash, marry the boyfriend, and get off because you were at a movie and nowhere near the scene of the crime. Maura and I decided that if people knew we had been at the movie that just such a scenario might pop into their heads. They might say we bought the tickets as a convenient alibi, then spent the afternoon chopping the adulterers into little bits and pieces.

But we really did go to the movie. And I'm not her boyfriend.

I explained this all to Wanda and she listened like she understood. The nachos were gone and the main dishes sat in front of us. I took a deep breath and dug in.

She said, "So you're really doing this to save your own ass, not hers, right?"

"She will eventually break down and tell someone where she was. If she doesn't they'll find her guilty. When she tells there will be a good chance it comes back on me."

"Like I said, you're trying to save your own ass," she said.

"Yes, I am."

"And I want to help," she said.

"Why would you want to help?"

"Let's just say I like your ass."

I don't think I blushed. Do I have a nice rear? How would I know? I can't see the damn thing and wouldn't know how to judge a male bottom anyway. If Wanda thought it was fine, then fine it was. And why all the talk about asses?

"Have you got a plan? For helping me, I mean. Have you thought about what we should be doing, to whom, and when?" I asked.

She smiled, which could have had any number of meanings.

She said, "Yes, I've got a plan."

She slid a piece of paper and a picture across the table to me. The paper had Donnie's address and phone number written on it. The picture was of his sister, Annabella. What was she thinking, exactly? I said, "Who's the girl?"

"Annabella Silvestri. She's Donnie's sister. I think Grant told you about her involvement in the family business. Do you think she's cute?"

Her plan began to form itself in my head. She was going to work on Donnie, and I was going after the big sister. I could think of tougher jobs, and my end was actually already in the works.

"She's cute, but pictures can lie."

The fact of the matter remained that Maura had only actually been with Donnie Silvestri for about an hour of the four she needed covered. And if a person really thought about it, how long would it take to stab two naked adults and a dog? Maura could have done it. Wouldn't it make more sense for us to look for whoever really did kill Sam and Shannon? Probably.

She said, "I've got a date with Donnie tomorrow night. I'll find out what I can."

I wanted to tell her to take a chaperone, maybe a big bodyguard. Instead I said, "Annabella is coming to a party I'm throwing, Saturday night. Or at least she's invited."

"Do you know her?" she asked.

"Not yet. You and I were thinking in the same direction. I'm not sure it's the right one, though."

"We shouldn't be looking for an alibi. We should be looking for a killer."

"Something like that," I said.

"And how do you find a killer?" she asked.

"You look for a motive," I answered.

"Like twenty-five million dollars?"

"Just like. And I don't think Maura's daughter could have done it."

"But you don't think Maura did it either, do you?"

"No." I said.

"If not the money, then what? Jealousy? Revenge? Customer complaint about the popcorn?"

"Money and sex. It always comes down to money or sex, sometimes both."

"Was Shannon Powell married?" she asked.

"No, never married."

"What about a jealous boyfriend?"

"Sam was her boyfriend, and I don't think he's the guy we're looking for," I said.

"I'll have to think about it some more," she said, and that was the end of that.

In the cab I said, "You're place or mine?"

"Jake, I know who you are. Why are you asking that question? You're the janitor that won the lottery. Your girlfriend is that Leslie Watson from the morning news. That's why you've never thought about Maura Ferguson romantically, and that's why you shouldn't be asking me a question like that."

"I used to be a janitor, that's true. I won the lottery, that's also true. Leslie Watson was my girlfriend, past tense."

"There's something that always bothered me about your story when you won the money. Why was a television news lady dating a janitor? How does she even meet a janitor? No offense, Jake."

"None taken, Wanda. I met Leslie at a restaurant, actually. She was doing a live remote broadcast from the place, and I had stopped there to eat breakfast after work. When she wasn't on the air, she talked to the patrons, myself included. She asked me where I worked. I told her I worked at the Westlake Building, which wasn't a lie. She assumed I worked as an office professional of some sort. It wasn't until the third or fourth date that she asked what I did there. By then it was too late. She'd already fallen for me."

"And now you're broken up?"

"She left me, for another man. And now she left him too. I think she might want a second chance with me."

"So why would you want to take me home then, Jake?"

Aside from the obvious? "It's like a forest fire. Sometimes the firefighters will light a controlled burn on purpose, to sort of head off the original fire. They have no intention of fighting the controlled burn, but it stops the big fire from getting out of control. Understand?"

"Sure. That's very romantic. You really know how to touch a girl's heart. You're still in love with Leslie the news lady but she's burned you before. You don't think you want that fire to get out of control again, so why not stop it with another fire? Nice plan."

"Thank you," I said.

"You'd be using me. You know that, right?"

"That's an ugly way to put it, Wanda."

"But it's the truth, isn't it? Not that I'm not flattered," she said sarcastically. "If you still love the woman you need to let her know that. The woman needs to hear what's in your heart."

"You're right, I suppose," I nodded.

The cab pulled to a stop in front of a canopied entryway that must have led up to Wanda's apartment. I waited for her to say goodbye, but she didn't.

Instead she said, "Look, I probably shouldn't do this, and please don't read anything into it, but would you like to come up for a drink? It really is a spectacular view. You should see it."

I'd seen plenty of views since my lucky strike, but I threw two twenties at the cabbie anyway and followed Wanda onto the curb. It was a high-rise building and a doorman greeted her by name as we stepped into the lobby.

"You'll have to excuse the mess when we get up there," she said in the elevator. "My roommate moved out a couple weeks ago and she hasn't cleared out all of her stuff yet. I need to call her and jumpstart her ass."

"No problem," I said, doubting I would notice. "I'm a guy who lives alone. I know what a mess is."

Her apartment was on the twenty-fourth floor, with a picture window facing west. The lights of the city were in full glow. It was very impressive indeed, maybe too impressive. She was just Grant's secretary, right? Would it have been inappropriate to ask how much he paid her? Would it have been okay to ask what kind of rent she paid? Was she looking for a new roommate?

Wanda planted herself on a black leather couch and flicked on a big screen television. She scanned the channels quickly before stopping at BET, where they were in the middle of some sort of black music video countdown.

I said, "There's a Billy Joel concert on VH-1. It's from Moscow I think."

"That's funny," she said, and I really think she thought I was joking.

She kicked off her shoes and put her feet up on a glass coffee table. Next to the television there was a compact disc rack that was less than half full. The room was scattered with several cardboard boxes, some taped shut, some not. She was right about one thing—this place was a mess.

What she needed was one of those private cleaning services. I never worked for one, but I heard talk. Sure, a house is cozier than an office, but people who can afford private janitors usually demand certain efficiency. I wanted nothing to do with that situation. Just give me my broom and a dark hallway and leave me alone.

"Liquor's on a counter in the kitchen," she said. "Why don't you go in there and fix us something to drink? Lemons and limes are in the fridge if you need them."

If the living room was a mess, the kitchen was a disaster area. Plates, glasses, Tupperware, utensils, and silverware were spread out all over the counter and table. There were more boxes, both opened and sealed, on the floor. And tucked into a corner of one counter, right next to the microwave, were several bottles of alcohol.

I found the tequila and poured a dose into each of two relatively clean glasses. I found a lemon in the fridge and grabbed one of three chef's knives that were sitting together in the sink. I put the slices on a plate, grabbed the drinks and a saltshaker, and returned to the couch.

She pushed two coasters at me with her naked toes and held out her hand in the direction of the glasses. Her eyes never left the television. I gave her one of the glasses and a slice of lemon, but she waved off the saltshaker. She slammed back her drink, swallowing it hard with a shake of her head.

"Where's the bottle?" she asked.

"In the kitchen," I said with a nod in that direction. "I think one drink might be my limit tonight, though."

"Suit yourself. Could you get it for me?"

I brought it to her and asked, "Are you just going to watch TV and get drunk?"

"That's the plan," she answered. "Join me if you want. I told you downstairs not to read anything into my invite."

"I'm not, Wanda. I just don't think I should stay. Not tonight. I should go. Will you be okay drinking by yourself?"

"I think I can manage," she said, pouring another tall one. "I've done it before."

"Don't you work in the morning?" I asked.

I could feel my stomach starting to squirm as I watched her down her second tequila, knowing she wasn't close to done. Where do these women put it?

"Mmm hmm. Five o'clock," she said. "I'll be fine. I'm better when I'm hung over. I'm more of a bitch to the clients and they seem to like that."

She walked me to the door of her apartment, but not downstairs. She asked me once more if I wanted to stay longer, but I declined. She gave me a quick kiss and closed the door without another word.

Outside, I hailed a cab. The driver, who might not have known he worked for the Silvestri crime family, asked me where to. It had been a long couple of days and I wasn't sure I'd accomplished anything useful. I was proud of my forest fire analogy, though it hadn't had the effect I'd hoped for.

I said, "The Plaza."

CHAPTER NINE

The lobby of The Plaza is a brightly lit, gold-plated masterpiece. High-backed chairs sit everywhere, mostly two by two. The reception desk is more mirrored gold, and all the people behind it were dressed in suit and tie, or dress, depending on their gender. Off to one end is the restaurant, elegant American cuisine of the best kind available. To the other end is the bar, the darkest place in the building, as it should be.

I found a little round table in the bar where no one would bother me, and where I could see the front door of the hotel and the elevators in the distance. My nerve had disappeared during the cab ride away from Wanda Gaines, and I was trying to get it back through the consumption of alcohol.

The margaritas from hell had given me a fairly good start down the road to decreased inhibitions, but I wasn't there yet. I ordered a tequila shot to keep with the Mexican theme for the evening, and a beer chaser.

As I waited for my drinks to come, I thought about what Wanda had said. Was I here to talk to Leslie? Would I be able to tell her how I really felt? Was Leslie even here anymore? What if she had gone home to Lance? Could I handle that setback? And what about Maura? Did I want to go upstairs and tell the grieving widow that she had a very nice butt and we all thought so?

And then Maura Ferguson walked by, from the front door toward the elevator. She was not alone, and I didn't know the man next to her, though his face looked strangely familiar. Donnie? No. Grant? No. Frank Silvestri? No. But I'd seen that face before, somewhere.

The elevator door opened and Maura got in. He didn't. He bent and kissed her, one hand on her elbow. It wasn't a passionate kiss, I wouldn't say, but it was on the mouth. She smiled and thanked him, I think, and then the doors slid shut.

I watched the man closely. He had graying, curly hair and a beard. He was wearing a tie and a tweed jacket and Dockers. He was a handsome man who was just heading toward aging. Distinguished? I guess you could say he was distinguished, though I've never particularly liked that description. I think it's because I don't want anyone to ever use it to describe me. But that's the word. He looked distinguished.

And then he was gone, through the door and into the autumn night.

I pulled out my cell phone and dialed the front desk. When they answered I asked for Maura Ferguson. A lump rose in my throat briefly when I realized she may have registered under a different name, but she answered on the third ring.

I said, "Maura, where's your daughter staying?"

She said, "Who is this? Jake? Is that you?"

"Yes. I'm not at my computer, so I thought I'd call. Is that okay?"

"Sure, Jake. My daughter is staying with my sister-in-law."

"Sam's sister?" I asked. I thought that was a little strange.

"No, with Kathy, my brother's ex-wife. He doesn't live here anymore, and she loves Brittney. Kathy doesn't have any kids of her own, which I guess helped the divorce sail through so easily. Anyway, she takes care of Brittney all the time. Britt loves going over there. I'm pretty sure she gets spoiled."

"What have you been up to tonight?" I asked. "I tried calling earlier." This was a lie, but one I knew I couldn't get caught in. She had just walked in.

"I was with Grant. He just dropped me off," she said. Apparently it was her turn to lie. Unless, of course, she was in the habit of kissing Grant's underlings each time they dropped her off.

Why was she lying to me? Did she kill Sam and Shannon? Was I her patsy? Should I be worried about my own lifespan and it's possibly shortened length? Should I ask her about the guy in the tweed jacket?

I said, "Have you heard from friends since this happened? I would think they'd come to your aid, if they're really your friends."

"You mean like you did?" she asked.

"Help can come in many ways besides money. An encouraging phone call, a reassuring note, maybe a dinner date or a quick drink, just to let you know they were thinking about you during this crisis."

"I've had one or two calls, but most of my friends were Sam's friends too. They probably want to make sure I didn't kill him before they come to my side."

Should I have thought of that myself? Hindsight's a bitch.

I said, "That makes sense."

"Grant really doesn't want you poking your nose around anymore, Jake. He says it's only going to mess things up. And he doesn't want you to get hurt."

How nice.

I said, "I'm not poking my nose around anymore. Why should I? I found Donnie and that's it. I'm not inclined to stick my neck out too far anyway, so Grant doesn't have to worry about me. And where would I begin even if I chose to?"

"He'll be glad to hear that. I'll tell him tomorrow morning. He wants me back at the office at seven o'clock, if you can believe that."

"Time's not exactly your ally, Maura."

"I'll keep you informed with what's going on," she said as she hung up.

There's a movie poster hanging in my living room. It's framed and autographed by the three stars. Maura Ferguson had it sent over after our first afternoon together. It was the poster for the movie we had both tried to rent, and ended up renting together. It came with a note that said I shouldn't expect a poster from her for every movie we went to together, since she was hoping there would be quite a few.

How many had it been? Maybe a dozen? They were always in the afternoon and always on Monday. Was that long enough to set someone up? Had she really been setting me up? I hoped not.

My cell phone chirped.

Leslie said, "Tequila and beer?"

I didn't look around, but wanted to.

I said, "Tequila's no good by itself. You know that."

"Fourteen-sixteen," she said and hung up.

I walked to elevator, punched the button for the fourteenth floor. I even rode it all the way up. When the door opened I couldn't move. I let the doors close and the elevator took me back to the lobby. I scribbled a note at the desk, handed it with a twenty to the guy working there. He looked a question at me.

"Room 1416," I said.

It was raining when I climbed into another cab and pointed it toward home. It was still raining outside the next morning when I woke up. A rather loud thunderclap brought me back to a state of sort-of-conscious. I was sitting in my big chair in the middle of my home theater that I like to call a living room. I looked at the clock; saw that it was one minute before five.

I picked up the remote and turned on my sixty-four inch monster of a television. I went to the station I'd been avoiding for four months. Leslie came on with a smile, greeted all of us she couldn't see, and read the lineup for the morning show. Her face looked big on the screen and she looked rested. She wouldn't have looked that way if I'd gone up to her room. Eventually they went to a commercial and my mind headed back toward sleep.

The phone rang, very loud in the still of the dark room. It took me three rings to locate it, and another two to actually pick it up. Who the hell calls at five in the morning?

"I waited and waited, Jake. You never came up. Now I've got a case of beer and a bottle of tequila, but no one to drink them with."

"Leslie, I'm sorry. Did you get my note?"

"I got your note this morning. Plenty of good that did me. I waited up for awhile. I thought maybe you were finishing your drink, or gathering your nerve, or something. Your note said you were too drunk and it wouldn't be right. It said you might say things the wrong way. What did you want to say, Jake?"

"Did you get your stuff out of Lance's place?" I asked.

"That's what you wanted to say? That came out fine. Yes, I got my stuff out of Lance's house. It's mostly in a storage garage now. Is that what you wanted to say, Jake?"

"No, but I wanted to make sure."

"Make sure of what?"

"I wasn't going to tell you that I still love you if you were still with Lance. It didn't seem right."

There was a long silence on the other end.

Finally she said, "That's what you wanted to tell me? Seems to me like you would tell me that even if I were still with Lance. If you love me, I mean."

"You left me, Leslie. Remember? You need to make the first move."

"I did, Jake. I did. I'm back on the air. I'll call you later."

I looked at the screen and there she was, smiling like nothing had happened. You couldn't fault her professionalism. Where was her phone? Just under the desk? Off to the side? She turned to a monitor behind her and started talking to the weather guy. They acted like they were in different rooms, but he was actually twenty feet to her left. The magic of television.

Had she made the first move? Sure, showing up at my house could be called that, though she said she was concerned about me. She said Annabella Silvestri had called her about me, and that's why she was at my house. Maybe that's why I hadn't seen it as a first move. Did she want it to appear somewhat disguised, in case I wasn't interested?

Was she coming back? Did I want her back? Would we have to re-christen each room, or does that sort of thing keep for a long time? How did she look so good so early in the morning, especially with major life changes hanging over her pretty blonde head?

Leslie was introducing a story about animals, and it took me a couple minutes to realize it was because of Joe, Maura's murdered mutt. It turned out to be an interview from the pound, talking to a director of some kind, about the screening process people go through before they can adopt an animal. The gist of the story, I think, was that maybe the pound should be just a wee bit more selective with whom they let take animals home.

This whole attention to Joe thing was getting tiresome, and fast. I dozed off and on through the show, which runs an exhaustingly long four hours. Occasionally I surfed to other channels, just to see what might be on. ESPN was talking about the baseball playoffs and the just heating up football season. MTV was actually playing videos, though I couldn't stand to listen to the music. CNN said the President was somewhere in Asia trying to stop someone from making atomic weapons.

At nine o'clock Leslie and her team signed off for another day. Two minutes later, the phone rang. I figured it was Leslie, naturally.

It wasn't.

"Jake, I've got some stuff for you," Wanda Gaines said to me through my confusion.

"What kind of stuff?" I asked.

"Last night after you dropped me off I was sitting in my apartment thinking. I got an idea and so I'm sending you some stuff."

"Is it bigger than a bread box, Wanda?"

"Grant's got a big file on this case. He has police reports. He has statements from possible witnesses. He's got everything the prosecution has. They have to give it to him, you know? It's probably three boxes of stuff."

"You're sending me Grant's files on Maura's case? That's got to be a serious crime of some kind."

"I was sitting in my apartment trying to think of a way to let you have a look at those files. The police wouldn't let you near them, I'm sure. Why would they? Grant doesn't want your help. He's got his investigators and they do a good job. I just don't think they're looking in the right places, like we talked about last night. They should be looking for the killer, not an alibi. Anyway, I went to the office last night about midnight and fired up the copy machine. It took about five hours. I got everything boxed and back where I found it about ten seconds before Grant came in."

"At five o'clock?"

"He starts early when he's got a case like this," she said.

"And you're sending me those copies?" I asked.

"They should be at your house before noon," she said.

"What do you want me to do with them?"

"Look through them. See what Grant has. See what the police have on Maura. Maybe see what they have that would point to someone else besides Maura. You're a smart guy. Find something."

"Wasn't Grant a little surprised to see you at five o'clock in the morning?" I asked.

"Not at all. He expects me to be in the office when he gets there. He starts early and he works late. The man earns his money. So do I."

"Wanda, does anyone else know about this? Are the boxes marked with the firm's logo or anything?"

"It will be three plain cardboard boxes. They're fairly heavy, but they're not marked. I told the delivery guy that picked them up that they were my boyfriend's books and he forgot to take them when I kicked his butt out."

"So I'm your boyfriend now?"

"Don't you listen? I kicked you out. Did you talk to your news lady?"

"Yes," I said.

"Did you tell her how you feel?"

"I'm not sure what I told her. It didn't come out the way I planned."

"Try again, Jake," she said.

"Wanda, these boxes full of files could get you fired, couldn't they?"

"Definitely."

"And they could put us both in jail, right?"

"Probably," she said.

"You're sure about this? We should be doing this?"

"We'll be fine. I'll see you tonight, after my date with Donnie. Study hard."

After her date with Donnie? How late would that be? Would I be alone? Would she? Did I want to risk going to jail for Maura Ferguson? Why did Wanda want to risk her career for this woman?

Or was she indeed doing it for me? And isn't that really why I was doing it? Three boxes of stuff to look through?

I needed some sleep.

CHAPTER TEN

The kid who delivered the boxes showed up a little before eleven. He wasn't cut from a cloth of intelligence, I noticed right away, so I wasn't too worried about him putting things together on his own.

He said, "You're that janitor who won the lottery, aren't you?"

"How did you know?" I asked. No, I didn't blush.

"I read the paper. I watch the news. I thought you dated that chick from the news. Leslie what's-her-name?"

"I used to. She left a few months ago," I said, not sure why I was telling this kid any of this.

"And then you hooked up with the gal with these boxes?" he asked.

Oh yes, I remembered Wanda's cover story about the books. I said, "That's right. It didn't work out either. These rebound things never do."

"What happened? Is it because she works and you don't?" he asked.

"No. I came home and found her in bed with my best friend's wife."

"No shit?"

Plenty, actually, but who did it hurt?

I said, "My friend actually took his wife back, if you can believe that."

"And the bitch kicked you out? That figures. Too bad, man."

I thanked him with a hundred dollars and sent him on his way. The boxes were heavy, but I managed to get them upstairs to what could be described as my office. There's a desk in there, and a chair, but not much else. I don't have all that much office work to do.

There's a phone on that desk, and it rang just as I cracked open the first box. It was my party planner, Helen Roth.

She said, "Jake, darling, everything is coming together for tomorrow night. It's going to be a grand evening."

"Thanks, Helen. I knew you would give me nothing less. Is there anything I can do to help? I feel a bit like an outsider at my own ball."

"I thought that's the way you wanted it, darling. But there is one little thing you could do for me. Are you busy this afternoon?"

I looked at the three boxes on my floor. I never much cared for studying. It's not that I wasn't capable; I just didn't like to do it. Maybe that's why I wound up a janitor.

Anyway, I said to Helen, "Nothing I can't get out of. What's up?"

"Well, I got a curious phone call. You asked me to put Annabella Silvestri on the guest list, and I did. Do you even know her, Jake?"

"No, we've never met. She's Leslie's friend, from college."

"Well, most everyone on the list has called to confirm their attendance, including the Ferguson woman and your Leslie. But this Annabella seemed, oh I don't know, suspicious I guess would be the word. She wanted to know why you were inviting her to a party. She wanted to talk to you. She was very persistent. I told her I'd call you and get back to her. I just got off the phone with her. Can you help me out there, darling?"

"Sure, Helen. Give me the number and I'll call her myself."

She said, "Jake, I don't need to tell you who she is, do I? She's a dangerous woman."

"No, I'm fully aware of who she is," I said.

"Be careful, darling. I'll see you tomorrow night."

"God willing," I said.

Would He be? I sure hoped so. What did Annabella need to talk to me about? Was she really that dangerous? I hadn't done anything to her, had I? Why had I invited her to my party? Did I see that flashing caution light?

Not a chance.

"Annabella Silvestri," she said, answering her phone.

"This is John Jacobs. Jake. Helen Roth and Leslie Watson both told me you wanted to talk to me. What about?"

"Do you know Guilianos? The Italian restaurant?" Her voice was like sandpaper on gravel, and low.

"I ate there on Wednesday," I said.

"Meet me there at one o'clock. We'll have lunch. Okay?"

"One o'clock, Guilianos. I'll be there."

Did she know what I looked like? Could I gain an advantage by spotting her first? Did I need to gain an advantage? Would she come alone? Would she have a gun? A knife? A hired goon? More than one? Did I mind eating Italian twice in the same week? Had she been there Wednesday, when I was with Maura? Would she let me order my own food?

I dialed again.

Wanda answered, saying, "Spencer Law Office, can I help you?"

"I've got a date this afternoon with Annabella Silvestri. I'm meeting her at one."

"I thought you were on for tomorrow. What happened?"

"She called and wanted to see me. Apparently my snooping around her brother has struck a nerve of some kind."

"What do you think she wants, Jake?"

"I don't know, but you don't say no to the mob, do you?"

Wanda was the second person to say, "Be careful."

I drove the Lexus to my lunch date. I didn't want to rely on an employee of the Silvestri family for my getaway, so no cabs. Not that I'd be able to make one if she didn't want me to. I gave the valet twenty bucks and the keys and hoped I'd see my car again.

Annabella was already seated in a booth in the back when I arrived. She was alone. If she recognized me, she didn't show it. I went to the bar and ordered a Coke and sat where I could see her. After ten minutes she was still alone, so I made my move.

She saw me coming and stood. She was wearing a pair of denim overalls with a white tank top underneath. Her hair was black and wavy and two bright gray eyes held me tight. She smiled a nice, white smile.

"John Jacobs?" she said, offering me her hand.

I took it, told her to call me Jake, and suggested we sit down. She said that sounded like a great idea, and then did just that. She said I could call her Annie.

I said, "Leslie tells me the two of you went to college together."

"Yes, in Boston. We were both in journalism. She's actually using her degree now, isn't she? I don't watch those morning news shows too much. I hadn't talked to her in several years before a couple days ago. You do lose track of people, don't you?"

"That's for sure. I never talk to anyone from college these days."

This was true, but only because I'd never gone to college. I was going to. I was accepted at the University and everything. I had a vague dream of being a history teacher. I even met my roommate on check-in day at the dorms. I don't think it was his fault, but something snapped inside me that day and I knew I couldn't stay. I made it one night and was gone before the first class began. Two weeks later my mom made me get a job and my janitorial career was born. The rest, as they say, is history.

"You never went to college, Jake," she said.

"You do your homework, Annie," I answered.

We ordered our lunches, fettuccini for her, spaghetti for me. We small-talked our way through the salads, but they sat emptied in front of us, and the main course hadn't yet arrived.

She said, "Tell me what your interest is in my brother Donnie, Jake."

"He was with Maura Ferguson the night she allegedly killed her husband and his mistress. You know about the murders?"

"Yes, I know about the murders. Donnie was with her the entire day?"

I explained to her how Maura had picked Donnie up and used his young body. I laid out the time frame for the murders, and the time Maura and Donnie were together. And I knew what was coming next.

"Where was she those first three hours?" Annabella asked.

Was lying to a known mobster a good idea? Probably not.

I said, "She was with me at a movie."

"I get it now. You want Donnie to be her alibi so you don't have to. Right?"

"More or less," I said.

"You have some reason? Are you hiding something? Maybe you're involved?"

"No, I'm not hiding anything, and I'm not involved. It's just that the police might not see it that way if they find out where she was and whom she was with. Let's just say that it would be in my best interest to not get my name brought into it."

"Because you would be each other's alibi. Because you were dating a married woman. Because there's a lot of money to be made here, even if you already have plenty. Because you bailed her out and ate lunch with her here on Wednesday."

"You're good," I said.

And I meant it.

"It's interesting that you felt you needed to sit at the bar for ten minutes before you came back here. Why is that? You thought I'd have a car with a trunk big enough for your body, a shovel, and someone with me to dig the hole. Am I close?"

"You sound like you've done that sort of thing before," I said.

She smiled but said nothing. She finished her fettuccini and drank the last of her water. She got the attention of the waiter and asked him to clear the table. He did.

She said, "My family has an interest in not having Donnie's name involved with this case."

"This case, or any case?" I asked.

"We get enough bad press as it is, Jake. Some of it we deserve and some of it we don't. We would just like to keep the stuff we don't deserve to a minimum when we can. You can understand that, can't you Jake?"

"Was the press about your fiancé deserved?" I asked in a moment of daring.

She thought for a moment, then two.

She said, "My fiancé, his death, it was an unfortunate thing. A terrible accident."

"Was it?"

Did I really think she would tell me the truth? Did I know what I wanted the truth to be? Would I believe her? She did look sad, didn't she?

"My father has maintained that it was an accident, and he doesn't lie to me," she said. "Okay?"

"Fine," I agreed.

The moment of blind courage had passed and I let it go.

"You don't think she killed them?" she asked, obviously wanting to change the subject back to the present. "Maura, I mean. You don't think she did it?"

"No, I don't."

"And you didn't kill them?"

"Definitely not," I said.

"Someone did. And they need to be found."

"I couldn't agree more. The one little problem there is that the police aren't looking anymore. They already have their arrest, so they're happy to go back to the donut shops or whatever."

"Okay," she said.

"Okay? What does that mean? Okay?"

"It means that you and I have a similar interest in finding the person who did this. And it means that I have certain resources that might help us do just that."

"Okay," I said. "I've got resources too."

I told her about the boxes Wanda Gaines had sent over. It occurred to me that my most truthful moments of the week were coming in the presence of a known criminal, but it seemed like my best option.

"You need help with those?" she asked.

Did I?

I said, "It wouldn't hurt."

"Leslie won't mind my being there?"

"Leslie left four months ago," I said.

"I have another question for you. Why did you invite me to your party? You don't know me. Leslie and I no longer talk. Why did you invite me?"

"When I took Donnie in to see Grant Spencer, I didn't know anything about his family. I quickly found out. I do my homework, too. I'm not sure what made me invite you. I think I just liked your picture."

"And my family business didn't scare you off?" she asked.

"I'm too stupid to scare easily. Besides, people have to work, don't they?"

"You don't."

"I'm the exception. I'm lazy and rich. It's a fortunate combination for me."

She raised her eyes in the direction of two different tables. Within seconds four rather large men were standing next to our booth. She didn't do any introductions, but in my head they were Tony, Vinnie, Lou, and Dom. I was probably fairly close. She told them she was fine, that they could go, and that she could be reached on her cell phone. The boys looked happy to have the afternoon off and shuffled away.

"I knew they were there the whole time," I said.

"Liar," she said with a smile.

CHAPTER ELEVEN

The last thing Leslie Watson had said to me on the phone was that she would call. As of the time I left to meet Annabella Silvestri for lunch, she still hadn't done so. If I was accessing the correct file from my memory, this meant she wasn't going to call at all. She was just going to come over. Wanda Gaines was coming over after her date with Donnie. And Annabella was sitting in the passenger seat of my Lexus.

I felt like George Clooney in *The Perfect Storm*. Was I steering my boat into three deadly storms all coming together at my house? And what about Maura? Would she be the fourth storm? Is bringing a mob boss home ever a good idea? How about re-firing an old romance? Flirting with a suspected killer? Accepting documents from a lawyer's secretary that I knew I shouldn't have any access to? Where's the rewind button?

My car, a just-off-the-line black Lexus, was returned to me unmarked. I gave the kid another twenty bucks and asked him if he'd seen a nicer car all day. He said he hadn't, but he didn't sound sincere.

My new friend Annie didn't have a car. She had ridden over with her goombahs and was now officially in my hands. This meant, of course, that I had to return her to her compound, or wherever it was she lived, once we were done examining my resources.

I said, "So which one of those guys digs the holes? Tony?"

"No, Tony drives. Vinnie's the hole digger," she said with a straight face.

I had two names right? I had to go for it. I said, "What's Lou's job then? Does he hold the flashlight? Honk the horn when trouble's coming by?"

"Lou? Lou wasn't with us. His wife just had a baby. He's got maternity leave right now. We've got a nice insurance plan for the guys."

"But there is a Lou?" I asked.

"You're funny," she said, smiling. "They're not all named Tony, Vinnie, and Lou."

"I had the fourth guy pegged as Dom," I said.

"Tony, Vinnie, Stan, and Allan," she said. "Stan and Allan are brothers. Their mother isn't Italian. I think she's Jewish, but I'm not sure."

"That's right, you're mother isn't Italian either, is she? Didn't I hear she was from somewhere in Central America?"

"What? She is if you consider St. Louis to be Central America. My mother is full-blooded Italian. She moved here when she was ten. Central America? Who told you that?"

"Grant Spencer told me," I said.

"St. Louis," she said.

"And here I sit with all these questions for you about life in the jungle with a dictator for a leader. Thanks a lot."

"Sorry," she said, smiling. I wondered if mafia people got to smile very often.

I said, "Let me ad-lib some St. Louis questions for you then."

"Okay."

"How tall is that arch on the river?" I asked.

"I have no idea," she said. "I've never even been to St. Louis."

She really had called off her dogs. I had driven at varying speeds and turned numerous corners between Guilianos and my place. I kept checking my mirror, but no one appeared to be there. It occurred to me that if she wanted someone to come along, they'd be in the car with us. I assumed she trusted me and wished I felt the same about her.

There was a red Porsche parked in my driveway as we pulled up, and it wasn't mine. It did, however, belong to Leslie. I should know, since I bought it for her with my lottery money. She had two bad habits. Driving fast was one of them. Talking on the phone, constantly, was the other. She had some good habits too, one of which we've already discussed that involves full nudity. Anyway, she had to be inside.

Let the fun begin.

"Leslie's here," I said to Annabella. "That's her car."

"Didn't you say you broke up?"

"We've called all the king's horses and all the king's men. We're trying to put Humpty Dumpty back together again. At least I think we are. Neither one of us is committing to too much yet. There's been plenty of hinting and innuendo, but neither of us has actually said we wanted to get back together. I think pride might be getting in our way."

"I see," she said. "It always does. Get in the way, I mean."

"You still want to come in?" I asked.

"It'll be awkward," she said.

"I live for awkward," I said as I turned off the ignition.

Leslie was sitting at the kitchen table, cell phone cradled against her ear, eating a cantaloupe. It hadn't come from my refrigerator, which meant she brought it. More hints and innuendo. There was a magazine in front of her, and a glass of water next to it. She was wearing the same thing she had on when she was on the air earlier.

She looked up and saw whom I was with and just about choked as she got rid of the person on the other end of the line. Her eyes kept switching from one of us to the other. Could you blame her? It was Annabella who broke the ice.

She said, "Leslie, it's so good to see you after all these years. How long has it been? Too long, too long."

Annie walked over with her arms open, asking for a hug. Leslie stood up and gave her one. I said a silent prayer of thanks.

Leslie said, "I wasn't aware you two knew each other. I talked to you both the other day about the other and neither one said anything."

"That's because until a couple hours ago we didn't know each other," I said. "Annie took me to lunch. We have a lot in common, really. We have the same objectives; maybe that would be a better way to put it."

I was sure Leslie had plenty she wanted to say to me. I could see that much in her expression, in her eyes. She looked a little afraid of Annabella, like the guy in the wedding scene in *The Godfather* whose asking Don Corleone for a favor. He knew he was in the presence of potential danger, and so did Leslie now.

Leslie said, "Jake, I just came by to see if you wanted to have lunch, maybe talk. You weren't here, so I went ahead without you. And you went ahead without me. Anyway, I've got to be back at work. We're taping some promos this afternoon, so I should really get going. Can you walk me to my car, Jake?"

Annabella hugged Leslie again. They promised each other to have lunch sometime. They both knew they would never do it.

Next to her car, Leslie said to me, "What the hell, Jake?"

"She called. I figured I had to go see what she wanted."

"Okay, I can see that much. Why the hell is she at your house?"

"We're doing each other a favor. I've got access to some information and she's got access to . . ."

"Thugs? Killers? Hit men? Take your pick, Jake. That's what those people are."

"You think I'm making a deal with the devil, don't you?" I asked.

"His daughter, anyway. Jeez, Jake. She's in the mafia. Do you get that? Do you understand that? Organized crime, Jake, with emphasis on crime. Do you know that she's not going to do you any favors just because you're cute? She's going to expect you to reciprocate with a favor of your own. Maybe a lot of favors. Are you listening to me, Jake?"

"I'll take it under advisement," I said.

"Under advisement? You better do a lot more than that with it. What did she want anyway? Is it about her brother?"

"She would just as soon not involve her brother in this, if at all possible. I would just as soon not get my name brought into it either," I said.

"Both of those are completely understandable viewpoints. Shouldn't you tell the police about them? Or at least Grant Spencer?"

"Probably."

"Probably? Probably hell, Jake. What are the two of you planning to do? Go on a manhunt or something?"

"Well ..."

"Tell me that's not it," she said.

I couldn't, because that was it. She knew, and I knew it.

She said, "Maybe we should wait a little bit. With us, I mean, maybe we should wait until this is over. It's more than I bargained for maybe. I'll call you, okay Jake?"

"Okay Leslie," I said.

"Please don't get killed, Jake," she said with a quick kiss and hug.

There were tears pushing to the front of her eyes and she didn't want me to see them. She turned away quickly, hopped in the Porsche, and left with a squeal of rubber, back out of my life again.

"Your girlfriend's upset," is how Annabella greeted me back in the kitchen.

She was sitting in the chair Leslie had just vacated. She was working her way through a bag of chips from my private stock.

"Leslie isn't my girlfriend. Didn't I tell you that?" I said.

"She's acting like your girlfriend, Jake. Is she afraid I'm going to break your legs or something?"

"Yeah, something like that. You aren't, are you?"

"No. Lou does the leg breaking."

She smiled and I wasn't sure how serious she was. I smiled back. We hadn't actually used the word 'mafia' in our conversations yet, but she wasn't exactly trying to hide her affiliation with organized crime. Did she just like to play it up, maybe? Did she like to see what sort of reaction she could get? Probably.

I took the seat across from her and eyeballed the chip bag. She gave it to me after taking a big handful herself. She reached into the refrigerator and pulled out two sodas, popped the top on each, and handed me one.

"Wanna go jogging?" I asked.

She laughed and grabbed the chip bag back from me. She was not a big woman, rather lean actually, so I didn't picture her as the junk food type. What's that about a book and its cover?

"I don't jog," she said. "I swim."

"No pool, sorry. I've got a hot tub out back though. We could swim a thousand really little laps."

"That's okay. You have any chocolate around here?" she asked.

I pointed to a cabinet behind her where she found a bag of miniature sized candy bars. They were supposed to be for Halloween. She ripped it open and pulled out a half dozen pieces. She set the bag down and tore into the first bar.

"Do you always eat like this?" I asked. "You're in good shape, it looks like, so you can't do this all the time."

"Only when I'm nervous," she said.

Interesting.

Why was she nervous? Had she told me too much about her business? Did she feel threatened without her bodyguards nearby? Had Leslie upset her? Had her soap opera had a riveting cliffhanger? Was she worried about the partnership we were about to embark on? Did she have a crush on me?

"You think I'm in good shape?" she asked.

Oh yes.

I said, "Very good shape. Do you swim a lot?"

"I try to every day, but things come up that I need to deal with from time to time, so I don't always get to."

What did she look like in a swimsuit? How about out of one? Did the thugs watch the pool while she swam? Was that considered a good job in their business? And she did look good in those overalls, didn't she?

"What are you looking at?" she asked, busting me.

"You, Annie. You asked if you were in good shape. I was just making sure I hadn't fibbed."

She smiled.

"You remind me of my fiancé," she said.

"How so?"

I hoped it wasn't because I'd look good at the bottom of a lake surrounded by airplane debris.

"The way you talk, your mannerisms, your sense of humor, your smile, and the fact that you aren't afraid of me," she said.

"I'm a little afraid."

"It doesn't show. And you don't need to be afraid of me," she said.

Was that sadness creeping into her eyes? Melancholy? Remorse? Loneliness? It sure wasn't lust, was it? Did she regret being a mafia kingpin? Or would that be queen-pin in her case? Maybe princess-pin?

"Don't take it personally. I'm afraid of all women on some level. Especially when they start smiling at me like you've been doing," I said.

She smiled again.

"Jake, I don't give the guys the afternoon off very often."

"Only when you're really hungry and want all the junk food to yourself?" I asked.

"Something like that," she said.

"The boxes are upstairs in my office," I said.

"What boxes?" she asked.

"My contribution to solving our little problems. Remember?"

"Can we forget the boxes for now?"

"I thought that's why we were here," I said.

She stood up and took my hand, pulling me up too.

She said, "Where's that hot tub, Jake?"

I pointed to the sliding glass door that led out to the back deck. This is one of those unforeseen circumstances that a person can get into every now and then. True, it usually isn't with someone in the mob, but here we were. And she did look good.

"I don't have a suit for you to wear," I said.

"I don't need one," she said.

She kicked off her shoes, peeled off her socks, unsnapped the overalls and lowered them to the deck. She climbed into the tub in her panties and tank top. I found the switch, flipped on the pump, and stripped to my boxers. I joined her in the warm water, but took a seat on the opposite side.

She leaned back against the wall, her dark arms stretched out to each side. Her head was tilted back against the edge, the ends of her hair dripping, and her eyes closed. Her feet were alternately going up and down, first one, and then the other.

"My father's dying," she said, her eyes still closed. "He's got cancer and it's going to win. And the stubborn bastard still hasn't quit smoking."

"Maybe he doesn't see the point in quitting at this stage," I offered.

"Yeah, maybe. I take over when he dies," she said.

"How long?" I asked.

"By Christmas, probably. He's already outlived the doctor's guess by six months. He's on borrowed time as it is."

"I'm sorry, Annie," I said, because I really didn't know what else to say.

"He's sticking with it right to the end. He told me to check you out. He told me to 'take care of you' if I thought you were a problem. He should be praying his ass off, making his peace with God, but he's telling me to check you out. It doesn't seem right, does it Jake?"

"That you should take care of me? No, that doesn't seem right to me," I said.

"I'm not going to do anything to you. Stop worrying."

"Okay," I said.

"After he dies I'm going to dissolve the business," she said.

"What does that mean, exactly? What would be involved with that? You don't just sell off the shares on Wall Street and retire to the country, do you?"

"Actually, yes. The corporate end is legitimate. It'll take me a couple months to find some compensation for all of the guys, and then I'm done. The Silvestri family will be out of the business world."

The way she said business, I knew she meant crime. How much money is a mafia kingdom worth? How many guys needed to be compensated? Would they look for jobs? Could they? Does that sort of thing look good on a resume'? Would the taxi service in town still be good? Why was this news making me happy?

"And then?" I asked.

"I find a nice guy who doesn't hold my past or my family's past against me, and we settle down. Maybe we have kids, maybe we don't, but I'm for sure going to get a dog. Something big, but not too big. Maybe a German Shepherd. I'm used to a certain level of loyalty, and I hear they've got that. Good looking would be nice, too, but I'm not that particular. I mean the guy, not the dog."

"You've thought about this a lot," I said.

Was I a nice guy? Did Annabella think so? Did I hold her family's past against her? Did I want kids? What about dogs? Was I good looking? Could I pass if someone wasn't too particular? Why was she telling me this?

"You understand there is a certain amount of confidentiality that I'm trusting you with here, don't you? You can't tell anyone about my father."

"I won't," I promised.

She slid around to my side of the tub. She sat next to me, pulled my arm around her shoulder, and leaned her head back again.

Did I want to lean over and kiss her? Should she make the first move? Had she already done that? Was there much of a future for a retired janitor and a retired mob queen as a couple? What would Helen say? Good luck, darling? What would Leslie say? Hello? Wasn't I just in love with Leslie an hour ago? Wouldn't she say, "What the hell, Jake?"

And then Annabella said, "Jake, someone's watching us."

CHAPTER TWELVE

Nothing can pull a person out of restful reverie like the knowledge you're being spied upon. It's also the kind of thing that makes you glad you weren't quite naked. I might not have seen them, were it not for Annabella. Paying attention must be more useful in her line of work.

"See the van, across the street? It's a red van, facing the other way about halfway down the block. Do you see it?" she asked.

And there it was, halfway down the block, facing the other way.

I said, "How do you know there's someone in there watching us?"

"You get a feel for stuff like this after awhile," she said with a shrug. "The windows are a little too dark. It's too convenient. It's parked on the other side of the street, so we wouldn't notice, but it's facing the wrong way. Things like that make you take notice. Do you know anyone who drives a van like that?"

I didn't and I told her that.

"What do we do?" I asked.

"Act naturally, for one thing. Keep doing what we were doing."

What was that again? Flirting? Cuddling? Getting ready to make out? Was she thinking the same thing I was thinking?

No.

She said, "I could call Tony and Vinnie and have them come up here. They'd take care of it. Hand me my pants over there. My phone is in the pocket."

"That might not be our best option in this neighborhood," I said.

"No? Those guys can be very discreet when the job calls for it."

"What would they do, exactly?" I asked.

"They'd knock on the window. They'd talk to the people inside. They'd ask them to move on. Then they'd kill them if they were still getting static."

Kill them? Didn't that seem a bit excessive for parking on the wrong side of the street? Could she tell I thought so? Had we crossed a line by actually talking about murder?

"Mrs. Henderson next door would crap in her diaper," I said.

"Mrs. Henderson?" she asked.

"She's about three hundred years old. She lives on the other side of this fence here with a couple dozen cats."

"I'm kidding, Jake. Lighten up."

Was she kidding? Did I know her well enough to be able to tell? Did I trust her yet? Was she just backtracking, covering what she had said?

I said, "How long have they been there?"

"I don't know. I just moved over to this side. You're the one with the view. You didn't notice them?"

"No. I think I was distracted by you," I said.

"We're going inside. I'll call Tony after a shower," she said.

She lifted herself out of the tub onto the deck, picked up her overalls, shoes, and socks and went back into my house, water trailing behind. I turned off the pump and did the same.

I handed her a towel and a dry t-shirt, told her I was fresh out of women's underwear, and pointed her toward the bathroom. I could hear the shower start up and went upstairs to dry off.

I called The Plaza and asked for Maura Ferguson. She wasn't in. Was she with Grant, working on her defense?

"Maura left about an hour ago," Wanda told me. "She said she had something she had to do and she'd be back before dinner."

"Was she alone?" I asked.

"When she left she was. What's up?"

"I'm not sure if anything is up. I just haven't talked to her today, that's all."

I went downstairs to talk to Annabella, but the shower was still running. I started picking through the chips and candy bars while I waited. The phone rang and I jumped.

93

"Maura just got back here, Jake," Wanda said.

I thanked her and looked out the window. The van was gone. Coincidence? Thirty minutes later the shower was still running and I started to think that was a little extreme. Even rich people have to pay for their water.

I knocked on the bathroom door, but got no answer. I knocked again, called her name, and still got no answer. I slowly pushed open the door and was choked by a wall of steam. I reached for the vent switch and flipped it on.

"Annie, it's Jake. Are you okay?" I called into the steam.

No answer.

I took a step toward the shower and tripped over something on the floor. Looking back I saw the naked body of Annabella Silvestri, face down, covered in blood. Alive? Dead? She sure looked dead to me.

Oh shit.

The fog cleared enough to see a lot of blood in the shower, on the walls, and all over the floor. Annabella was holding something in her right hand. Lipstick? On the mirror was a red letter M. Lipstick. It was starting to run from the moisture on the glass. There was a knife still stuck in her ribs. There were a couple footprints in the blood. There was probably a lot of other evidence in the room that I would never think to look for.

I leaned over the toilet and threw up a stomach full of chips and candy.

Had I touched anything? Should I call someone? Who should I call? Was the person who did this still in the house? Was I next? Why hadn't she called Tony from the deck? Wasn't it actually lucky for me she hadn't? Were Wanda's boxes still upstairs? Would the police find them? How long had she been in the bathroom? An hour? Why did I wait so long to check on her? When had this happened?

Who should I call?

She was dead for sure, so calling 911 could wait a couple minutes anyway. The daughter of the biggest mobster in the city was lying dead on my bathroom floor. This was not good. I turned the shower off and sat down on the toilet seat.

I looked at the knife to see if it came from my kitchen. It hadn't. It had a 'G' on the handle. Where had I seen that knife? I was shaking too much to think clearly about it. But I had seen it somewhere.

I lifted myself to my feet, grabbed a towel, and did my best to wipe the blood from my shoes. I didn't want to track it all through the house if I could help it. I stepped into the hallway and pulled the door closed behind me.

Was I imagining sirens in the distance? They were in the distance, weren't they? Were they getting closer? Had someone called the police? Mrs. Henderson, maybe? The murderer? How far away were the sirens? A mile maybe?

The phone rang and I picked it up before it could do it again.

Leslie said, "Jake, I've been thinking."

I interrupted her, "Please don't ask me to explain, Les, but would you meet me at the park? Right away? Sooner if you can?"

"Jake, what's wrong? You sound positively terrified."

"The park, Leslie. Please?"

"Okay, Jake-"

I hung up and sprinted upstairs. I grabbed a bag and threw some clothes into it. I grabbed my passport. I grabbed a wad of cash and my checkbook. I tossed the bag over my back and picked up the three boxes.

The sirens were closing and I was pretty sure they were coming to my house. I gambled that I had enough time to get to my car and get out of there. I was right, but just barely. As I turned the corner at the far end of my block I could see in my rearview mirror three squad cars, lights flashing, pull up in front of my house.

It was getting dark as the little red Porsche pulled up beside my Lexus. Leslie got out wearing sweatpants and a t-shirt, and her hair was pinned back. Off in the distance, under some lights, a group of kids were playing basketball. Lucky bastards.

Leslie climbed into the passenger side and said, "Jake?"

On the court one kid, pretty tall, did a nice crossover dribble that left his defender swinging at air. Two steps later he dunked, rattling the rim and the chain netting. I stared, transfixed by their posturing, and avoiding Leslie's eyes.

"Jake?" she said, noticeably louder this time. She put one hand on each of my shoulders and turned me towards her. "What happened, Jake?"

"Annabella is dead," I said, just above a whisper.

"Dead? Where? When? How? Why?"

"She's dead. Someone stabbed her in my bathroom. I must have been upstairs changing. It was about a half hour before you called probably. I don't know why, though I can guess. Someone is setting me up."

I explained to her everything that had happened since she left Annabella and me at my house. I told her about the hot tub and the flirting and how Annabella's dad was sick. I told her how Annie planned to sell off the business and retire once her father died. I told her about the van. And I told her about the bathroom.

"The knife is still in her back, stuck between a couple ribs," I said. "It had a capital letter G on it. Does that sound familiar to you?"

"Vaguely," she said.

"She was holding a tube of lipstick in her hand—red lipstick. On the mirror she had managed to write an M. It was running pretty bad by the time I left."

"You think that was a message?"

"Don't you?" I asked.

"Did you call the police?"

"I didn't have to. Someone else did that for me. They were pulling in as I was pulling out."

"Jake, why did you run?"

"Are you kidding? I had to run," I said.

"Let's go to the police and tell them what you just told me. You can leave the boxes from Grant's office out of it if you want. No, wait; don't leave anything out. Honesty, Jake. Tell them the truth and let them figure it out."

"Oh, they'd figure it out alright, but it wouldn't be the real truth. It would be the truth that someone out there wants them to see."

"Which is what?" she asked.

"That I killed Annabella, Sam, and Shannon," I said.

"Okay. Now what? Do we go into hiding? Do we know who we're hiding from?"

"Well, Frank Silvestri and his people for one. The police. A murderer."

She said, "Oh Jake, the M on the mirror-you don't suppose?"

"Maura Ferguson."

CHAPTER THIRTEEN

Leslie said almost no one knew she was staying at the Plaza. We decided it would take awhile for the police to connect me to her, and then awhile longer to track her down, so the Plaza seemed like our best bet.

We decided against leaving one of our vehicles at the park. We weren't in a bad part of town so much, but one doesn't need to tempt fate more than necessary. I told her I would follow behind a couple blocks and just meet her at room 1416.

Leslie caught a green light that I didn't, so we were each on our own. I turned on the radio and tried finding some local news. I had found only static when the light changed, so I ignored the dial and eased back into traffic. It was dark, and all headlights look the same in a rearview mirror, but I got the distinct feeling I was being followed.

Maura? Frank or his thugs? The police? Was it my imagination? I turned right from the left-hand lane and watched the lights behind me do the same thing.

Oh no.

I sped up, and so did they. I turned three more corners, and so did they. By the time this little chase became officially that, I was pointed away from the Plaza, not toward it. I caught a ramp onto the freeway, ducking between two cars. I thought I had lost my pursuers, but the lights popped back into view seconds later.

I didn't want to go fast enough to draw the attention of law enforcement, but I didn't particularly want to let the lights catch up to me either. This sort of thing doesn't often happen to janitors.

The only chase I ever got involved in was after a cat that had found its way into my building. His bodily functions were stinking up the place, and no self-respecting professional cleaning person can stand for that.

I caught the exit pointing back downtown and in the general direction of Leslie's hotel. When the lights did the same, I made a decision. I pulled into the next convenience store I saw, parked, and watched them do the same, right next to me.

I didn't say it was a wise decision.

Behind the lights sat a black limousine with tinted windows. I opened my door and stepped out into the cool night. I kept the door of my Lexus between the limo and me, with my hands on top so they could see them. The back window of the limo whispered down, and a hand came out. It waved me over.

Leaving the door to my car open, just in case I needed to sprint toward it and dive back in, I edged slowly toward the open window and the beckoning hand. I stopped almost in mid-step when the door opened. It was one of those doors that open backwards. Why do they have those, anyway? The hand was waving again, and I continued toward the shadows of the backseat.

I climbed in, sat down, and found myself face to face with someone I knew. I just didn't know if I should take it as good news or bad. I was leaning toward bad.

Donnie Silvestri said, "Jake, we need to take a ride."

"Take a ride as in go out in the woods and bury me alive take a ride?" I said.

"No, Jake. Take a ride, to my father's house, so we can talk."

He nodded to the tinted window between the front seat and us. I heard a door open and watched the guy Annabella said was Tony getting out. He walked over to my car, sat down behind the wheel, and closed the door.

Donnie said, "This neighborhood's a piece a shit. That Lexus wouldn't make it the night. Tony will follow us so you can get home when we're done."

"Talking," I said.

"Right, when we get done talking."

"My girlfriend will miss me," I said, meaning Leslie.

"Your girlfriend?"

"We had a date," I said.

"The red Porsche?" he asked.

"Yes."

Where had they picked up my scent? They knew about Leslie? Had they been at my house the whole time Annie was with me? Had they followed me from there? Did they get a call, telling them to bring me in? Did Frank know his daughter was dead?

Donnie said, "Don't worry about her."

"She'll worry about me," I said. "It's been a strange evening."

"Yeah, no shit. Don't worry about her. Okay?" He said it in a way I knew meant that was the end of it.

It probably was okay. Leslie would blame me, think I'd blown her off again, and we'd be two steps further from reconciliation. At least I got to ride in a limo.

Donnie was dressed in what he must have thought were stylish clothes. They reeked of seventies retro to me. It appeared he was ready for a night on the town.

"Going out?" I asked.

"Not anymore," was all he said.

Great, I ruined his plans. Or whoever decided to kill his sister in my bathroom ruined his plans. Was he blaming me? It sure seemed like he was. He had very little to say as he stared out at the passing city. After twenty minutes or so of freeway driving the lights began to thin. We were heading south, away from the city. Another ten minutes and we exited.

Did they always tell a guy they were about to bury alive that they were just going somewhere to talk? Did people actually live this far out? Was that a shovel I heard rattling around in the trunk? And what kind of cologne was Donnie wearing? Magnificent smell, wasn't it?

I did my best to hold my composure as they drove me toward what I was sure would be my death. Donnie picked up his phone and dialed.

He said, "It's Donnie," then hung up.

The driver turned off the country highway onto a dirt driveway. Ahead of us an electronic gate was just swinging open. We passed through and it closed behind us. The little road twisted up a hill through very dark woods before emerging in a well-lit parking area in front of a gigantic house.

Two guys in dark suits and sunglasses stood on either side of the front door. They must have been the mafia's version of secret service. Secret thugs? We rolled to a stop right in front of them. The thug to the left stepped to the car and opened the door. Donnie motioned, so I climbed out first and he followed.

Tony screeched the Lexus to a stop inside a garage in a string of about ten, off to the side of the house. He got out, pulled the garage door down, and walked over to our little group.

He threw me the keys and said, "Nice car. How much?"

"Sixty," I said. He seemed to nod his approval.

"Your father is waiting in the library," agent thug number one said to Donnie. Tony and I followed behind as agent thug number two opened the door for Donnie.

The house was as beautiful inside as out. Like I said, money can buy a lot of things. The library turned out to be on the third floor, and in the rear of the place. Tony was huffing and puffing pretty well when we finally reached the summit. He positioned himself to the side of the closed door, arms crossed like the guys outside.

As Donnie opened the door, I prepared myself for another scene from *The Godfather.* I expected Brando to be behind the desk with jowly cheeks and a quiet, hoarse voice. Pacino, Duvall, and the rest would be lurking in the shadows. I prepared to pucker up and kiss the Don's ring, ask for his kindness.

What I got was more like Michael Keaton at the end of *My Life*. A hospital bed was sitting where the desk should have been. The head was raised to a sitting position. Frank Silvestri was in the bed, though he was a shell of the man I'd seen in the pictures at the library.

The cancer was certainly doing its work on his body. He couldn't have weighed more than a hundred twenty. There was a tube of something running through a needle into his arm, and a small line of oxygen was hooked to his nostrils. A nurse sat in a chair to his left, reading a *People* magazine. She didn't even look up as we walked in.

There were three chairs positioned to face Frank Silvestri. Donnie took the middle one and waved me into the seat to his left. A retired janitor was sitting in the library of the most dangerous criminal in the city. Frank was in his pajamas and slippers. The place smelled like a cigar store more than a hospital. I was happy to still be alive, but this was kind of weird.

And who was that third chair for?

My question was answered when the door opened behind us. Stan and Allan, the half Jewish goombahs, had Leslie Watson with them. If they were the police she would have probably been cited for resisting arrest. She calmed down when she saw me though, and took the seat on the other side of Donnie. She spent a few seconds straightening her blonde hair, then settled in to listen.

Frank started her off with a compliment.

He said, "Miss Watson, I watch your show almost every morning."

He had to swallow hard every few words, so it came out more like this: "Miss Watson—hard swallow—I watch your show—hard swallow—almost every morning." I wondered if the swallowing was a result of the cancer, thought it probably was.

Leslie said, "Thank you, Mister?"

"Silvestri," he said. "Frank Silvestri." Two hard swallows; one by Leslie.

"We try to put on a good show every day. Some days are better than others. You know how it is," she said, maintaining her composure.

"Some days are better than others. I certainly do know how that is. And this one hasn't been particularly good, has it Mr. Jacobs?"

"Not particularly," was all I could think to say.

"You had lunch with my daughter, Annabella, today. Is that right, Mr. Jacobs?"

"Yes. And some of your employees were there as well. At Guilianos."

"Did you have the tortellini? No? Best damn tortellini in town."

"I had spaghetti. Your daughter had fettuccini, I think."

"Why did you meet Annabella for lunch, Mr. Jacobs?"

As he asked, he pulled a cigar from a box on the table beside him and lit it with a match. The nurse didn't even twitch. She must have given up.

"To talk about your son," I said with a nod toward Donnie.

He kept puffing on the cigar and staring at me. My answer must not have been complete enough for him. I assumed he knew some of this, but maybe not. Maybe the kids were telling daddy only enough to keep him posted. And certainly Annabella never made it home to tell him about lunch.

I said, "Donnie was with a friend of mine on Monday. That friend is now being tried for murdering her husband and his mistress. The murders also took place on Monday. Donnie is my friend's best alibi."

"Donnie?" he said to his son.

"Yes, sir. I was with her for part of the afternoon and evening on Monday. She didn't kill anyone when I was with her."

"You said best alibi, Mr. Jacobs," Frank said. "What do you mean by that?"

"I mean he wasn't with her the entire time in which the murders were possibly committed. There are a few hours still unaccounted for."

"My son will be no one's alibi. Is that clear, Mr. Jacobs?"

"Your daughter told me as much at lunch," I said.

Was Frank just trying to figure out what his daughter did with her last few hours of life? Was he trying to come up with a good reason to kill me? Why was Leslie here? Did Frank even know Annabella was dead?

"Are you talking about the Ferguson murders, Mr. Jacobs?" he asked me.

"Yes. Maura Ferguson is a friend of mine."

"Is she a friend of yours too, Miss Watson?"

"No. We've never met," Leslie said.

"My people tell me that Maura Ferguson is guilty, Mr. Jacobs. You don't agree?"

"No. Well, I'm not really sure. She's my friend, so it would be hard for me to see her as a killer."

"I know killers. For the most part they're no different from the rest of the citizenry. Most of the time you can't tell by looking at someone if they are capable of killing. And when you throw in a cheating spouse, well, all bets are off."

He had to swallow a whole bunch of times to get through that speech. I had to grant him that he knew more about killers than I did. Unfortunately I've got this stubborn streak that sometimes doesn't let me listen to a reasonable argument.

I said, "I'm sure you're right, Mr. Silvestri. I just don't think she did it."

Leslie broke in with, "Mrs. Ferguson was with Jake that afternoon. He is her alibi for the rest of the time in question. For some reason he doesn't want that known."

Thanks, Leslie.

I said, "That's true. We were at a movie. I think I'd be a suspect myself if they knew it was me she had been with. That's all."

"You didn't kill them though, did you Mr. Jacobs?" Frank asked.

"No. I didn't kill anyone," I said.

"Anyone? Is there someone else I would think you had killed?"

"Well, Annabella. Isn't that why we're here?" I asked.

He raised his eyebrows and squinted in my direction. He picked up the phone beside him and mumbled something into it. He quickly set it back down and peered at me through his cloud of cigar smoke. He said nothing. I imagined a man with a Tommy gun was about to walk through the door and blow me away. I just hoped they would spare Leslie.

I said, "Leslie wasn't there. She wasn't at my house this afternoon when it happened. It was just me and your daughter."

The door opened and it wasn't a man with a Tommy gun.

It was Annabella Silvestri.

CHAPTER FOURTEEN

"Jake, that sure looks like Annabella to me," Leslie said to me across our friend Donnie. Sarcasm didn't sound so bad coming from her mouth.

Donnie was kicked back, one leg crossed over the other, hands behind his head. He was wearing the grin of a shit eater.

"It sure does, Les," I said.

"What the hell, Jake?" she asked.

I just shrugged and turned to Annabella.

"You didn't check the body very closely, did you Jake?" asked Annie.

"It was foggy in there. The body was face down. It had hair about like yours, and it was female. I just assumed. I didn't want to touch it and leave prints or anything."

"It wasn't me," she said.

"I figured that out, Annie," I said.

"I was in the shower when I heard the door open. It needs a little shot of WD40 or something, because it's got a sort of squeak to it. Anyway, I thought it might be you, getting your nerve up or something, so I looked through the curtain at the mirror. I saw a woman with a knife. I stepped to the back of the tub and grabbed her when she threw open the curtain."

"Did you have to kill her?" I asked.

"As it turns out, yes I did. She was like a female terminator or something. She just kept coming and coming. I hit her a couple times, but she took it. The killing part was actually kind of an accident. I grabbed her hand with the knife and pulled it hard behind her back.

She did a quick spin right into the damn thing. I dropped the body to the floor of the tub and it didn't seem to want to move anymore."

"Dead people usually don't," I said.

"Right."

"Why was she naked?" Leslie asked, which I thought was a very good question. She's such a reporter.

"I took her clothes off," she said.

"Why?" was Leslie's follow-up.

"The van outside. I guessed they would be looking for that woman to come out of Jake's house. I put her clothes on so they would think I was her."

"But wouldn't they have been waiting for her to come back to the van?" I asked.

"Maybe. I just waved in their direction when I came out and they took off. There's probably a car around there somewhere that she was supposed to get into and drive away in."

"You didn't look for it?" I asked.

"No. Tony and Vinnie were just around the corner, keeping an eye on things. I just went and hopped in the backseat and left."

"So you didn't trust me as much as I thought you did," I said.

"Trust is earned over time, Jake. Especially in my world."

"I'm a little bothered that you didn't say anything to me when you left. It would have made my day a whole lot less stressful," I said.

"I called upstairs. You didn't answer. I figured you were dead. I didn't know if she was alone in the house, and I didn't want to snoop around too much to find out."

"Did you call the police?" I asked.

"No. Why would I call the police?"

"I don't know. Someone called them. They were pulling in as I was pulling out."

"Which means you are now a wanted man, Mr. Jacobs." It was Frank, retaking control of things. "You must be wanted at least for questioning in this murder, since it took place at your house. And you are nowhere to be found."

"Wonderful," I said.

"You must truly disappear, Mr. Jacobs. You know that, don't you?"

Annie said, "Daddy, be careful what you say to him. He has a habit of interpreting everything we say to mean we're going to kill him."

The old man let out a throaty laugh. "I'm not fucking Marlon Brando," he said, followed by laughs from everyone in the room but Leslie and me.

"Why is Leslie here?" I asked. "She surely isn't going to be wanted for this."

"She's here because you called her, Mr. Jacobs. You told her about this. If you were to disappear, she'd start asking questions. That would do no one in this room any good. So she disappears too." Frank was obviously a man used to getting his way.

"You don't think a missing news anchor will raise some questions?" I asked.

"We've got the weekend. We'll deal with it when we need to deal with it," he said between a couple very hard swallows.

This talking was taking a toll on the man. Christmas was still two months away. It didn't look like he was going to make it.

That was the end of our summit meeting with Frank Silvestri. His eyes closed and his breathing relaxed and before I knew it, he was asleep. Annabella took the cigar from his hand and stomped it out in an ashtray. She took the glasses off his face and set them on the table beside his bed. She turned off the light behind him and led us all back into the hall. She said something quietly to the nurse, and then closed the door on her father.

The hallway was wide and tall, but there were several of us crowding the space. Donnie was dressed like an extra from *Saturday Night Fever*, and he was starting to fidget. And then I remembered Wanda. She was Donnie's date. Poor thing, she probably had no idea what she had in store.

I said, "Donnie, I see you've got on your boogie shoes."

"Remember the secretary? From the lawyer's office?"

"Your lucky day, huh?" I said.

"We shall see," he said. And then, to his sister, "Can I go now?"

"Stay out of trouble, Donnie," she said. He was around the corner before she finished the sentence.

"Are we prisoners here?" Leslie asked Annie.

"That's an ugly way to put it, don't you think? It's for your own good to not be found. Or at least it is for Jake. You're our guests."

"What would happen to us if we tried to leave?" Leslie asked.

"Please don't," Annie answered.

Annie proceeded to tell us there were rooms waiting for each of us, down on the second floor. She said we could eat, that we just needed to call the cook, who was on twenty-four hour call. The Silvestri Inn, at your service.

"Can we just share a room?" Leslie asked.

"If you want to. Just pick one of the two," Annie said.

"It's been a weird day. I'd feel better having some company around. You understand."

"Sure, I understand. Look, we were the same size in college and you don't look like you've changed too much. I'll send some clothes up later. You probably don't want to wear sweatpants the whole time you're here."

Were they the same size? Would Leslie want to wear Annie's clothes? What sort of clothes was she going to send up? Jeans? Dresses? Naughty nighties? And why did Leslie really want us to share a room? Was she not planning on wearing much clothing?

Annie didn't even take us to our room. Tony did. He wasn't that bad of a guy, I guess, for a professional criminal. He did say he liked my car. Maybe he was looking forward to claiming it when I was dead.

He left us alone after showing us the phone and the television controls. The room was set up with a satellite dish and a big screen. I wondered if the pimply kid who sold me my home theater had sold to the Silvestri family. Maybe they just took what they needed, as a favor.

Leslie disappeared into the bathroom to do what women do in there. I found the news and waited to see my house and maybe my smiling face. Neither ever showed up. A murder, especially as gruesome as this one, should have been the top story. It wasn't even the human-interest piece that comes on after the sports. Leslie agreed with me that it seemed a little mysterious. She suggested calling people at her newsroom, but didn't do it. Paranoia was taking over a little, and we both thought the conversation wouldn't be a private one.

"Where did they get you?" I asked her when the news was over.

"The elevator. They grabbed me before I could get on. I didn't even know I was being followed. And they wouldn't tell me who they were or where they were taking me. Would that have been so hard? I was scared to death. Couldn't they have just said I was being brought out here? These people are different."

"They're crooks, remember? I think you're the one who told me," I said.

"Oh, yeah. Where'd they get you?"

"I picked them up behind me almost right after I lost you. Stupid me, I stopped to see who it was."

"They would have just grabbed you at the hotel too," she said.

"I suppose," I said.

"I was happy to see you in there, Jake. I've never been so happy to see you."

I smiled and said, "Why are we in the same room, Les?"

"I don't trust them. I'm not letting you out of my sight again if I can help it. And you should be damn glad that I'm not. You don't seem to be doing a very good job with this whole thing."

"What do you mean? It's not exactly my area of expertise," I said.

"I mean that everything you've done since Sam Ferguson got murdered has been wrong. Tell me that isn't the truth."

"I found Donnie, to help out Maura and Grant," I offered.

"Which is why we're in this bedroom right now," she said.

"It's also why you came to see me last night. That's a good thing, isn't it?"

"That's not why I came to see you, Jake. Try to pay attention. I came to see you because I miss you. The whole thing with Annabella was just a convenient cover."

"But it got you moving, didn't it?" I asked.

109

"Okay, we'll call that one a wash," she said.

"What else have I done that's so awful?"

"Well, you haven't told anyone the truth about Monday; at least not anyone that can help you out. You took legal documents that weren't yours. Three boxes of them. That's illegal as well as dumb. You were in a hot tub with a mafia leader. You let her kill someone in your house while you were upstairs blow drying your hair or something."

"Okay, Leslie, I get the point."

"Do you? Are you done? Are you all done playing cops and robbers? This is for real, Jake. Ask the corpse in your bathroom. Do you want to end up like her?"

"Can I ask you something? It's been bothering me since Annie told us what happened in the bathroom. Do you mind?"

"Do I have a choice?" she asked.

"The lipstick. Where did the lipstick come from? Annie took the woman's clothes, and she took her own. Where did the lipstick come from?"

"Maybe it fell out of one of their purses. Who cares? Does it really matter?"

"Not as much as this. When did that dead person right the M on the mirror? Annie didn't mention it."

"Because it wasn't there when Annie left. Jake, it couldn't have been there."

"Which means the woman wasn't dead yet when Annie left, right?" I asked.

"I guess that's true. Annie said she dropped the body on the floor of the tub. Is that where you saw it?"

"No. I tripped over it when I walked in. She was lying right in the middle of the room, in front of the sink," I said. "How did she get there?"

"You've got to stop asking so many questions, Jake."

We both jumped a little and turned toward the door where Annie was standing, a stack of clothes in her hands. How long had she been there? Hadn't we locked that door? How did we not hear it being opened? Did she forget the nightie?

Leslie's hand grabbed mine instinctively as we both sat silent, staring at Annabella. She walked over to the bed and set the stack of clothes on it, next to Leslie. She stepped back and smiled, and then she laughed a quiet laugh.

She said, "I'm on your side, remember? Relax. Get some sleep. Or don't. Lord knows you could both use a good fuck." And then she left, locking the door behind her.

Leslie turned back to me, eyebrows raised above a grin.

She said, "You can't say no to the mafia, Jake."

And calling it good would be an understatement.

CHAPTER FIFTEEN

Did this mean we were a couple again? Had Leslie made her peace with my multimillionaire lifestyle? Was she going to allow me to continue hanging out at the courthouse? Or, was this just maintenance sex? And what exactly is being maintained with maintenance sex? Were Tony and Vinnie sitting somewhere listening to the heavy breathing, screaming, and grunting and so forth from our extended lovemaking, through the magic of a microphone? Had they ever taken part in maintenance sex? Had Annie? Was there a video camera somewhere? Were they watching? Was Annie? Was I destined for porn stardom? Would that be porndom? Is the woman required to stop when you finally drop from exhaustion? Or, is that more of a general guideline for women to follow at their discretion? And does it really come into play that often? Did I really care?

No. I had just gotten laid and that was that. Good night, over and out.

Saturday started with cartoons. I wasn't watching them, Leslie was. I woke up and she was cackling like a three-year old, watching Bugs Bunny and his pals. She had already showered and was dressed in a pair of Annie's jeans and a tank top. She was barefoot and sitting cross-legged on the floor, not more than five feet from the set. Her hair was still wet. She didn't have the look of someone who wanted to join me, so I hit the shower alone.

When I got out, Bugs had turned into George Jetson, but not much else had changed. I dressed in the same dirty clothes I had worn the night before. Annie's clothes didn't fit me.

Leslie said, "You're not wearing that same shirt, are you?" Which meant, of course, that I shouldn't. "Annie brought a couple things for you, too."

I went to the pile and found a green polo shirt and a New York Yankees t-shirt. I went with the Bronx Bombers. There was also a package of boxers that hadn't been opened and some socks that looked and smelled clean. I changed quickly and presented myself to Leslie.

"At least you won't smell bad," was all she said.

I considered discussing the implications of our late night romp in the hay but voted myself down. That's a conversation men shouldn't go into when still caught in the haze of the post-coital thankfulness stage, or PCTS. Leslie would bring it up, I reasoned, when Leslie was ready.

"Jake," she said, "What did last night mean?"

Damn, I guess she was ready now. The PCTS, I should tell you, tends to be much shorter for most women than men.

"I think it means we still like each other," I said, trying to stick with the safe road, not committing to anything too soon.

"That's it?" she asked, obviously hoping it wasn't.

"It also means we fit together good. Really good," I said.

She smiled, but still didn't seem satisfied.

She said, "Jake, am I going to have to start looking for a place to live?"

"Why don't you ask Annie? It looks like they have room."

"Be serious. I can't keep paying two hundred dollars a night for a bed to sleep in and cable TV. I don't care how good the room service is or how many clean towels they bring me. That starts to add up pretty quickly."

I was the one paying the two hundred a night, but why nitpick?

I said, "I would be happy to have you back at my house, but you left me without much explanation. And now you've left Lance without much explanation. I won't feel comfortable with you moving back in until you do some explaining."

"That's fair. When this is over I'll tell you everything and then you can decide. Okay?"

If I had said those words I would be labeled a commitment-phobic or something, because that's the way the world sees us men. It's not fair, but life is like that sometimes. For all the men of the world, I should have called her on it. I chose to let Leslie slide though, because I really wasn't ready for that discussion yet.

"Breakfast?" I asked.

"Starving," she said.

She stood and kissed me, straightened my hair a little, took my hand, and led me into the hall. Tony was there, magazine on his chest, asleep in a chair. Leslie gave me a "shh" sign and we tiptoed past the big, snoring Italian. We found the steps and took them down to the first floor. A goon we hadn't met yet was waiting for us when we reached the front door.

He said, "Can't let you leave. Boss' orders."

"We're looking for something to eat," I said.

"Kitchen's in the back. Just follow that hall back beyond the steps, all the way back, then turn left. You can't miss it."

Before I won the lottery I lived in apartments that were smaller than that kitchen. It was all shiny stainless steel appliances, wood floors, and hard-marble countertops. If I cooked, I'd have thought I had died and gone to heaven. My kitchen consists of a refrigerator for beverages and a phone to order take-out.

Leslie tends to be a bit more domestic than me, so she found some eggs and cheese and stuff and whipped us up a couple of omelets. We tore into them without speaking, the way couples that have been together awhile do.

As we finished Donnie joined us. He hadn't showered and looked a little rough around the edges. He smelled like a bar, all cigarettes and beer. Poor Wanda.

I asked, "Good night last night, Donnie?"

"Not bad," he said. He grabbed a carton of orange juice and stumbled back out the door he had come in. Poor Wanda.

Perceptive as always, Leslie said, "You know something about his date?"

"Wanda Gaines. Grant Spencer's secretary. She gave me the files and was going to help me go through them last night after her date. Her date with Donnie."

"You weren't home, though. What do you suppose she thought of that?"

"She thought you might be dead," came a new voice on the far side of the room. It was Wanda Gaines, in the flesh. Poor Wanda.

I introduced Leslie to Wanda, but was too stunned to say anything more. Wanda didn't have that problem.

She said, "Why are you here? Did your date go better than you had planned?"

"I might want to ask you the same thing," I said.

Leslie said, "Jake, what date?"

"With Annie," I said. "I was supposed to be with her and Wanda with Donnie so we could find out what the underworld knew of our neighborhood murders."

To Wanda Leslie said, "Jake is here with me. They grabbed us up and brought us here. It wasn't an optional thing. You too?"

"Not exactly," she said.

Was this the same Wanda that had ridiculed Donnie every time we had spoken of the boy? Was that ridiculing a mask for her true feelings? Was she just using her assets to get the information we needed? Was she doing it for me? Was she ashamed?

She said, "That boy can dance, let me tell you. Oh my, can that boy dance."

She started to shake her own groove thing right there in the kitchen. Leslie's eggs had tasted too good to throw back up, so I had to act quickly.

I said, "So, did you find anything out?"

"No, I didn't. But I didn't really ask. Did I tell you how that boy could dance?"

And then she danced through the door and back to who-knows-where to do who-knows-what with Donnie. Poor Wanda.

Alone again, I said, "Wanda's crossed over to the dark side."

"You mean she isn't normally like this?"

"Hardly. She's the one who told me to get you back. She saw that I was heartsick and told me to grow some balls and tell you about it." *Oops.*

Leslie must have filed that for later use because she said, "Where are those boxes? Weren't they in your car? Where's your car?"

"My car is out front of the house in one of the many garages they have here. The boxes were in there last night, so I would assume they still are."

"Can we see?" she asked.

"How are we getting by the goon out front?" I asked.

"Leave that to me," she said.

She told me to let her go out the front door first and give her ten minutes. To set the hook, she said. She reached inside her tank top and unsnapped her bra, snaking it off without undressing. She rolled it into a small pile and shoved it in my front pants pocket. She reached up and gave me a kiss and said, "Ten minutes," as she tapped my watch.

A woman can do plenty to a man in ten minutes. I tried not to think about that. It was a very long six hundred seconds, but I waited for them all to pass.

I opened the door a crack to see what I could see. There was no one standing right there, so I opened it enough to squeeze through. The line of garages was off to my right, and Leslie was off to my left.

One of the limos was sitting there with the hood up. Leslie was leaned over, looking at the engine like it was the most fascinating thing she'd ever seen. The goon kept pointing at things, in between trying to look down her shirt. I could have driven a tank from the front door to my car and that guy wouldn't have noticed.

Men are such pigs.

Lucky for me, I picked the correct garage stall on my first try. I tried to raise it as quietly as I could, just in case someone else was around. Inside I found a light switch, flipped it on, and pulled the door closed behind me.

My keys were in my pocket, padded nicely by Leslie's bra. I dug them out and let myself into my car. The boxes were there, right where I had left them. I grabbed all three, opened the garage door, shut off the light, and closed the door behind me on the way out.

Leslie must have seen all this, because she was at the front door of the house by the time I got there. Her new friend was too. He stepped toward me, like maybe he didn't think I should have those boxes, but Leslie was quicker.

"James," she said to the goon, "He's just got some work to do. Annabella said it was okay. She said we shouldn't leave, but we could sure get our work done."

She smiled, leaned a little forward, and he caved. She thanked him and followed me back upstairs.

"I don't think I want to know what the two of you talked about," I said.

"Pistons and horsepower and the proper way to lube an engine. I never knew cars were so sexual."

"At least he'll have a nice story to tell about the celebrity he met. The one who doesn't like to wear underwear," I said.

"Might help my ratings," she said.

Back in the bedroom we spread the three boxes out in front of us on the floor. They weren't labeled, so we really didn't know where to begin. And even if they had been labeled, we both knew enough to know that we still wouldn't know where to start.

"What are we looking for in here?" she asked, which was a good question.

"Lightning," I said. "A spark. Something that might tell us where to look or what to do. I was hoping Wanda would be able to explain some of it to me, but I guess we'll just have to wing it."

I fell back on the bed and wished this would all go away. Leslie opened up one of the boxes and started pulling things out. Then she opened the second, and finally the third. I stared at the ceiling.

She seemed to be going through the files fast. I heard paper shuffling very quickly. I figured she was organizing the mess, assuming it was a mess.

And then she said, "What the hell, Jake?"

I sat up and looked at the boxes. All the file folders I could see had a heading typed onto the little tab, which wasn't unusual.

Leslie handed me one of the files and said, "Look inside."

It was a thick file, full of paper. I looked at every sheet.

I said, "What the hell, Leslie?"

Every single sheet was blank.

CHAPTER SIXTEEN

The question at this point became quite simple. Who was yanking our chain, and why were they tugging so damn hard? Every sheet in every file in all three boxes was blank. I'm sure because we checked them all. A random sample wasn't going to be enough for us. There was only one possible explanation, and I didn't like it.

Someone in the Silvestri household had taken the real files and replaced them with the blanks. It would have been a tedious job, but Leslie and I had been preoccupied with being naked, so they had the time. And I bet most mob soldiers do what they're told without asking too many questions.

Why? Why were the Silvestris doing this to me? I'd have gladly shared my files with them. Isn't that why Annabella was at my house in the first place? Did this mean she wouldn't be sharing her resources with me after all? Or anything else?

"We're leaving," I said to Leslie as we put the last file back into its box.

"Those files are here somewhere. They're in this house, aren't they? Why leave?"

"Those files *might* be in this house. They also *might* be shredded. And no matter where those files are, we aren't even sure there's anything in them that will help us. Not only that, I know where there's another set of the very same files."

"Grant Spencer's office," she said, coming to the same conclusion.

"Let's go," I said as I helped her to her feet.

Leslie went first, flashed some more cleavage at James, and lured him into the back of the limo. When the door closed, I ran to the driver's door, jumped in, and was overjoyed to find the keys in the ignition. I fired it up, slammed it into gear, and kicked up pebbles all the way down the twisting driveway. The gate was closed, but no one was standing watch. I just gunned the engine and hoped for the best. The gate barely put up a fight.

When I was on the pavement I pushed the car to ninety miles per hour and lowered the shaded window so I could make sure Leslie was okay. She was. James' jacket was off, and Leslie was holding his shoulder holster. She had another, smaller gun in the other hand. James had the look of a dead man.

Leslie told me to pull over, so I did. There were no other cars around on a Saturday morning a million miles from anywhere. Leslie made James get out and he complied without a single word of protest. He seemed resigned to his fate.

Leslie climbed through the open window into the front with me, throwing the guns on the floor at her feet. She stared back at James' shrinking body as we raced back toward the city.

"Wasn't that the exit for Grant Spencer's office?" Leslie asked as I drove by that very thing.

"We're not going to Grant's office," I said.

"Where are we going, Jake?"

"To get Maura," I said.

"Are you insane?" It wasn't a scream, but it only missed by one or two decibels.

"Maybe I am," I said.

"And all this time I thought when people said they had their brains fucked out it was just an expression," she said. "Next time I'll have to show a little more restraint."

"Please don't," I said.

"Jake, this is crazy. You know that, don't you?"

"Why? What has Maura done to us? Nothing, that's what. Someone else wrote a letter that just happens to be the first one in her name on a mirror with red lipstick, but that doesn't mean she was there. She might have been, but how am I supposed to know who's telling me the truth and who's lying?"

"I still say it's crazy," she said.

"This whole thing is crazy. Why is this really any more crazy than the rest? I have questions and I think Maura has answers. I want those damn answers. Is that crazy?"

"Strangely, that sounds fairly sane, unless I'm as crazy as you. Where's Maura? She's not at her house, is she?"

"She's staying at the Plaza," I said, "Just like you."

I pulled the limo into the valet area and told the guy to keep it handy. I gave him a fifty, which he seemed to like. Leslie had stashed the firearms into one of the liquor cabinets in the back. As we walked toward the hotel, I wondered if maybe we should have kept them with us.

"Do you know what room she's in?" Leslie asked.

"Fourteen sixteen," I said.

"Asshole," she said with a playful punch to my arm. "That's me."

"You're right. I never made it to her room either. We'll find out where she is at the desk if we can."

We couldn't.

The stuffy bastard on weekend duty wasn't the same one who had passed my note to Leslie. This guy couldn't be bought. And I tried. He said there were privacy issues and safety issues and so on. He kept using the word issues.

So we went to the bar. Leslie said she needed a beer and I sure needed something. We ordered two cold drafts and settled in. By the time we were on our fourth round nothing had happened. Well, I shouldn't say *nothing* happened. Leslie was drunk and I was on my way.

We had started in chairs on opposite sides of a small table and had worked our way to a small booth in the back, sitting on the same side. I suppose someone could have seen us if they had wanted to, but no one seemed to be looking that hard. If I would have been watching us, I might have suggested getting a room. We already had one of those.

"Wanna get lucky, Jake?" she asked, one hand on my thigh, the other around my shoulders. Her mouth was in the process of visiting every spot on my face and neck.

"Yes," I said.

Simple answers are best when dealing with someone in that never-never land of drunkenness where they've had enough to lose their inhibitions, but not enough to pass out or throw up.

"Room fourteen sixteen," she said. "The key is in my purse."

I fumbled through her purse, which would be more accurately described as a backpack with some style. I found the key eventually and we were on our way to the exit when Maura finally showed up.

I saw her before Leslie did, so I pushed Leslie down into the nearest booth. She wobbled on the way down, but survived. I slid in behind her and pointed to the elevator doors where Maura stood, waiting for them to open. When they did, she stepped in and the doors closed behind her.

"If she hasn't done anything to us, why are we hiding from her, Jake?"

"A simple safety precaution," I said.

We staggered to the spot she had just been standing and watched the numbers keep going up. They stopped only once, at the fourteenth floor.

"What the hell, Jake?" Leslie asked. I think she burped too.

"Just a weird coincidence?" I offered, half-heartedly.

We looked at each other and back at the floor counter. It was on its way back down. We stepped to the side where she wouldn't have been able to see us, but we needn't have bothered. When the doors opened, she didn't get off.

"Now what?" Leslie asked.

"I don't suppose getting lucky is an option anymore?"

"It's always an option, Jake. Is that what you want? Or should we go snoop around up there and look for Maura?" Against my better judgment and years of lessons to the contrary I said, "Maura."

122

On the way up Leslie said she was getting cold in her tank top, could we please go to her room first so she could change clothes. I said yes. Leslie then decided it was a good time to become unconscious as she passed out, just outside the sliding elevator door. Lucky for her I already had my arm around her. I caught her before she hit the floor, and lifted her up into my arms. I chose to drop her off in her room and continue the search for Maura on my own.

I shouldn't have.

When I opened the door to her room, I recognized the reddish-brown hair at once. Maura Ferguson was sitting on the couch, watching television, like this was her room or something. To say I was surprised would be selling it a bit short.

"I think your girlfriend's tired, Jake," Maura said. "She is your girlfriend, isn't she? Some people think I am though. Isn't that cute? You're getting quite a reputation up in the neighborhood, or so I hear."

I didn't say anything. I don't think I had it in me. Didn't Leslie tell Frank Silvestri she had never met Maura? Was that a lie? Why was Maura in this room? Were they staying together here? And if they were, what exactly did that mean?

"Do you always get so quiet when your lady love passes out?" Maura asked. "I'll have to remember that if I'm ever in her position and want some peace and quiet. Just fake a little blackout and you'll finally shut your mouth."

I didn't say anything. I was too busy deciding if Leslie knew Maura would be in this room. And if she did, was I screwed?

Maura kept talking, "Poor Jake's been through quite a bit this week, hasn't he? Is that why you're so quiet? Murder can be so tiresome sometimes, Jake."

"Excuse me," I finally blurted out. "What?"

"What? Is that the best you can do, Jake? Leslie, you've slept with the man. Talk to him. Oh, I'm sorry, she's a little unconscious. I said murder's tiresome, Jake, isn't it?"

I looked from Maura to Leslie and back again. There were connections being made in my head, I just wasn't in any sort of position to access them as I stood in that hotel room. These two should not, could not, be together. I tried to set Leslie on the couch as softly as I could and turned her head to the side.

I said to Maura, "How did you get in here?"

"Just like you. I used a key," she said. "I just told the guy at the desk I was Leslie Watson and he handed it right over. He must not watch the morning news."

"How long have you two known each other? You and Les—how long?" I asked.

"Oh, we don't technically know each other. I met Leslie at the big New Year's Eve bash at Helen Roth's place. Isn't that right, Les? I keep forgetting. She's not going to talk to us right now, is she? She may not remember anyway. It wasn't a long conversation, just two jilted women at the bar, getting a drink. Were you there, Jake?"

"No, I missed that one," I said.

"That's right. You were sick that night. I remember Leslie telling me about it. She said you stayed home and watched Dick Fucking Clark on the television and she had to go to the party all by herself. Those were here exact words, too. Dick Fucking Clark."

She laughed to herself, and I knew she was telling the truth. Leslie had used those same words as she slammed the door on her way out that night.

"I *was* sick," I said.

"Sure you were, Jake," Maura said. "So was Sam. Or at least, so he said. He was with Shannon Powell, that fucking whore."

"And so the two of you . . ." I let my insinuation trail off.

"No Jake, I didn't sleep with your girlfriend. We just talked, real quick and short. We aren't lovers or anything, not that Leslie's not a good-looking woman. I think you'd agree with me that she is. But this isn't your lucky night, if that's what you were thinking." She had a good chuckle at my expense with that one.

"Why are you here again?" I asked.

And what was with the attitude? Had I done something to her that I was too insensitive to notice? Wasn't she supposed to be my friend? Aren't women confusing?

"I'm here to talk to Leslie. I didn't expect you. I have a proposition for her," she said. "It's business."

"What kind of business could you possibly have with her? And what could you possibly have in common?"

"Well," she said coyly, "I should really wait and talk about this with Leslie."

"I'll get her the message," I said. "What do you think you have in common?"

"Well, you for starters, the way you brutally killed my husband and his girlfriend," she said.

"What?"

"I won't miss *her*, so don't sweat it. But Sam was my husband. *Him* I'll miss. At least his income; that's a hard thing to replace."

"I didn't kill them, Maura. How could I have? And where is this coming from?"

"You've been ignoring me, Jake. It's given me plenty of time to sit around and think. I thought of this."

"And what is *this*, exactly?"

She said, "Suppose this is what happened Monday afternoon. I dropped you off at your house and you went to the door and opened it. You waved at me and I left. I assumed you went inside. I was a little bit disappointed. I thought Monday might be the day you finally asked me inside and made your move. Leslie here had been gone several months and you seemed interested. God knows I wasn't being subtle about wanting it.

"But I went home anyway because a girl doesn't like to be too pushy. I stopped at the market on the way to pick up some milk. In the meantime you must have gathered the nerve you needed, because when I rounded the corner in front of my house, I saw your black Lexus parked on the street in front of my house."

What in the name of Columbo was she talking about? I didn't like the sound of anything she was saying, and I sure didn't like where I thought it was heading.

Maura kept talking, "Well, I watched your car, out of curiosity more than anything. I guessed you would ring the bell, find out I wasn't home, and leave. I was set to intercept you in the driveway. But you never got out of your car. I know. I waited for forty-five minutes, more or less. I figured you were waiting for me to come back, so I went ahead and went in and parked in my garage.

"I figured Sam would be home any minute and it would be no good for us to be found naked in bed when he arrived. I pulled into my garage, got out, saw that Shannon and Sam were already inside, and left. I forgot all about you—sorry—and I spent the night with the pretty boy from the bar.

"The next morning I went home, and the police were there, waiting for me. It wasn't hard for me to put two and two together once I figured out who was dead and when they were killed."

"You think I killed them?" I asked.

"Yes," she said. "Or, at least that's what I'm going to tell the police. Why else would your car have been there, Jake? You killed them."

"Won't they wonder why you didn't tell them about it right away?" I asked.

"Sure, they might. I think they'll understand the stress I was under and how forgetting something like your car was a simple thing to do. They'll believe me, Jake, because I'll be telling them the truth. They'll check the evidence in my house and they'll believe me."

I hadn't killed anyone. And I was fairly sure she knew that. Those two facts, when put together, equaled frame-up. She thought she and Leslie were going to frame me for murdering Sam and Shannon? I understood why Maura would want to do that, to clear her self and get Sam's money, but Leslie? I thought she loved me still and would never go for it. I thought—it doesn't matter what I thought. And Leslie was in no condition to answer for her self.

"What's in this for Les?" I asked.

There was nothing for her to gain, was there?

"You've been kind of busy at the courthouse, haven't you Jake? I bet you never bothered to actually stop and talk to a lawyer, did you?"

"Why would I?" I asked.

"Your will," Maura said. "You talked about needing one that first Monday we spent watching movies, at your house. Did you ever get around to drawing one up?"

Damn, damn, damn. Procrastination is all well and good—until it jumps up and bites you in the ass. Leslie and I had been together more than two years. In this state, that means common law marriage. If I were to die, she'd inherit my estate, assuming we were still together.

"We broke up. Leslie left. Remember?"

"Details," she said, "And the kind that can be smoothed over with plenty of cash. The kind we'll have if this plan flies like I think it will."

"So you're after my money?" I asked.

"No, not directly. Leslie will be. I'll get Sam's pot of gold once you're convicted," she said. "And Leslie will give me half of your money as the creator of this grand plan. We'll call that a finder's fee or something."

"They'll have to convict me," I said. "If they don't, neither of you gets paid."

"They'll have to do more than convict. They'll have to give you the death penalty," she added. "I think they will, don't you? Does a grieving, crying widow help with that sort of trial?"

I hadn't killed anyone. Not yet. Which meant . . .

"When did you kill them? Was it right after you dropped me off?" I asked, calling her bluff.

"You're not listening, Jake," Maura said. "*You* killed them."

"I'm not talking about fabrication. I'm talking about fact. Make up all the stories you want. Lie to the police, the press, and everybody else if you'd like. The fact remains that someone killed those two people. And that someone, if they're in this room, is you. But I don't think you did it, probably because I'm too stubborn to see the truth. But someone did kill them, because they are certainly dead."

"And you still want to find them?" Maura asked. "How noble of you."

"Now more than ever," I said. "Don't you? You've sort of made it a priority for me. I don't see that I have much choice. If I don't find them, you frame me."

"That's true enough," Maura said, "but then if you do find them, Leslie doesn't get paid, which means my checkbook is slightly lighter than I'd like it to be."

This is where I would find out how much Leslie loved me, and how much she loved my money. I wasn't betting on the money, but Leslie wasn't in a talking mood.

"Leslie," I said to her snoozing body, "Is the money more important to you than my life?"

She didn't answer of course, which I took as a good sign. I was looking for one, so it wasn't that hard to do.

I said, "Leslie seems undecided. She has shown a renewed love for me after all. Give me a week, Maura. If I've got nothing, frame me like a picture and see if I hang."

Maura said, "I was thinking about letting you have twenty-four hours, just for the sport of it really."

"That's not enough time," I said.

"Monday night then. You've got until Monday night, midnight. Okay, Jake? That's a little more than forty-eight hours. Okay?"

I glanced at my watch. It was fifty-four hours and twenty-two minutes—a bit short of a week. Oh well.

"Monday at midnight," I said.

Is a janitor capable of conducting a manhunt? A retired janitor, with lots of cash, probably wouldn't do much better, would he? Who was on my team? Did I have a team? Did I need weapons? Why does it never seem this hard in the movies?

Maura Ferguson, and if she had her way Leslie Watson, were trying to frame me for murder. At least that was Maura's plan. I didn't like it, and didn't think Leslie would go along with it, but you never know.

I considered a drive over to Grant's office. I could lay it on the line, tell him my situation, and see if he could help. Laying it on the line, of course, meant I had to tell him he wasn't defending a murderer, technically, just someone who had conspired to frame a person for murder. I figured he wouldn't care what she had done, and that he wouldn't be able to help me even if he believed me. "Conflict of interest" kept running through my head, and it sounded like Grant's voice.

128

His secretary, Wanda, seemed willing enough to help just a day earlier. I had a hard time imagining her as any more useful searching for killers than me. Not to mention, she was last seen dancing back to Donnie's bedroom.

Which left me alone in the world, with fifty-four hours and counting on my clock. Or was I? Maura left me alone with my deadline and an unconscious blonde. I put Leslie into bed and left her there. I found a hotel employee, peeled off ten hundred dollar bills into her hand, and asked her to sit in the chair next to Leslie, to make sure she would be okay. I wasn't sure that was money well spent, but it was the best I could do.

I gave the valet another hundred bucks and I jumped into the limo when he brought it to me. I checked to be sure the guns were still there, and pointed it back toward the country. I had to know why they switched the files. I had to know what they knew. I had to know why they were screwing with my life.

The gate hadn't been fixed, and that surprised me a little. As I maneuvered up the winding driveway to the front of the compound, everything looked calm. Maybe, I thought, the Silvestri family and their henchmen were all out somewhere looking for me.

They weren't.

CHAPTER SEVENTEEN

Annabella was sitting on a bench on the porch as I walked to the door. I threw her the keys, which she caught without having to move her arm more than six inches.

"You've got balls, Jake, I'll give you that," she said. She slid over a little to give me room to join her, so I did. "Or is it Leslie that's got brass down there?"

"Maura's the enemy," I said, getting down to business and ignoring my anatomy.

"Oh, so you're finally caught up?" she asked.

"You knew?"

"Sure, I knew. I thought everyone knew."

"You knew about Maura?" I asked again. "You know what she's up to?"

"I told you, I've got certain resources that can be very useful," she said. "Why do you think I wrote the M on the mirror? I was just trying to nudge you in the right direction, that's all."

"So you know she's trying to frame me?" How could she know that? I only found out within the hour.

"She what?" Annie asked. "She's trying to frame you? No, I didn't know that."

"She thinks she's going to get Leslie to go along with her, make her story that much stronger. When I'm convicted and executed, Leslie gets my money. Maura figures they'll split it."

"What does Leslie say?" she asked.

"Nothing. She passed out in the hall on the way up to the room. She would never go for it though."

"Don't be so sure, Jake," she said, sounding like a warning.

"What do you mean?"

"Resources, Jake. I've got 'em."

"I'm not sure I want to hear this," I said.

"We've kept tabs on Leslie for years. We had to. I could never be sure what she really knew about my family and our business. And she's kind of in a position to do plenty of damage if she so chose. As for Leslie and Maura, well, that's a recent friendship. At least as near as we've been able to find out. They met at a New Year's Eve party."

"Maura, maybe, but Leslie? I can't believe it."

"You sure know how to pick your women."

"Leslie won't go along," I said.

Annie just shrugged and continued, "Grant Spencer knows about the two of them, too. At least he knows they know each other. He's got plenty of notes on your blonde news lady. Wanda was saying inside earlier how he had assigned one of his people just to Leslie Watson research. He wouldn't have done that if he didn't think she wasn't somehow involved with Maura."

"Maybe Maura's telling him lies to get him to look into Leslie more, just in case she needs the information down the line."

"Maybe," she said skeptically.

"You think he knows what she's up to?" I asked.

"I would guess he has no idea about her intentions, though you can never really be sure with lawyers."

"So you've looked at his files?" I asked.

"No. How would I have gotten a look at his files?" she asked.

"The boxes," I said.

"Boxes?"

Maybe she really didn't know. I explained to her about the boxes of files and how they were full of blank paper. I told her how we assumed someone at the compound had switched them and was looking through the files.

"If someone switched those files, it wasn't on my orders," she said.

"Your dad? Could he have done it?" I asked.

"I suppose, but I doubt it. He's more worried about keeping you in hiding here. I was told to find you and bring you back. Daddy thinks I screwed it up the first time."

"You were successful this time," I said. "You could have put a little effort into it."

"I knew you'd come back. I knew you had no one else to turn to. You're next best bet, I'm sure you thought, was Wanda, and she's been in my brother's bedroom for most of the day. You had to come back. I'm the only one that can help you and who's willing to do it."

"I came back because of the files. I figured you had switched them and I wanted to know why you felt it necessary to further fuck up my life."

"Not me," she said, holding both hands up, palms out.

"I'm sorry about the limo," I said, nodding toward the scratched fender.

"Forget it. I'll get your thumb later to pay for the damage."

She smiled when she said it, so I'm pretty sure she was kidding.

"I thought you were dead last night, Annie. It wasn't a good feeling."

"Thanks, Jake, I think. Are we having a moment?"

I ignored her sarcasm and said, "Why wasn't the murder on television? Les and I watched the news last night and this morning, and it's not mentioned anywhere."

"They can't report something that never happened," she said.

"I saw the blood. I saw the body. I saw the police. They were too close, too soon, for you to have been able to get rid of that body."

"We didn't have to get rid of the body," she said, "Because no one was killed."

"I just told you, I saw the body. And you told me last night that you killed someone. There *was* a body," I said.

"No, Jake, there wasn't. I was the body on your bathroom floor."

"You were?" I asked, I'm sure sounding confused.

"You didn't check real close for a pulse, which I figured you wouldn't. I see you as the squeamish type around blood. I had a hard time not laughing when you puked, though. You're gonna have to get tougher or this just won't work."

Again, she was smiling when she said it.

"What about the cops?" I asked.

"Ours," she said matter-of-factly.

"Where'd all the blood come from? And what about the knife? It was stuck in her back. I mean your back. I think."

"Special effects," she said, "Just like in the movies. The knife I had put in my purse when we were at lunch at Guilianos. The blade was broken off real short. Why did you think I was in the bathroom so long? No one could shower that long."

"Well, once I went in I figured it was because you were too dead to turn off the water. Silly me. I guess you were just napping."

"I know it doesn't seem like a nice trick to have played on you," she said.

"Why'd you do it?"

"To see whose side you were on. To see what we could expect out of you. To see whom you'd run to and where that would lead. To see if we could trust you."

"What'd you find out?"

"You ran to Leslie, which seems like a natural enough thing to do. But didn't it seem odd to you that she had just shown up back in your life? Anyway, you came back, and without her. That Jake has saved your ass."

"And why the big story last night?" I asked.

"For Leslie. I still don't trust her, Jake. And she still doesn't know there wasn't a murder, I'm guessing, though calling her station could probably clear that up pretty quickly. She's smart, so it won't be long."

"It'll be a little while," I said. "I just left her passed out in her room."

"Really? How'd you find out about Maura's plan?"

"Maura was there, in Leslie's room. She had let herself in. She had a very nice version of what took place at the Ferguson place on Monday. It ends with me killing Sam and Shannon. She gave me until Monday at midnight. If I haven't found the killer by then, she goes to the police with her lies. And so much for my ass I just saved by coming back here."

"Why do you keep saying 'her,' and not 'them'? It could be Maura *and* Leslie, couldn't it?"

"I hope not. I'm trying to keep an open mind about her involvement."

"The eternal optimist," she said.

"Maybe."

"Okay, we've still got tonight and two more days. We might not get much sleep, though. Are you up for this?"

Did I have any choice? Was I sure I wanted to align myself with the mob? How many people would be helping me here? Ten? Twenty? A hundred? No sleep? Was she kidding? Who doesn't sleep? Once again, did I really have any choice?

"I'm in Annie," I said.

"I won't let you out of my sight, Jake," she said, again with a smile.

"Who was in the van? The van we saw from the hot tub. Who was in it?"

"Tony and Vinnie," she said.

"You're some boss. I bet guys like working for you."

"They don't complain, though my dad might have more to do with that than me."

I didn't think so. I said, "I've seen you naked."

She smiled and said, "The first time's always the hardest, Jake. That's true of anything."

"So what do we do now?" I asked, trying to ignore her implied meaning.

"Go to your party," she said. "I have a feeling we don't want to miss it."

I had forgotten all about my own party. The reason for having it in the first place was to meet Annie, and that was now a moot point. Leslie and Maura were both invited, but I didn't really want to see at least one of them until I had to.

"Do we have to go?" I asked. "I mostly set it up as an elaborate way to meet you. That's no longer necessary."

"You couldn't have just picked up a phone and called me? Don't get me wrong. I think it's sweet that you went to so much trouble just to meet me, but it's kind of extreme. Does the word subtle mean anything to you?"

"I'm new at this whole money thing. And I'm kind of shy with women."

"It's your party so, yes, we have to go. If you don't show up at your own party, don't you think that will seem a little suspicious to people? It would to me. You have nothing to be hiding from, as far as everyone that will be there will know, except for your two girlfriends. If you aren't there, you'll be missed. And you never know what we might find out once we're there."

"You're right, of course. Are you my date?"

"Well, you have seen me naked. Are you asking?"

"Yes, I'm asking," I said.

"Do you have a costume yet?"

"No, I haven't found the time. Can we find a shop on the way or something?"

"Wear Donnie's. He's not going to be going anywhere tonight. Did you put those two together?"

"Accidentally, I guess I did. I would have never thought they'd like each other, though. No offense, but your brother's a little vulgar, and I figured someone like Wanda wouldn't like that."

"Surprised me too," she said. "I'll send the costume up to your room while I go change into mine. When you're dressed, come on down to the kitchen and we'll eat. And then we'll go. Okay?"

"So you are my date?" I asked.

"I'm all yours. I hope you can handle me," she said, again smiling.

"I should call Helen Roth," I said, again trying to ignore the implications of her smile. "It's my party; she might need some help."

Annie handed me a cell phone and went inside. Didn't she just say she wouldn't let me out of her sight? Maybe she meant it in the figurative sense. Or maybe she was watching me from behind the curtain or something. Or was this a *1984* type of place?

Helen answered on the second ring, and she didn't sound like she'd been drinking. Yet.

She said, "Jake, darling, where have you been? I've been calling your house all day, but I just keep getting that dreadful answering machine. I loathe those things. Where have you been? Stitching your costume together, I hope."

"I've got a costume, all sewn up. Is there anything you need me to do?"

"That's why I've been calling, Jake. I was calling to gloat about my sheer greatness at putting a party together. Two days were plenty of time, though I noted the look of concern on your face when you told me the time frame. It was more time than I needed, really, but this way I've been able to double-check all the little details. Everything is ready to go. The band is setting up by the pool right now, and the catering service just arrived. It's going to be fabulous, Jake, darling. Are you excited?"

"I'm excited, Helen. Listen, I can't thank you enough for putting this together, and for letting me use your house and yard. I'll owe you for this."

"That you will, darling," she said. "Have you heard from Leslie? Is she coming?"

"I spoke with her earlier today. I'm not sure if she's coming or not."

"Well, be careful. Your heart can be a fragile thing."

I promised her I would watch myself. If only she knew the truth. That information, in the hands of a woman like Helen Roth, would make for a very interesting party indeed. But I kept my mouth shut. Besides, what was the truth?

"Helen," I said, "There's a small chance I'm not going to make it tonight."

"Jake, no. You must come. It's your party."

"Well, it's been a crazy week and I've got some deadlines and I just don't know if things are going to allow me to come. I want to, I just don't know if I can."

"Jake, darling, here's a little riddle for you. Are you ready?"

"I hate riddles, Helen. Is it easy?"

"Humor an old woman, would you? When is a party not a party?"

I thought about it for a little less than three nanoseconds before saying, "I don't know Helen, when is a party not a party?"

"When there's no host, Jake. Do come. We'll carry on without you, but it is your party. No deadline can be that important, right? At least think about it, will you?"

A light turned on somewhere in the dark shadows of my mind.

Before I hung up I said, "Helen, you just might be a life saver."

I skipped the part where I was supposed to put on my costume and ran straight to the kitchen. Annie had done the same thing, unless her costume consisted of the same blue jeans and sweater she had been wearing on the porch. She was poking a fork through a plate of ravioli, and there was another plate sitting next to it untouched. She pushed that one toward me, and kicked the chair next to her back from the table.

I sat down, but ignored the food. Ravioli always made me think of Chef Boyardee and I always hated that crap. Besides, I had to tell Annie what I had just discovered, before it slipped back into my unconscious.

I stared at her until she took the hint and set her fork down. She didn't seem too happy about doing it, but she did it. She folded her arms across her chest in a defensive sort of way and leaned back away from me. Her eyes were saying that what I was about to say had better be more important than Mama's old ravioli recipe.

Her patience was evaporating quickly and she said, "Well?"

"I'm not sure I can explain this to you in a way that will make any sense at all. I'm not sure it makes all that much sense to me. But it feels right, in my gut. Aren't I supposed to go with my gut? I'm new at this, so I'm not sure. Anyway, am I making any sort of sense?"

"You haven't told me anything yet," she said.

Her eyes drifted back to her plate. They had the look any man would like focused on them.

"Haven't I? Well, Helen and I were talking and she said something that tripped a wire in my memory or something. I had one of those moments of clarity you hear people talking about all the time. It was great."

"You're not exactly transferring that clarity over to me. It's about as clear as my ravioli, and not as tasty. Tell me what you remembered."

I said, "Helen asked me a riddle. I hate riddles because they never make any sense to me. They're so subjective really, when you think about them. Hey, except for this one. You want to hear it? How do you sell a duck to a deaf man?"

"Jake, is that what your moment of clarity was about? You remembered an old riddle from seventh grade or something?" "Actually I think it was tenth or eleventh grade, but those years all kind of run together. So, how do you sell a duck to a deaf man?"

She shrugged her shoulders. They said either she didn't care or she didn't know. Probably both. Or was she just surrendering?

I yelled, "WANNA BUY A DUCK?"

She stared at me without even a small chuckle. Not even the hint of a smile on her lips. She looked positively pissed off. Her patience was officially used up. She licked her lips and then smacked them together. Everything about her expression and posture told me that had better not be it.

I said, "That's not it, Annie. I remembered something I read a long time ago, and then connected it to something I saw recently and the old synapses started firing like a machine gun."

"Okay. What did you read long ago? What did you just see? How did you put the two together?"

"Well, there were some murders a few years back. Bloody things. Major headlines. Even I read them, and I was still working back then."

"And?"

"And then I saw Maura Ferguson with a man the other night. A guy in a tweed jacket, with a nicely trimmed, graying beard."

"And?"

"And they were the same guy," I said.

"You're sure?" she asked. Finally, I had her attention and the ravioli did not.

"Pretty sure," I said.

"A few years ago, you said? There aren't that many murders that get much media around here. Was it one that was blamed on us?"

"No. At least I don't remember that it was."

"Why would that guy be with Maura? Shouldn't he be in jail? How would they know each other?" she asked.

"He got off, first of all. And they have the same lawyer, Grant Spencer."

"You're talking about . . ."

"Theo McAlister."

CHAPTER EIGHTEEN

"Theo McAlister?" Annie asked. "The teacher who killed those girls? He's the guy you saw with Maura Ferguson? He's the guy in the tweed jacket?"

"Yes. I knew he looked familiar when I saw him at the Plaza, but I didn't know why. For some reason, it came to me when I was talking with Helen. She said a party isn't a party without a host. And I thought of him."

"Why?" she asked. "I don't see the connection."

"Annie, do you remember the case? McAlister was a professor and the four victims were all attractive female students in his class. One died each semester for four straight semesters. It was sort of a tuition deal, or maybe faculty hazing. He killed one student each semester."

"So?"

"They were stabbed and stabbed and stabbed some more. Some of them were nearly impossible to identify they were so hacked up. Sam Ferguson and Shannon Powell and the poor dog were also stabbed a whole bunch of times. He, they were able to identify by his face. Shannon, I heard, they had to check the records of the surgeon that did her implants."

"She had fake boobs?" Annie asked.

"Nice big ones too, if you like that sort of thing. I don't."

"So you think because McAlister sliced up some girls a few years back he sliced up these two on Monday? Connect the dots for me, would you please."

"Helen said a party's not a party without a host. When McAlister was being tried, his lawyer said the same kind of thing."

"And his lawyer was this Grant Spencer that's defending Maura?"

"Right. Grant said a murderer couldn't be a murderer if he was never at the scene of the crime. The prosecution couldn't put him physically in any of the hotel rooms where the murders had taken place. His evidence was in and on all the women, from having sex with them, but there was nothing specifically at any of the crime scenes to prove he had ever even been in the room."

"I get it I think," she said.

Just in case she didn't, I finished, "Grant said that McAlister admitted to having sex with all four of them. He even admitted to doing it on more than just the day they were killed. But he adamantly refused to say he had anything to do with the hotel rooms. His claim was that someone was jealous, or angry about a poor grade, or something, and they were killing his girlfriends one by one, and trying to make it look like he had done it."

"And the jury bought it," she said.

"That's why he's free to be seen in a hotel downtown with Maura Ferguson."

"Which means what, do you think?"

"Well, Maura's doing the old guy. Or maybe she used to."

"Was she a student of his?" Annie asked.

"I'm not sure, but I think we should find out. Can we?"

She scoffed softly, picked up her phone, and punched in some numbers. She explained to the ear on the other end what she needed and that tonight wouldn't be too soon. I got the impression the ear was on some sort of mafia retainer program.

"He'll call this number," she said, regarding the cell. "What else?"

"I guess we go to the party," I said.

I went upstairs and found my costume. It was one of those rubber masks people pull completely over their heads. I was going to be Ronald Reagan. There was a suit laid out next to it, and a jar of jellybeans. I slipped into the suit, stashed the beans in one of the pockets, and yanked the mask over my head. It was hot inside, but a quick look in the mirror assured me that no one would be able to recognize me.

Was Theo McAlister our man? If he was, or even if he wasn't, would he be stupid enough to be seen in public with a woman on trial for committing a double murder of her own? If he did it, did Maura know he had? Did Leslie? What kind of communication was taking place between their merry little band? Was there truly a merry little band, or had Maura made it up? Did McAlister do it to free Maura for himself? Did he do it to get her money? Did it have anything to do with the murders he almost got juiced for? And what was Annie's costume going to be?

Her costume, as it turned out, was much like mine. She too was a Republican President, Richard Nixon. She had on a gray men's suit, a white shirt, and a black tie. She managed to give him a certain sexiness I had never noticed before.

The mouth of her mask didn't move, obviously, but I heard her voice in my ear saying, "Jake, you look great. These masks have little microphones and earphones. We can talk to each other and no one will know we are. They won't see our mouths move and they won't hear us. They pick up fairly low volumes."

The last sentence she said just above a whisper, and I heard it in my ear, loud and clear. Impressive. Richard Nixon was whispering in my ear in a very husky, feminine voice and it was turning me on just a little, I have to admit.

"No one else will be listening?" I asked.

I didn't want to say the wrong thing and have it end up in father Frank's room on the loudspeaker.

"No, Jake. It will just be us. They have pretty good range. I could hear you telling yourself how good you looked when you were still up in your room."

Damn impressive. I was blushing, but she couldn't see, could she?

"Don't blush," she said. "You do look pretty good."

"Where's your prop?" I asked. "I've got my jar of jelly beans. What have you got?"

142

She reached in her pocket and pulled out a cassette tape and a pair of scissors. Funny. She stuck them back in her pocket and took my hand. She started toward the door, pulling me behind her.

"So, we're going as the gay Republican President's?" I asked. Her throaty laugh sounded too good in my earpiece.

It was eight o'clock as we climbed into the back seat of the same limousine I had driven into town earlier. I was at fifty-two hours and counting on Maura's clock.

Tony was our chauffer for the evening, and that made me feel safer. We drove down the drive to the gate. It was fixed, and two guards were on duty. Tony stopped long enough to tell them who his passengers were, then hit the road toward Helen's house.

It was a nervous ride, at least for me. Annie seemed cool, but she wasn't such a novice at this game, was she? We sat in silence for a few miles, just holding hands and thinking. She has nice hands.

"Do we have a plan?" I asked quietly into my mask.

"Not really," she said. "Keep your eyes and ears open and hope for the best."

The band was playing beyond the pool when we crossed over into Helen's backyard. She had lights strung all around, very orange and black everywhere. The food was on tables under one tent, the liquor behind a bar in another. A soft steam was rising up from the water of the pool, but so far no one had taken a plunge.

A large crowd was already in place, and all of them were in costume. Helen's parties were legendary, so people tended to come early and stay late. A few couples were dancing, but most were pacing themselves and filling up on food.

I found Helen and introduced her to Annie. Helen didn't let on that she knew what my date did for a living. She was the consummate host.

"Isn't it grand, Jake?" she asked with a big smile. Helen was dressed, strangely enough, like Barbara Bush. She had even gone to the trouble of dying her hair a very bright white, and she had on a blue dress that came right out of the Rose Garden, 1990.

"It's very nice, Helen. It's more than I expected even. I could have never done this on my own."

"That's what friends are for. If we could all do everything ourselves, well, we wouldn't really need anyone else, would we? Jake, darling, this just happens to be what I'm good at."

And Annie was good at crime, so she was my date. Which was the more valuable skill? That would depend on your needs. Mine dictated staying close to Annie and begging away from Helen. We told her we needed to mingle.

We split up and worked the crowd. I could hear conversations taking place where she was, through my earphone, and I'm sure she could hear those near me too. We said very little to one another, and even less to anyone else.

I saw Maura Ferguson before Annie did. She was dressed as Little Red Riding Hood. Her date was in a fox suit, covering him from head to toe. And no, I couldn't tell for sure who it was, or even if it was a man. The fox head made the height hard to judge, and the suit was loose and padded, so body type was anyone's guess as well. It could have been anyone.

"Maura's twenty feet off your port side, Annie," I said quietly into the mask.

I watched her head turn to the right.

"The other port side," I said, "To your left."

"Little Bo Peep?" she asked.

"Little Bo Peep is a blonde, and usually has sheep with her. Little Red Riding Hood wears the red cape and is usually seen with a fox who wants to eat her."

"Sorry, Jake. I didn't much like nursery rhymes and fairy tales when I was growing up. They're so violent and scary. Wolves huffing and puffing, foxes eating girls, and stuff like that. It's scary when you're a little girl."

I think she missed the irony in her own words.

As she was talking she was walking. She had maneuvered herself into an excellent position just a couple feet from Maura. Annie sat at a table where she was in fact back-to-back with Maura.

"Are we eavesdropping?" I asked.

"Gathering evidence," she whispered back. "Shut up, would you please?"

So I did.

Maura looked pretty good. Grandma would be so proud when Red arrived with her basket of goodies. She had on the requisite red cape, but I don't think much more. There was a hood hanging down her back, and plenty of cleavage showing up front. The cape ended at her waist, where a very tight red leather skirt began. She had red stilettos on her feet. All twenty nails were painted red as well.

Her date had disappeared into the food area and Maura was left to talk to a guy who had spent plenty of time in the drink tent. He was in a Superman outfit that was meant for someone about thirty pounds lighter than him. He was giving stretch nylon a very bad name. He, naturally, thought he was the man. I could hear the conversation like I was sitting at the same table.

Superman said, "Little Red Riding Hood, huh?" It was slurred badly.

"Perceptive," Maura said. "Is that because of your x-ray vision?"

"No, honey, but if you'd like to undress and climb on the table here I'll give that a shot."

"You gonna join me?" she asked.

"Sure, honey. Should we find a private table, somewhere inside?" Super asked.

"I'd rather not, Superman. That suit you're wearing? It's a little tight. Maybe you hadn't noticed. It's not really that flattering. And it's tight in some places you don't want it to be tight. Do you know what I mean? At least I know where my straw ended up. You keep it. I'll get me another one."

"Fuck you, little red riding bitch," he slurred, standing up. "Fuck you to fucking hell."

As he started to walk away Maura said, "See you later Superman, or is that Supergirl? It's hard to tell from where I'm sitting."

Annie was laughing in my ear, all scratchy and low.

And then she said, to me, "Here I go, Ron. Have some jelly beans and pay attention."

"What?" I said too loud.

But there she was, tapping Maura on the shoulder.

Annie said, "Nice brush off. Very nice. Can I get you a drink?"

"Sure," Maura said.

Her eyes said she was trying to decide if Mr. Nixon was man, woman, or beast. With Annie's voice, it wasn't easy to tell. Annie waved to one of the circulating waitresses and held up two fingers when the girl looked at her. Annie got out of her chair and took the one next to Maura.

Maura said, "I came with someone."

"Yeah, me too," said Annie. "Men. They serve a purpose, I suppose, but I can't figure out what it is."

She laughed her deepest laugh, and it sounded sincere.

"I'm not a lesbian," Maura said. Her tone didn't sound like it was a firm choice.

"No? Me neither." The waitress came and set down the drinks. Annie told her to bring two more. "To lesbians," she said, raising her glass.

"Okay," Maura said, lifting her glass to Annie's.

They both drank. Maura looked confused, but interested. Annie looked like Richard Nixon, but with a nice, female body. Annie leaned in a little, and Maura didn't back up. Not an inch.

"Do I know you?" Maura finally asked.

"Sure you do," was all Annie said.

"Do I like you?"

"You seem to," Annie said.

"Where's your date?" Maura asked.

"Probably somewhere inside with the easiest woman at this party," Annie said.

"That would be Leslie Watson," Maura said, "You know, from the morning news. She'll sleep with anyone."

What? What? What?

"Leslie Watson? The blonde? She does commercials for that halfway house for the homeless, doesn't she?" Annie asked without skipping a beat.

"That's the one," Maura said.

146

"She's easy?"

"Very easy," she said.

What?

I said to Annie, "Ask her to prove it."

Annie said, "You know for sure, or are you just spreading gossip?"

"She used to live with a guy that lives around here, but she was cheating on him with this other guy. So she left the first guy for the second, but then cheated on the second with the first."

I said, "That's not easy, it's confused."

Annie said, "That sounds more like confused than easy."

"The hell with her," Maura said.

"Okay, where's your date?" Annie asked.

"Very good question," Maura said. "What did you say your name was?"

"Nixon," Annie said, "Richard Nixon."

"Alright, Dick, call me Red. Do you want to get out of here?"

"I thought you'd never ask."

They both stood and I watched them walk through the door into Helen's house. They weren't talking, because I'd have heard that. A light came on in the room I remembered was old Abe's den, and I guessed that's where they were.

What did Annie have in mind? Was she just trying to get lucky? Was this some sort of mafia interrogation technique that's not widely publicized? Did Annie go both ways? Did Maura? Or would the actions fail to live up to the talk? As a guy, wasn't I really looking forward to this?

I said, "Does she know what you look like? Will she know you when you take off your mask? What the hell are you doing?"

She whispered, "No, she won't know. She's in the bathroom down the hall right now. It's okay. I've never met her before tonight."

"She could recognize you from pictures. I did."

"It's too dark in here. I'm not sure I could recognize me. Stop worrying. Here she comes. Shh."

The light in the window went out a few seconds later. I heard someone say something about taking off the mask. And then things went kind of muffled. I tried to find a quiet corner but it didn't help. It seemed like I heard some breathing, of the heavy variety, and what I interpreted as moans. I listened to what I assumed was two women making out. Guys will do that, you know. It could just as easily have been aerobics I was listening to. Or pain.

And then I heard the screams. Four or five of them, followed by crying, which was followed by silence. The screams weren't loud enough to hear without my microphone, as if a pillow or something covered them.

Heavy breathing was next, but this time definitely not of the sexual variety. It was more from the exhaustive exercise family. Stuff was being knocked over, I think, and someone or something was being dragged. It all took about five more minutes.

The last thing I heard was a car door slamming, an engine starting, and tires squealing as the signal slowly faded away.

I had fifty hours to go.

CHAPTER NINETEEN

There was no sign of anything out of the ordinary in the den. Anything that might have been tipped over, either during a struggle or a tryst, had been put back. Any pillow that may have been bloodied was gone. There wasn't so much as a water ring on the coffee table. Annie's mask wasn't there. No one, as far as I could tell, had been in that room. And it had only taken me a couple minutes to get in there after the tires squealed away from my ear.

That's what my quick once over told me. My intuition was saying otherwise. I found the bathroom off the den. There were two or three reddish hairs on the vanity. It had to be the bathroom Maura had gone in, which meant this had to be the room she and Annie were together in. It had to be, so what had happened?

My mask was still pulled tightly over my head. If any sound came through from the microphone in Annie's mask, I wasn't about to miss it. I was fairly certain she had had a plan when she started talking to Maura, I'm just not sure if it went the way she thought it would. I told myself she could handle herself in a situation like this, and hoped I was right.

I went to the parking area to get Tony, let him know what had happened to his boss. I didn't know what had happened, but I knew Tony couldn't be kept out of the information loop. There was one small problem, though. The limo was there, but Tony was nowhere to be found. He might have been somewhere catching a smoke, but I couldn't find him if he was.

I went back to the party and found Helen. It wasn't late yet, at least not for a get-together at the Roth's house, and there was a large crowd surrounding the pool. I tried to find the fox suit that had walked in with Maura. There was a chance, I figured, that it might be Leslie. I was hoping to reason with her if it was.

I found Helen and asked, "Have you seen someone in a red fox costume?"

"Yes, I believe I have. They were over in the bar tent last I saw them. Is that someone you know?"

"It's Leslie, and I need to talk to her. Could you have one of your people find her and send her into the den? It's important."

"Right away, Jake, darling," she said.

"Helen, I don't want her to know it's me in this costume, okay? It's kind of a special surprise for her," I said.

"Oh Jake, I do love it when love blooms at my parties. Are you sure the den is where you want to meet? The guest room is just down the hall. Help yourself if you need it."

I promised her I would and retreated to an oversized leather chair in a dimly lit corner of Abe Roth's den. Twenty minutes later I was ready to chuck the whole thing, hail a taxi back to the Silvestri compound, and throw myself at the mercy of Frank. Lucky for me, that's when the fox walked in.

Sure, lucky for me.

She seemed to be walking pretty steadily for someone I left passed out on a hotel bed just a couple hours before. I scored it as just another optical illusion in a week full of them. I told her to close the door, and she did. She came over to me in the leather chair and sat on the sofa that was next to it. She put her feet up on the coffee table and let out a rather large sigh.

"Feeling better?" I asked.

The fox head nodded an affirmation.

"How'd you get here? With Maura?" I asked.

Again, the response was a silent nod.

"She left. At least I think she did. She was with Annabella last I saw her, walking into the house. Annabella's car is gone, so I'm assuming so are they."

There was no nodding this time. I could feel the human eyes staring at me from inside the head of the fox suit. I knew it was going to mean I'd possibly be out of contact with Annie, but this whole mask thing was starting to bother me some. I peeled mine off and set it in my lap. She did the same, but instead of the blonde head of Leslie Watson, inside was the graying beard of Theo McAlister.

Damn.

I fumbled with my composure, grabbed at it, and managed to blurt out, "You're not who I was expecting. I don't think we've had the pleasure. I'm John Jacobs. Most people just call me Jake." And I stuck my right hand in his direction.

"Theo McAlister," he said, taking my hand and shaking it. "Who's Annabella?"

"What? Oh, Annabella. She's my date. Or she was anyway. I saw the two of them, Maura and Annabella, leaving together. You came with Maura?"

"I sure did. You say they were leaving together? As in, *together* together?"

"It sure seemed like it, but I couldn't say for sure. Women can be strange that way, showing one emotion and meaning another."

"They sure can," he said.

I got the feeling my usefulness to him was about at its end. He seemed to be looking inside for answers he was probably not going to find. I felt his pain, but I didn't have the time to share in it.

I said, "Do you know Leslie Watson?"

"The news lady? Not personally. Why?"

"I thought you were going to be her. She was supposed to be in a fox suit tonight. Have you seen another one of those out there?" He shook his head and said, "Sorry, no."

I told him it was nice meeting him but I had to find Leslie Watson. He didn't need to know why, and I'm sure he didn't care. I tugged the Reagan mask back over my head and dove back into the sea of people out back.

By midnight I was convinced Leslie wasn't there, and that Maura and Annie weren't coming back. I went to the parking lot and walked amongst the cars. There wasn't a bad one in the bunch. Tony must have finished his smoke, because the limo was gone. There was a red Porsche, though. I reached in my pocket and prayed I had the ring with Leslie's key on it. For once, my prayer was answered.

I walked to the driver's side door. I stood there a few seconds scanning the perimeter. I wasn't sure I had the right car, and I didn't want anyone thinking I was trying to steal it if it wasn't I slipped the key in and turned. The locked tumbled over. I think I may have shrieked with joy. I climbed in, pulled the door closed, and locked it with a slam, as if the harder I pushed it down, the safer I'd be.

I left without a clue where to go. Strangely enough, my house seemed like a good idea. I only live ten blocks from Helen, so it figured to be a nice quick drive, the kind where I wouldn't be spotted.

Halfway there I was idling at a four-way stop when I heard a groan. A female groan. And it was coming from the backseat of Leslie's Porsche. I turned to see who it was, sure it wouldn't surprise me.

Wrong again.

Both her hands were rubbing Leslie Watson's blonde head. Her eyes were squinty, and she appeared disoriented at best. There was no way she had driven this car to that party, not in the condition she was in. She pulled herself up so her mouth was next to my ear, her breathing uneven and hoarse.

"Jake? Where are we Jake? Why does my head hurt so much?"

"We're in your car, and you've been drinking. Too much on your empty stomach I guess. You went down like a sorority girl during pledge week."

"Jake, there's a bump on my head. Did I hit my head when I fell?"

She hadn't. I had caught her before she came anywhere near the floor. She was rubbing up near the crown of her skull.

I tipped her head slightly and turned on the dome light. There was some crusted blood in her hair, and a bump the size of a golf ball in the center of the blood. It looked fairly fresh, and it had to hurt.

Now what do you suppose that meant?

"Jake, is there a bump there?" she asked, letting herself fall softly back into the seat.

152

"Yes, a pretty good one. You didn't get it when you passed out. Someone must have clubbed you."

"Clubbed me? Who the hell would club me?"

"I don't know. It's been too strange a night for me to have even a small clue. And you obviously don't remember much. Let's go to my house and get some ice on that thing, get you some aspirin, and see what we can piece together. Okay?"

She didn't say no, which I took as yes. Silence is agreement, at least when you want it to be. We rode in that silence the last few blocks, except for the occasional groan from the back seat.

Who had hit her? Maura? McAlister? Why had they hit her? Why had they brought her to the party in the condition she was in? Had she agreed to get involved with Maura in her plot? Had Maura made the offer? Where had Maura and Annie gone? Were they both okay? Was Tony? Was I any closer to the end of the maze?

I was busy contemplating those and other questions when Leslie woke me up. We were rounding the corner and my house was at the end of the block.

She said, "Are you expecting company, Jake?"

"No, why?"

"You've got some," she said, pointing at my driveway and the big, black limousine that was sitting in it.

Forty-seven hours and counting.

CHAPTER TWENTY

I knew I couldn't pull into my driveway. Not yet. Tony and Maura and Annie and whoever the hell else was in there would just have to wait. I hoped they were all still alive, and I hoped none of them were there to kill me. I had to know what had happened back at Helen's house. I had to stop the Porsche, go inside, and let destiny takes its course.

Not yet, though.

Not until I knew if Leslie was with me. Was this the Leslie I loved? Was this the Leslie who seemed very happy to be naked with me twenty-four hours ago? Was this the Leslie who was wearing her jealous eyes the first time she saw me together with Annie? Or, was this the Leslie who was now in cahoots with Maura? Was this the Leslie who was after my millions? Did that Leslie even exist, or had Maura made me believe something that wasn't true?

Will the real Leslie Watson please stand up?

"Jake," she said from the tiny back seat, "Who hit me on the head? Did you?"

"No, it wasn't me. And I don't know who did it. I left you passed out on the bed of your room, from liquor, not violence."

"Where was I when you found me just now?"

"In this car, in the parking area, at my party at Helen's house," I said. "I didn't know you were even in here when I started driving."

"You were stealing my car?"

"Borrowing would be a better word, I think."

"If I was passed out, how did I get the car to the party? I wasn't at the party, was I? How was the party, by the way?"

"The party was a huge success. You were not, as far as I can tell, at it. And I'm not sure how you got to the party, though I have some theories."

"Theories?" she asked. We were pulled to the curb, my driveway and the limo half a block in front of us. Leslie squeezed through and into the passenger seat next to me. "Tell me your theories."

"Maura Ferguson brought you," I said, "Or maybe Theo McAlister."

"Maura? Theo McAlister? The murderer? How would I know him? What the hell, Jake?"

I figured I had nothing to lose by telling Leslie my version of the day's events. If she was working with Maura, why not let her know I knew? She would be free to stop acting out the charade. If she wasn't working with Maura, I reasoned, I'd be able to tell by her reaction to my story.

"Maura told me she wanted the two of you to be a team. She said you would be after my money, and the only way you could get it would be for me to die. Killing me would be too easy, too obvious, and too risky. But framing me for killing someone so that the state killed me seemed like a good alternative. Maura made a pretty convincing argument for the two of you. She said she'd ask you the first chance she got. And I couldn't ask you, because you were not conscious."

She looked bewildered, but with a splitting headache. I took it as a good sign. It took her a few seconds to process what I was saying.

She finally said, "What the hell are you talking about? I'm not after your money. I've never been after your money. You were a fucking janitor when I met you. How could I be after your money? You believed her? She said I would go after your money and you fucking believed her? What the hell, Jake? You believed her?"

"Look, I didn't know what to believe. I carried you into your hotel room. She was in there, like she owned the place or something. I assumed she had a key, and she said she did. I wanted to ask you. I really did. But you were gone by then."

"Okay, Jake, I'm going to tell you something and hope you believe me. It's the truth, so you should believe me. And I've never lied to you before, have I?"

Well, she had cheated on me with Lance. Is adultery lying? And is it only adultery if you're legally married? Is there such a thing as common law adultery? Oh hell, she cheated on me, and she did it in a dishonest manner, not that it's ever done in an honest manner, so she had lied to me. But just that once, right?

Right.

I said, "No, Leslie, you've never lied to me. What do you want to tell me?"

"I'm not after your money. I'm not in some sort of arrangement with Maura Ferguson. I don't even know Maura Ferguson. I've met her, at parties and things, but I've barely ever even spoken to the woman. I love you, and all I want from you is for you to love me, too. Cross my heart, and hope to die."

As she said that last bit, she actually did cross her heart with her right hand. I hoped she wouldn't die.

I took a few minutes to explain what she had missed. I told her how I was working with Annie now, and that we had gone to the party together. I told her about Annie and Maura and that it was their limo in my driveway. I explained to her how Theo McAlister fit in to the whole mess, but when I said it out loud it didn't seem real solid.

"So you think Maura and McAlister are lovers or something? You think she was his student back in school?" Leslie asked.

"We're guessing on the lovers part. Annie was having the student part checked out. She hadn't yet heard when I lost track of her."

"But you're sure they know each other, right?"

"I saw them together at the Plaza. The night you called me and told me to come up, when you had the tequila and beer, he was with her. I saw him, and I recognized him, but I couldn't place him. It came to me earlier tonight, though. And then at the party tonight, he came in with her. I'm sure they know each other, Les. How well I can't say."

"She could have been involved with him back in school," she said.

"Easily," I said.

"Did she have anything to do with the murders he was charged with? Did she help him by testifying? Someone did. Was it her?"

"I hadn't thought of that. Can we find out?"

"Journalism sometimes has its privileges. Do you have your phone?"

I reached inside Reagan's suit coat and pulled out the cell Annie had given me to call Helen. It was in the jacket because I thought it might come in handy. And now it had. She took it and started punching numbers.

It took her a few minutes to work her way through the various barriers at her station, but she finally reached the person she wanted. His name was Roger.

She said, "Roger, do you remember the McAlister trial a few years ago? Can you find out the names of the girls who testified on his behalf?"

She held the phone against her chest and said to me, "He's checking it out."

I think I could have figured that much out. She put the phone back to her ear and listened.

She said into the cell, "Hang on," then to me, "Paper and pen?"

"It's your car, Les," I said.

She nodded and reached into the glove box, producing a small spiral notebook and a black pen.

Into the phone again, she said, "Shoot, Roger."

She scribbled some things onto the pad, muttering a series of "Uh huhs," as she did. Finally, she thanked Roger and folded the cell phone closed. She kept it in her right hand, slipped the pen behind her right ear, and took the pad in her left hand.

"Well?" I asked, "Does it say Maura Ferguson somewhere on that pad?"

"No, Jake, it doesn't."

"Damn it. I thought we might be catching a break."

"Jake," she said, "We did."

She handed me the notebook, then leaned back in her seat, arms crossed on her chest, a satisfied smile on her lips. I smiled back, out of habit probably, and then looked at her scribbling. There was Louise Zeller, Theresa Smith, Hannah Jackson, Bailey Anthony, Liz Sanchez, and Rita Lester, but no Maura Ferguson. Where was the damn break?

"Help me, Leslie. Where's Maura Ferguson?"

"The teaching assistant that testified as his alibi, Jake, did you get that far?"

I looked back at the bottom of the page. It said, "Teaching assistant-Maura Winters."

"Well I'll be," I said.

"Yes, you will. She wasn't married yet, so she was obviously not Maura Ferguson. She seems more like a Winters, don't you think?"

"Like an icy bitch, you mean?"

"Something like that," she said. "She knew McAlister. She helped him get off. And now he's got to be helping her do the same thing."

"Aren't we clever?"

I thought we were, and I'm sure Leslie agreed. But had it helped us? Had he helped Maura with the murder, or just the escape? Was this background information useful or just juicy gossip? Was she seeing him all along, or did she simply call in a favor?

And then the cell phone screeched, loud and piercing in the quiet Porsche.

"It's Annie's phone," I said to Leslie as she looked from me to the phone in her hand.

"It might be her, calling us," she said.

"She probably doesn't remember I've got it."

"So someone is calling her?" she asked.

I took the phone from her and flipped it open. I didn't say anything, not wanting to tip my hand. I expected someone from the Silvestri estate. It wasn't.

"Are you coming in?" the voice asked me.

"Coming in?" I asked.

"It's your house, Mr. Jacobs. Come on in."

"I'm not sure that's such a good idea. Why are you inside my house? How did you get in? Who else is in there? Should I put on my body armor? Should I come alone? Can I call the police? How did you know I was out here?"

The voice interrupted my string of questions by saying, "No police. Bring Ms. Watson in. You'll find out who is here when you get here, and all those other nasty questions will be addressed in due time. You do ask a lot of them, don't you? Just as well, come in."

"I'll be safe? Leslie will be safe?"

"You're both safe, if you get inside here. Out there, I can't promise anything."

"Okay, we're on our way," I said before folding the phone closed.

Leslie said, "We're going in?"

"Yes."

"Who was it? Who called us?"

"Grant Spencer," I said.

"Grant Spencer?" she asked. "What the hell?"

I was down to forty-six hours.

CHAPTER TWENTY-ONE

"Leslie," I said into the quiet of the Porsche, "There's a good chance the person that killed Sam Ferguson and Shannon Powell is inside my house."

"Why do you think that? Did Grant say something? Do you think Grant killed them? Who's in the house?"

"It's just a feeling I'm getting. Grant's not alone in there, though he didn't actually say that. I didn't hear anyone else, but that doesn't mean anything. He knew this number, which means he at least knows Annie or the Silvestris on some level. Maybe Annie's in there, maybe she's not. We won't know until we go in."

"And you've got a feeling the killer's in there?" she asked.

I nodded. "It's been that kind of day, Les," I said.

She leaned over and kissed me, soft and tender, and said, "I love you, Jake."

"I love you, too," I said, because sometimes the truth is the best thing to say.

"Are we sure we want to go in?" she asked.

I was sure of something. I said, "No."

"Let's go," she said, ignoring me. "Piss or get off the pot, isn't that what they say? You coming?"

She opened her door and stepped into the cool October night. I'm not sure if I expected bullets to start ricocheting off the fender or something, but I hesitated just the same. When none came, I took a deep breath and joined her on the street. I took her hand in mine and led her to my front door.

Grant Spencer poked his head out, looked up and down the street, and gave us a nervous "hurry up" wave. So we hurried up, though obedience to his wishes wasn't something he had yet earned. He opened the door just wide enough for us to sneak through and slammed it closed behind me, flipping the dead bolt into place.

Walking into my living room I wasn't sure what I expected to see. I only know that what I saw wasn't it. No one was there. Not one soul, besides Grant.

"You're alone?" Leslie asked him.

"Yes, I'm alone," he said, leading us into the kitchen where we all took a seat. Leslie wrapped some ice cubes in a towel for her head before she cozied up next to me on the right. Grant was across from me, his briefcase on the table between us. He pulled some supplies out of it before setting it on the floor at his feet.

"I don't get it," she said to him, and then, with her look, to me.

"Annabella Silvestri is a friend of yours, right?" he asked me.

"Recently, I guess so," I said. "She's a new friend, let's say."

"Annabella called me at my office around dinner time. She gave me the number of the cell phone you have. She said if I hadn't heard from her by one o'clock I was supposed to come over here and then call you at that number. She said if she didn't call she was probably dead and you were probably in need of some help."

"How'd you get in?" I asked.

"It wasn't locked. Did you leave in a hurry or something?"

"Something like that, yes," I said.

"And she didn't tell you anything else?" Leslie asked. "Annie didn't tell you what the two of them were up to? She didn't tell you why she would be dead? She just told you to come over here and call Jake?"

"That's it," he said, palms turned up.

He seemed very calm, probably from all the years of staring down an opposing witness. He'd most likely been in tougher spots than this. But I hadn't.

"Do you know her?" I asked him.

"Not personally. I know who she is, if that's what you mean. I told you, remember?"

"Yes, I remember, and that's not what I mean. What I mean is, are you friends? Acquaintances? Have you represented her in some sort of criminal proceeding? Is there more to your relationship than you're letting on?"

"I've never met her, so there's no relationship to let on about," he said, sounding a little annoyed with me, not that I particularly cared.

"You could have told me about the connection between McAlister and Maura Ferguson," I said. "Why didn't you?"

"You aren't the police. You aren't a lawyer. You aren't really anyone important, are you? Why would I tell you anything, except to get you out of my office and leave the real work to people who were used to doing it."

"I'm trying to help," I said.

"I've told you, more than once, not to help. I thought I was clear about that. Why won't you take my advice? Why don't you take some of your money and this girlfriend of yours and go somewhere warm, with an ocean and a beach, and spend about six months there. Work on your tan, read some books, see a few movies, and let this run its course. It will, whether you're here or not. But if you're here, it may chew you up in its path."

"Like it did Annabella?" I asked.

"You tell me," he said. "She's your friend and you were with her earlier tonight. You would seem to know more about what happened to her than I do. From what she told me when she called, I must now assume her to be dead."

Honesty seemed to be rearing its ugly little head more often than was healthy, and I felt it pushing at the tip of my tongue as we sat there. Grant was a prick, but it probably just came with his job. And he carried a certain amount of weight in legal circles; so lying to him probably hadn't been my best decision of the week.

I said to him, "I was at the movies with Maura Monday afternoon. She was the other ticket stub in my pocket. I am her alibi for most of the time the police think she was killing her husband and his girlfriend."

I figured I was only beating Maura to the punch by telling him now, and maybe I hadn't even done that.

"You're kidding," he said. The look on his face said he really thought I was.

"No, Grant, I'm not. I wish I was, but I'm not."

"And you think it's going to come back on you, don't you? That's why you're so interested in finding a smoking gun."

"Well, I was looking more for a bloody knife, but yes, that's the general idea."

He considered this turn of events for a moment, and then said, "Maura Winters, now Ferguson, was the teaching assistant whose testimony was the key in the acquittal of Theo McAlister. She provided his alibi. That's how they're related."

"They were together? They had a relationship?" I asked.

"I didn't say that. I only said that Maura testified to them having a relationship."

"So they didn't?" Leslie asked.

"I didn't say that either," he said.

Lawyers.

"In your opinion, off the record or whatever, did McAlister kill the students?" I asked.

Leslie nodded like she wanted the answer to that question as well.

He didn't say anything, which meant plenty. He wasn't about to admit to having defended a murderer, even successfully. And he wasn't going to admit that his key witness had committed perjury. But he wasn't going to tell us she hadn't either. McAlister had done it, if I was reading Grant Spencer correctly.

"Are we going to work together on this, Grant?" I asked, "Or, is it every man for himself? Because if it is, I've got a ticking clock to beat and I can't waste time sitting at this table with you right now."

"A ticking clock?" he asked.

"Your client, Maura Ferguson, gave me until midnight Monday to find the real murderer, or she was going to the police with a frame up of me."

"Why would she do that?" he asked.

"She told me it was because she was going to get Leslie to work with her. Leslie gets my money, Maura gets Sam's money, assuming the state kills me."

"And yet here you sit with Leslie," he said. "What could that mean?"

"It means, you stupid fuck, that Maura was lying to Jake."

Leslie's temper was starting to get the better of her. Her patience was gone. She probably had a splitting headache from that nasty bump on her noggin. Poor Grant. He is a lawyer, so I just let her go.

"At least you've told him that," Grant said.

"She. Was. Lying," she said, like it was three very distinct sentences.

"Or, just maybe, you are now," he said. He was more courageous than I thought.

"Fuck you, *Mister* Spencer. Fuck you."

"Do you talk that way on the air, too?"

"You're an asshole," she said. "A fucking asshole."

He didn't flinch. He didn't even blink. His expression was even and his eyes steady. Leslie's weren't. She muttered a blue stream of profanity that would make a rap star blush as she walked through the back door and out onto the deck, closing the door behind her.

"Can we trust her?" Grant asked me.

"My heart wants to," I said.

"That's usually not good enough. Not when the stakes are this high. She seems high strung and somewhat defensive."

"You noticed," I said.

"Tell her as little as you can," he said.

I nodded my acceptance of his terms but had no real plans to stick to them.

"She sure swears a lot," he said. "I wouldn't have figured her for that."

"I think it's her release after being on the air. She constantly has to curb that part of her speech, so she just lets it fly when she's off the air and not on the job."

"You'd think maybe the language would just sort of extinguish itself, wouldn't you?" he said.

"I'm no psychologist," I said, "but it hasn't worked out that way so far."

Grant took the chair Leslie had vacated, closer to me than I really wanted him. He pulled a yellow legal pad and a pen across the table so it was sitting between us. He jotted the names of the victims down in the center of the page and drew a circle around them. Then he scribbled the names of all the significant people he could think of, each in their own little circle around the one in the middle. Maura, Leslie, Annie, me, and McAlister were all there. I watched, but he didn't write down the names of anyone I didn't know, which probably meant he didn't know all that much more than I did.

Was Grant about to invite me into his ring of knowledge? Would that mean I'd be sharing mine with him? Was he a good guy to have on my side? Was I a good guy for him to have on his? Did he really not know any more? Or was he merely writing down all the names I had mentioned? And was Leslie in the hot tub? Naked?

Focus, Jake, focus.

When the great Grant Spencer spoke, it was in a voice that let me know I should see him just that way. Unfortunately the message didn't agree with the pitch.

He said, "Someone killed Sam Ferguson and Shannon Powell."

He tapped his pen several times in their circle in the center of the page while looking very earnestly into my eyes. I felt like a juror in his courtroom, but I'd seen this act before from his peers. I wasn't buying it.

I said, "No shit, Grant."

He looked perturbed, but it didn't slow him down.

"The police," he began, "think Maura Ferguson did it. You think Theo McAlister might have done it. Maura wants to frame you for it. And isn't it all a little too convenient that Annabella Silvestri just suddenly entered your life?"

Was it?

"I entered her life, Grant, and that's for the record."

"Did you? You may have stepped into her brother's life, but she then came into yours. It wasn't the other way around."

"True, but she wouldn't have done that had I not first brought Donnie into this."

"It's all a little convenient," he said.

Bullshit.

I said, "Annie didn't kill anyone."

He raised his eyebrows enough so I got the point.

"You know what I mean," I said. "She didn't kill Sam and Shannon."

"Who do you really think did it, Jake? Maura? McAlister? You must have some sort of educated guess. Let's hear it."

"My guess is it was someone not on this list, though I can't completely eliminate any of them but me."

"And Ms. Silvestri?" he asked.

"I can't completely eliminate her, but she didn't do it."

"You're not as much help as I thought you'd be. Haven't you found anything out the last couple days with all of your snooping around?"

"Haven't you? You're the lawyer. I'm nobody. You said so yourself. How am I going to find anything out, except by sheer luck? Where are your files? Don't you have police reports or something? Haven't you looked into this? Have you eliminated anyone from your list?"

"My files are at my office. I wasn't aware I would need them at your house. The police reports are there as well, though they showed nothing conclusive that we've been able to find. And unless I put you on my payroll as an investigator or something, I can't share what's in there with you anyway."

He had that superior look in his eyes again. This guy needed a good ass whooping. I couldn't wait until I saw Tony and the boys again. They would probably even do it pro bono. For now I would have to make do with my superior wit and charm.

"Hire me then, Grant. It's the only way we're going to get anywhere on this."

"As an investigator?" he asked.

"Call it whatever you want. I think I should be able to see what you've got. I'm willing to work with you, if that's what you want, but

I'm determined to work against you just the same, if that's the way you want it."

"I've got an investigator," he said. "He's out investigating right now."

"Call me a special advisor or something then," I said.

He considered this a moment, then tore a sheet from the legal pad. He scribbled some lines on it before signing his name on the bottom. He pushed it and the pen over to me. It basically said he was hiring me as a special advisor on all criminal proceedings, as of this night, for the salary of one dollar per day. I signed it and he seemed satisfied.

He said, "There are no prints in the Ferguson bedroom that belong to anyone but Sam, Shannon, or Maura. There are prints in higher traffic areas of the house, like the living room and kitchen, but they haven't bothered trying to match them. They don't think they're much of a lead anyway, because the Fergusons entertained quite often."

"Do they have a murder weapon?" I asked.

"Don't you read the paper?"

"Papers lie, Grant. Sometimes the police lie to the news people. Even I know that. Do they have a weapon?"

"No weapon," he said. "They both died from multiple stab wounds from a straight edged blade, like a large kitchen knife. The holes were all over the chest, neck, stomach, and arms of both victims. Whoever killed them would have had to be covered in blood from doing it."

"What about the dog? Same thing?" I asked, pretty sure it was.

"No. The dog was poisoned. He was dead before the murders took place."

Interesting, but I couldn't place why.

"What about the marks on Maura's arms? The press made it sound like they came from the dog. They didn't?"

"Papers lie, Jake. And sometimes so do the police. Sound familiar?"

"What kind of poison did they use?" I asked.

"Does it really matter?" he asked.

I shook my head no, but somewhere inside I knew it did.

I looked up and saw Leslie standing behind Grant. She couldn't have been there long, but I hadn't looked up in awhile either. She looked at me like she had something she just had to say, and right now. I looked at Grant quickly and then back at her. She shook her head slowly, no. Whatever it was, she didn't want Grant to hear it.

"I think I better go outside and check on Leslie," I said to Grant after she had slipped back out of the room. If Grant had noticed her there, he didn't let on. "She might be drowned in my hot tub."

He waved his hand dismissively, lost in thought, as I walked past him and onto the porch. Leslie was sitting on the steps heading into my backyard, knees curled up under her chin.

"What's up?" I asked. "You could have been nicer to the sleazy lawyer guy."

"Did he write his own name on that suspect list, Jake? The page with all the little circles of suspects—was his name on it?"

"No. Should it be?"

Very quietly she said, "Does he always drive a limousine?"

"What? I doubt it. Why?"

Her eyes grabbed hold of me and tugged hard. She wasn't going to say any more. She wanted me to make the same connection she had, so I started looking for it. I think Freud called it free association or something.

I rambled, "Does he always drive a limo? Annie and I went to the party in a limo. Tony drove it. It was gone when I came out. There's a limo in the driveway now. Damn, Les, how long did it take you to think of that?"

"How long was I out here? There are no other cars here, besides mine."

"So how did he get here?" I asked.

"Exactly my point. How the hell did that smug little fucker get here?"

"He commented on your eloquent way with words, by the way," I said.

"Fuck him."

"So, did they pick him up? Are they still here? And who is 'they' anyway?"

"All good questions," she said. "I have no answers."

"But there is a light on in the back bedroom," I said, pointing to its window above us.

She had to turn her head to look, but smiled when she did.

"Well, what the hell do you suppose that means, Jake?"

Forty-four hours to go.

CHAPTER TWENTY-TWO

The possibilities were staggering. Grant Spencer had to know there was someone up there. He just had to. Or did he? Could he have taken a taxi to my house? Wouldn't he have asked us about the limo out front? He had to know there was someone upstairs, didn't he? Was he trying to protect them by not telling us they were there? And was I sure there was indeed someone there? Could the light have just been left on? I had left in a hurry, so it could have happened, right?

"I just saw the shadows of two heads, Jake," Leslie said, her head tilted back.

"You're sure?"

"Yes, I'm sure. Who do you think it is?"

"Maura and McAlister," I said. "Annie's dead, and Tony too, and those two stole the limo and came over here. Grant was lying about Annie giving him the cell phone number. She didn't have anything to do with him being here. Maura and McAlister picked him up after the party. And now they're all three here."

"Sounds good," she said.

"The bodies might be out in the limo. Should we check?"

"That's kind of morbid, isn't it?"

"Kind of," I agreed.

"Let's go," she said. "You first."

She stood up and let me walk past her down the steps. The grass at the bottom was wet from the early morning dew and I slipped a little stepping on it. I put my hands on Leslie's waist to make sure she didn't do the same.

We sneaked around to the front, making sure no one was watching, or at least we made ourselves think that's what we were doing. Before we walked into the clearing of my front yard, I pulled my Ronald Reagan mask back over my head. Leslie shook her head and pushed me on toward the car. Her hand never left the small of my back.

"Try the back door," she whispered behind me, pushing toward it.

I nodded and did as I was told. It didn't open, so I proceeded to try all the other doors too. No luck.

"The doors are all locked," I said.

"Just a second," I heard, but not from Leslie. It was in the speaker in my ear, and it was definitely Annie's voice.

"Annie?" I said into my mask, "Where are you?"

"I'm right behind you," Leslie said, "And my name's not Annie."

I pointed to the mask and where the microphone was, but she didn't seem to get it. It didn't matter because just then the door in front of us opened, slamming into me hard. I caught myself enough to give Leslie a shove through the opening and into the back seat. I followed her as quickly as I could, pulling the door closed behind me, careful not to slam.

There on the seat across from us sat Richard Nixon, or at least Annabella Silvestri dressed up like the former President. I pulled off my Reagan mask and she peeled hers too. Leslie was busy picking her jaw off the floor.

"What the ...?" she said.

"It looks like Annie hasn't perished after all, and for the second time this week," I said to Leslie. "This is definitely good news."

"It is for me," Annie said.

"Where's Tony?" I asked.

"He's not here? He's not behind the wheel?"

"No one is," I said.

"AWOL, then," she said. "I haven't seen him since he dropped the two of us at this party. I didn't know Leslie would be here."

"We're not at the party," I said. "Are you alright?"

"We're not at the party? Where are we then?"

"My house," I said. "This is your car, and it's in my driveway."

"You don't remember anything?" Leslie asked her.

"No, but my head hurts." She was rubbing a spot roughly on the same part of the skull where Leslie's bump was. I pulled her head toward me and looked.

"Matching eggs," I said to the two of them. "Someone whacked you over the head in the same spot they whacked Les. What's the last thing you do remember?"

"Being in the den, waiting for Maura to come back from the bathroom. It was dark, and I thought I heard her coming so I was tugging my mask down over my face. And then I heard your voice in my ear, Jake. You said the doors were all locked."

"It had to be McAlister," Leslie said.

I nodded slowly, trying to remember if I had seen the fox costume by the pool while Annie and Maura were inside together. I couldn't say for sure. Finally, I knew what a witness must feel under cross-examination.

Leslie said to Annie, "Did you talk to Grant Spencer earlier tonight?"

"Spencer? The lawyer? No. I don't think I've ever spoken to him. Why?"

"He's inside," I said. "He said you gave him the number of the cell phone I had, and that he should call me if he hadn't heard from you by one o'clock. And that's how Les and I ended up here. He said you told him you'd be dead if you hadn't called by one."

"He's lying," she said.

"Fucking lawyers," Leslie said. "That's all they do."

"So how did he get the number?" I asked.

Annie started searching her pockets. Her hands came out empty.

She said, "My cell's gone, too. Your phone, the one I gave you, is on the speed dial. Maybe he just started punching through them, hoping to get lucky."

"Probably," I said.

"Now what?" Leslie asked us. "Who the hell can we trust? What are we going to do? This sitting around catching up is nice, but won't

Grant start to miss you pretty soon, Jake? What did you tell him when you came outside?"

"I told him I was coming to check on you."

"You'll both be missed soon, if you aren't already," Annie said. "We've got to get out of here and regroup. Are the keys in the ignition?"

Leslie stuck her head through the glass divider and came back with a "No."

"Where's your car? How did the two of you get here?"

"It's the Porsche down the street there," I said, nodding in its direction. Annie looked at it.

"That's no good. It's too far, with too much open space between it and us. We'll be sitting ducks if we go for it," Annie said.

"You sound like a General or something," Leslie said, "But I guess you are now, aren't you?"

"Sort of," she agreed. "It comes with the job."

"Some job," Les said.

"One of us has to go for it," Annie said. "Get the car, bring it up close, pick the other two up, and off we go. Any volunteers?"

It was a short but nervous silence, broken when Leslie said, "I'll go."

"No," I said, sounding almost like an order.

"Jake, it's got to be me. They'll notice Annie walking down the street. They think she's unconscious in here. They'd notice you too, because you're worth a couple hundred million dollars to them, though I don't see how. Me? I'm just the foul-mouthed blonde girlfriend. Grant didn't seem to care when I left you alone with him. He won't care if he thinks I'm leaving now."

"She's got a point," Annie said.

"No," I said again.

"Give me the keys, Jake," she said, her hand held out, waiting.

Reluctantly I pulled them from my pocket and dropped them in her hand. She flashed a nervous smile at us, took a deep breath and let it out, and kissed me on the cheek.

"Don't go anywhere," she said to us, just like she did the camera every morning. "I'll be right back."

173

And then she was off. The door opened and closed with barely a whisper. She stood up and walked at a fairly normal pace toward the Porsche. Her hands were buried in the pockets of her pants. Her eyes fixed on the sidewalk at her feet. Annie was watching me watch Leslie.

"That girl loves you, Jake," she said.

I nodded silently.

"She'll be okay," she added.

Again, I nodded.

Ten feet from her car a gunshot broke the quiet, still of the night. Leslie hit the ground with a belly flop, and then crawled on all fours to the far side of the little Porsche and the relative safety it provided.

Was Leslie hit? Could I live with myself if she was? Where did the shot come from? Who was pulling the trigger? Should I go help her? Could I help her?

"The shot came from the window right above the front door," Annie said.

"My bedroom," I answered, not taking my eyes off Leslie.

"Can't tell who's behind the gun, though," she added.

Two more shots were fired in that direction, one bouncing off the hood, the other hitting a tree on the curb. Leslie was out of my view, I hoped safe. As the next shot was fired, so was the engine of the Porsche. She popped it into gear and took off with a noisy screech of rubber.

"Here we go," Annie said. "You ready?"

"You go first, jump in the back. I'll be right behind you."

"Right," she said, already opening the door.

Leslie jerked to a stop, clipping the limo door, but didn't quite rip it off its hinges. Annie jumped out, yanked open the door of the Porsche, and dived into the back headfirst. I was so close behind that I caught her heel on my chin as she followed through. Leslie stomped on the gas before my butt was settled on the leather, and to the end of the block before I managed to close the door.

"Everyone alive?" Annie asked from the back. "Anyone hit?"

Leslie held up her right arm. There was blood streaming from a tear in her forearm. I've never been shot, but it had to hurt. She didn't say a word. Her eyes were focused on getting us to safety. She'd deal with the wound when she could.

"Here they come," Annie said after not long enough.

I turned my head and spotted the huge black beast round a corner with a nasty fishtail, right itself, and return to our pursuit. Leslie just kept turning corners and stomping on the gas.

The eastern sky was starting to brighten some and traffic was thickening just a little. Leslie just kept running. She weaved around the curves and up and down the hills, through the Market District as it was just coming to life, and then back and forth through another series of those damned curves. Couldn't they have built the city somewhere flat? Silly bastards just cared about the tourist traffic, or at least the scenery that attracted those tourists. I just wanted to get away from the limo as fast as we could, and the streets of this city weren't helping.

Leslie had the maneuverability advantage if nothing else. Every time she had to slow down for a bend in the road, they had to slow even more. We were pulling away, but not fast enough for me. I kept waiting for the movie chase-scene problems to develop, but no bus blocked our path, no workmen got in our way.

She hit the freeway, heading south. We lost them weaving through a neighborhood full of Bosnians, but she was taking no chances. She let up on the speed when Annie reminded her we didn't have time for the police to stop us.

Sixty miles away she finally stopped at a roadside motel, up a hill, just off the freeway exit. We got one room, two beds, and locked the door behind us.

Annie went to work on Leslie's wound like a battlefield medic who'd seen it all before. She was calm and precise and done in a few minutes. Leslie thanked her and went to sleep, curled up in a ball on one bed.

"I'll take first watch," I said to Annie.

She didn't argue. She stretched out on her back on the other bed. I turned the bathroom light on and all the others off. I planted myself in an uncomfortable chair and stared out at the quiet parking lot.

I was down to forty hours, and not much closer to the truth.

CHAPTER TWENTY-THREE

Annie gave me a gun before she climbed into bed. She called it an automatic something-or-other. "Just point and squeeze, squeeze, squeeze," she said. "Don't stop until they drop. And maybe not then."

I thought of Sonny Corleone in *The Godfather*. He drove to a tollbooth and the other guys just kept squeezing. Sonny was certainly dropped. He came out looking like a block of Swiss cheese.

It was a gray, misty day and there wasn't much to look at out the window of this motel. People with our kind of financial standing wouldn't normally pick a place like this, but we were trying to hide, so I guess straying from the expected was okay.

There was a Denny's restaurant across the lot and it had been awhile since I sat in Annie's kitchen and didn't eat. A Grand Slam breakfast sounded good, but I fought the urge. Was I slipping into hysteria? Maybe, but what's wrong with some shriveled sausage and stale pancakes now and then?

I have no idea what I expected to see through the window of our motel room. Certainly, I knew I wouldn't see a black limousine. We had lost them before getting out of town and they couldn't possibly know where we were now. I couldn't have been looking for that car, but that's exactly what I found myself doing.

A police cruiser, local, docked itself in a handicapped spot at the Denny's and two less than tough looking guys got out. They were laughing at something as they walked through the front door. None of us were wanted as far as I knew; yet I felt strangely compelled to avoid the officers. I even cursed their presence under my breath, thinking they would somehow impede our efforts.

"Cops are eating at Denny's?" asked Annie, still sleepy in her voice.

She was running both hands through her black hair, and arching her back to stretch out the kinks. She squinted in the direction of the illegally parked cruiser.

"They've been inside almost two hours," I said, looking at my watch.

"Probably not much crime to fight out this way," she said.

"I wish they'd hurry up and leave," I told her without looking away from their car.

"Why? We're the good guys, remember? If anything, I'm glad they're so close by. If something happens, help is right next door."

"They'll find out who we are," I said.

"Who we are? Jake, you're a rich, retired janitor. Leslie's a television celebrity. And they won't have anything on me," she said, avoiding mentioning her job again.

"But we're involved in the big murder trial in the city," I said. "They'll know that."

"No, they won't. Has any of your involvement been on TV? The paper? It hasn't. No one knows we're tied to that. Least of all local yokels like these guys out here. Relax."

I couldn't relax, but admitted to myself she was right. Just because we knew Maura was trying to frame me, it didn't mean anyone else knew. Just because there were people in my house, shooting live ammo at us, it didn't mean anyone else knew.

Annie offered to watch the window, so I traded my chair for her bed. Leslie kept sleeping, a soft snore rising from the sheets. When I woke up the cops were gone and it was closing in on lunchtime. Leslie was awake, and she and Annie were talking about Theo McAlister. They saw I was awake and included me.

Annie said, "Jake, what sort of teacher was McAlister?"

"College professor," I said through a yawn.

"What subject?"

"Biology. Or maybe physics. I don't remember. Something in science. Why?"

"Just wondering. Is he covering for Maura, or is it the other way around?"

"And which one did the killing and which one the covering last time?" Leslie added.

"I don't know," I said. "It's obvious they're involved with one another, or at least know each other. The crime itself, with the sex and the stabbing, is similar to last time. Maura told me at lunch the other day that her case was different because she was innocent."

"Meaning he wasn't?" Annie asked.

"That's the way I took it."

"But it was her testimony that was the key in his acquittal," Annie said.

"Which would lead me to believe that, at least that time, Theo did the stabbing and Maura the covering," I said.

"And this time?" Leslie asked.

"Maura's got the most motive. She will directly inherit Sam's money, assuming she's not convicted of killing him. And Sam was cheating on her."

"But she was cheating on him, too, wasn't she?" Leslie asked.

"With who?"

"You. McAlister. Who knows?"

"She wasn't cheating with me, unless a movie is now considered adulterous. McAlister? I just have a hard time seeing that as sexual. I think she's probably teasing him to get what she wants from him."

"So she killed them because she was jealous and jilted and stood to be rich?" Annie asked. We all nodded as one.

"Does she have the stomach for it?" Annie asked.

"Well, we know McAlister does," I said. "And he could have done it to impress her, to free her, to get some of Sam's money. Again, who knows?"

"Where does Grant fit in?" Leslie asked. "He had to know Maura and McAlister were upstairs, right?"

"I don't see how he couldn't have known," I said.

"So what's his part in all this?" she asked.

"Maybe he's trying to protect his two clients from our prying eyes," Annie said.

"Well, maybe," I said, "but I work for the man now."

I produced the yellow contract from the front pocket of my pants and showed it to them both.

"A dollar a day?" Annie chuckled. "After taxes you'll be lucky to see fifty cents of that, buddy. Did he pay you up front?"

"Let's assume Grant knew they were upstairs," I said. "That would mean he lied about being alone in the house. He lied about why he was there. He lied about why he called me."

"He's a fucking lawyer," Leslie said, "so he's a fucking liar. They all are. It's not a coincidence that lawyer and liar are so close to the same word."

"Wanda told me that Grant had a crush on Maura. Maybe he killed them, to impress her," I said.

No one seemed to think that was likely.

Leslie said, "It's got to be Maura. Occum's Razor, remember Annie? Occum's Razor from psychology?"

"The simplest explanation is usually the right one, or something like that, right?" she said.

"Something like that," Leslie agreed. "Maura is the simplest explanation, and we don't need to make it any more complicated than that."

"Something else bothers me," I said to them both. "Shouldn't whoever killed them be getting feted instead of fried? Sam Ferguson was a total shit head and everyone in the neighborhood knew it. Shannon Powell bought some boobs and let Sam play with them whenever he wanted, and never did much else. I'm not sure anyone has ever said anything nice about either one of them, so why does anyone care that they got killed?"

"Well, there are laws, for one thing," Annie said, her heart not in it.

"We did a feature on them this week," Leslie said. "Sam was actually very active in the community and wasn't afraid to spread his money around. He's paid for the development of a series of playgrounds around the city, he contributes to several charities, he's helped with city planning to help control urban blight, and he was actually a highly sought after motivational speaker. Other than

179

fucking Shannon, he wasn't that bad of a guy. Or at least that's the way we made him look."

"What about Shannon?" I asked.

"Fucking home wrecker," she said in a way that meant there was to be no discussion on that.

I was in an antagonizing mood, so I didn't let it go.

I said, "You mean to tell me that Shannon Powell never did anything worthwhile her whole life? She left behind no family? She never paid for life-saving surgery for someone's cat? She never helped an old guy with a cane across a busy street?"

"She's a home wrecker, Jake. Have you no sense of right and wrong? You used to be a blue-collar guy. I thought you all knew the difference between right and wrong."

"Sometimes it's a pretty hazy line," I said. "I bet Annie would agree with me on that. Annie?"

"Don't drag me into your mouth with your foot," she said.

"You're right about the family," Leslie said, "But she didn't have one, at least not around here. Her parents died five or six years ago, she was an only child, she's never been married or had kids herself."

"Fucking home wrecker," I said.

Leslie said, "Jake, have you ever saved a cat from certain death?"

"No, but some of the crap I used to throw in the dumpsters at the Westlake Building might have killed a few."

"It's Sunday, right?" Leslie asked. The days were kind of running together.

"Yes it is," I said. "Do we need to find a bar with a dish so you can watch the Packers' game?"

"Bye week for them," she said. "Otherwise your ass would be on the phone by now looking."

"How they doing this year?" I asked. I had quit paying attention with her gone.

"Six and two, a game behind the Vikings. They play next Monday at Lambeau." And then her relaxed expression tensed, and not because it was a big week for her team. She was looking at Annie, so I did too.

Annie's eyes were fixed on the lot at Denny's. She reached inside her jacket, still the same one she wore for her costume, and slowly pulled out a gun. She held it tight to her chest, both hands on it, pointed to the sky. Leslie saw it too and ran to the edge of the window so she could peak around the curtains.

"What's up?" Leslie asked.

Annie pointed with the barrel of the gun toward the lot. Looking for a spot to park was a black limousine.

"How the hell?" Leslie asked.

"There are a lot of limos in the world, Leslie," Annie said. "It might not be them."

"But it might. It might be Maura and Grant and Theo. They might have found us. They might be in there with guns, ready to take the rest of this arm off," she said, grabbing the bandage Annie had put there.

The black beast circled through the Denny's lot and didn't stop, though there were plenty of places big enough for them to park. They crossed over into our motel's lot at a slow crawl. They stopped behind Leslie's Porsche for a second, or was that my imagination? Finally, they swung wide into two open spots, behind Leslie's car, facing away from our window.

"It's them," Annie said. "That plate is one of ours."

We looked at the license on the back of the car. There's nothing like criminals with a sense of humor. It said, "MOBBED 4." It wasn't necessary to ask if she was sure, so we all braced for the worst.

Thirty-six hours to go.

CHAPTER TWENTY-FOUR

" Jake, what do we do now?" Leslie asked.

She looked worried, probably because she had already shed blood for the cause and didn't feel like she could afford to lose any more.

"I don't know. Why don't you ask Annie? She's the professional."

We both did just that. She didn't bat an eye.

"Well," she said, "we've got guns, too."

"Guns?" Leslie asked. "As in more than one?"

I showed her my automatic squeezing machine. It didn't thrill her; I can say that for sure, but I was glad I had it now.

"We should go out and meet them," Annie said. "Quickly, before they're out of the car. We might catch them off guard and gain an advantage."

"And do what with that advantage?" Leslie asked. "Shoot them?"

"Don't be silly. We'll only shoot them as a last resort," Annie said, like she had these sorts of conversations every day. Maybe she did.

I opened the door and said, "Are you coming?"

They both did, though Leslie didn't seem to want to.

Annie told me on the way out to put my gun in the pocket of my jacket, and to put my hand in there, finger on the trigger. She said split seconds were a matter of life and death sometimes and I didn't want to be fumbling with the one thing that could tip me toward the life end of that continuum.

What were those three criminals doing in that limo? Why was it taking them so long to come out? Were they watching the motel, or Leslie's car, and waiting for us to show ourselves? Were they cleaning their guns, getting them ready to kill more efficiently? Would a bullet really hurt that much? Did it depend on where it hit you?

We positioned ourselves a couple cars away and waited. Annie and I both had our right hands in our jackets. Leslie had both hers buried in the pockets of her jeans. It was cool, but the clouds had left behind a bright sky. All three of us were squinting in the direction of the bad people and their car.

The door on the back, right side opened and we all crouched a bit as Annie waved us down. Leslie had her back against the car and I think she was praying. Annie was peering over the trunk and I'm sure she was stalking. I tried to look through the windows, dirty as they were, and I was just watching.

After what must have been only ten seconds but seemed like ten minutes, Annie said, "It's okay," and waved us out from behind the car. Neither of us was too sure that was the right move, but she seemed committed to it, so we followed her, somewhat reluctantly.

Climbing out of the car, and buttoning her blouse as she did, was Wanda Gaines. I breathed a heavy sigh of relief and Leslie's face relaxed in an instant. She didn't see us at first, but when Donnie followed her out, he did. He didn't seem all that surprised, though we did startle him.

He said, "Annie? Jake? News gal? What are you guys doing out here?"

"Hiding," Annie said. "You?"

It was obvious to me what they had just been doing in the back of the limo, and now I understood why it took them so long to get out. But they wouldn't have had to drive all the way out here for that.

Wanda said, "It's such a nice day. I made Donnie take me for a ride. All that time indoors gets a little old after awhile. Kinda stuffy, you know? So we came on out, told James to just drive. Donnie got hungry, saw the Denny's sign, so we thought we'd stop for a bite to eat."

Annie looked at her little brother, sizing him up I think. He looked a little nervous, or embarrassed maybe, I guessed because his sister caught him.

Donnie said, "That's right, we're just out for a little Sunday drive."

The five of us decided to sit down and eat lunch together. It was Annie's idea and no one argued against it. Donnie ordered two meals, one a breakfast and the other a lunch. The waitress didn't seem to think that was unusual at all. I was sitting between Annie and Leslie on one side of an oversized booth, and Wanda had Donnie pushed into the corner of the other side.

Small talk ensued. Wanda and Donnie had spent the better part of Saturday inside Donnie's bedroom doing what people their age do best. We'd been hit in the head, shot at, and nearly killed. Well, not me, but the people I was with.

Wanda listened intently as the three of us took turns telling about our experience. Donnie didn't seem to care, but he did have two meals to eat, right?

Wanda said, "Grant always has been protective of his clients. This seems a little bit extreme, though. Are you sure he knew they were upstairs?"

"We're not sure of much," I said, "other than there were bullets flying at us from the house, he was in it, and so were they."

"You're sure of that?" she asked again.

"I think we are."

I looked at Leslie and Annie and they both nodded their agreement.

"Where do you think they are now, then?" she asked us between forkfuls of egg.

"Looking for us somewhere probably," I said.

Annie said, "My guess is they split up. Someone is at Jake's house to see if we go back there. Someone else is at the Plaza, since both Leslie and Maura have rooms. And the third person might be looking around wherever they can."

"Have you told the police any of this?" she asked us.

"Jake thinks they won't see it quite the same way we do," Leslie said.

"You all know why," I said.

"This is different, Jake," Wanda said. "A crime was committed against you. You were shot at. And you know who did it. You should tell the police."

"That's a good point," Annie said. "We wouldn't have to bring the rest of this into it. They'd probably ask, but we could be vague with the details. Maybe they'd get arrested. That would help me sleep tonight."

"You really think that's what we should do?" I asked.

She thought a moment before saying, "Absolutely."

The plan was to drive right to police headquarters, downtown. It would take us an hour or so to get there, so we'd rough out the details we would allow them to know as we drove. I imagined Andy Sipowicz rubbing his bald head before he went looking for the skells. I watch too much TV.

I paid the lunch tab for everyone, not to mention the motel. I paid for a second night and told Donnie and Wanda the room was theirs to use as they wished. They thanked me and we were on our way.

Was this the right move? Would we be able to pull it off, not telling them too much? I was the weak link here, wasn't I? Annie's a criminal, Leslie's on the tube, but I'm just a janitor, right? Was I sure Maura was one of the people in my house? Would her arrest mean I would forfeit my bail money? Would she have to get convicted for that to happen? Did it matter, as long as she hadn't run?

Halfway back to town Annie said she didn't think she should go in to see the police. She made a convincing argument that her family ties might cause us some trouble. She said a great looking couple like Leslie and myself would be more likely to get the sympathetic ear of the detectives.

She dropped us at the curb and told me to page her when we were done. She didn't say where she was going or what she was doing. I was too nervous to ask.

Inside, the desk sergeant, fat, with a shiny, red nose, was friendlier than I would have expected. Maybe Annie was right about the two of us.

"What can I do for you folks?" he asked from his seat.

"We've been shot at," I said, "and my girlfriend's been hit."

I pointed at Leslie's arm so he would know I was telling the truth, but that it wasn't life threatening just yet.

"Been to the hospital, looks like," he said.

"No sir, we haven't," I answered. "I was an athletic trainer in college. They teach you all kinds of first aid stuff. It finally came in handy."

"I see. Athletic trainer, huh? Where at?"

This lie was spinning out of my control already so Leslie short-circuited it by saying, "I don't mean to be pushy Sergeant, but I've been shot. Is there a detective we can talk to? Soon?"

He picked up his phone and asked for someone named Clint. He said "Uh huh" about four times and hung up.

To us he said with a point to our right, "Down that hall, third door on the left is the detectives squad. You'll want Detective Bildsten. Got it?"

"Yes, thank you. Detective Bildsten, third door on the left, down that hall," I said.

He nodded and went back to whatever he had been doing.

Leslie whispered, "Athletic trainer? Is that the best you could come up with?"

"I'm new at this. I thought about telling him I'd been a field medic in Nam. Athletic trainer was better than janitor, though, don't you think?"

"Sure, Jake," she said, just as nervous as me.

Detective Clint Bildsten looked like he might be the right age to enroll in the athletic trainer's program at the University. You did have to finish high school before they gave you a shield, right? He shook both our hands and led us back to his desk. He found an extra chair and wiped off the seat for Leslie. Mine he left dusty. His desk was covered with paperwork. He had a jar of black jellybeans wedged between his computer and the wall. He took a handful and tossed them into his mouth as he found the right form on his screen. At least the kid knew how to get around a hard drive.

He went through the usual sort of questions about name, address and so on. He wasn't impressed by my answers, but Leslie caught his ear.

"Leslie Watson? From the news? Oh, it is you, isn't it?" "In the flesh," she said.

In his dreams.

His cheery disposition darkened just a little when she gave him the same home address I had. Was she being presumptuous? Did I care?

"So what can I do for you, Ms. Watson?" he asked, ignoring me.

She proceeded to tell him the story of our little escapade at my— at our house. I was actually relieved it was her that had to fib about it and not me. She really wasn't telling lies. She just wasn't telling the complete truth. Then again, did we know what the complete truth was? Does anyone?

"Do you have any idea who might have done this?" he asked her.

"Yes. Maura Ferguson, Theo McAlister, and Grant Spencer."

He wrote down all three names.

He said, "Those are some pretty heavy hitters. Are you sure? Spencer's a lawyer, you know. You better be sure."

"I'm sure," she said in a way that even made me believe her.

When he asked where he could find them, Leslie pointed him to the Plaza, my house, or Grant's office. He offered to call a doctor for her, but she declined. He offered her coffee, and she declined that too. Finally he excused himself and left us at his desk.

"Nice job," I said. "You worked him just right."

"What do you mean? I was just doing what we agreed to in the car."

"That kid's so star struck you could have told him Jimmy Hoffa was in the trunk of the Porsche and he'd have believed you."

"Celebrity does have its privileges, Jake," she said. "You seemed a little star struck yourself the other night."

"I'll show you star struck," I said, but before I could go any further Detective Bildsten was back.

"Well," he said, "there have been some developments."

"Developments?" Leslie asked.

"Mmm hmm. I called up to the one-five, the precinct up where you folks live, and they said they were out to your house last night. Someone in the neighborhood reported the shots being fired and so they responded to that call."

"Well, what are the developments, Detective Bildsten?" Leslie asked.

"They found the lawyer, Mr. Spencer, in the living room. He was tied up and gagged, and he had a big old bump on his head. There was no one else there."

"Tied up? Hit on the head? Who did that? Did Maura Ferguson and Theo McAlister do it? Are those two in custody yet?" she asked.

"No ma'am, they're not. Mr. Spencer claims he was alone in the house except for the two of you."

"Which means what exactly?" Leslie asked.

I knew what it meant. It meant Maura and Theo came downstairs while the three of us were in the limo. They came downstairs, conked Grant on the back of the head, tied him and gagged him, and ran back upstairs to start shooting at us.

"It means," the detective said, "you two hit him over the head and tied him up. Or, at least that's what Mr. Spencer says."

And I only had thirty-three hours left.

CHAPTER TWENTY-FIVE

The good news, and I'm stretching here, was that Grant Spencer was not involved with the McAlister crime ring. The bad news, and there was plenty to pick from, was that he thought Leslie and I were.

The kid cop had excused himself again, but this time he made us promise not to go anywhere. Were we about to be booked? Could I bail myself out this time? What would the charge be?

"Grant couldn't have seen whoever hit him," Leslie said.

"Obviously not, since it wasn't one of us," I said.

"And he truly did not know they were upstairs."

"It looks that way. How'd he get to the house then? And why didn't he say anything to us about the limo? You would think he would have noticed it, wouldn't you?"

"I hope we don't have to wait until we're in court to get those answers," she said.

Junior came back and said, "We're gonna have to run you up to the one-five. They've got some questions for you, and they want them answered today."

Why had we come in again? Hadn't we been the victims just a few minutes ago? Weren't we still? What kind of questions would be asked at the one-five? Would we have to lie some more? Would we need lawyers?

"What kind of questions?" Leslie asked sweetly. "Can't you just ask us here? It seems like an awful trouble to take us all the way up there. We're already at a police station. Why can't you ask us the questions, then tell the guys up there what we said?"

He said with an emphatic shake of his head, "Doesn't work that way Ms. Watson. It's their case, so they get the interview. They know the details better than I do, so they'll know better what to ask and how to follow up on what you say. Understand?"

"Sure, but ..."

I interrupted her, "Detective Bildsten weren't we the victims of a crime? That's why we came in. Would we have come in if we had done something wrong ourselves?"

"Probably not," he said, "but you'd be surprised. There's a lot of stupidity out there."

"But we're victims," I tried again.

"Yes, I know Mr. Jacobs. I've taken your statements and will look into it. Actually, I'll forward those statements up to the one-five as well, since it's their neighborhood, not mine."

"Who did Grant Spencer say was shooting at us?" I asked.

"I don't know, which is why we need to get up there and get this cleared up. If someone was shooting at you, then we need to find out who it was. If Mr. Spencer was held hostage, we need to find out who did that as well."

We stopped arguing because it wasn't going to help us any. And I didn't like the way he discounted our story of being shot at. We had been shot at. Didn't the bullet hole on Leslie's arm count for something?

I used Annie's cell phone and dialed her pager number while the young guy was out rounding up someone to go with him to the one-five with his prisoners. Five minutes later the cell rang. I explained to Annie what was happening. She did an excellent job of hiding any surprise she may have felt. She said she'd move up to that part of town to be close by when we needed her.

She said, "Remember Jake, we're the good guys," and then she hung up.

Were we the good guys? Was Grant one of the good guys? More importantly, where were the bad guys? And who were they?

Detective Clint Bildsten was accompanied by a guy at the other end of the seniority list. And I thought Sheriff Taylor retired when he left Mayberry. I half expected the guy to grab a walker and shuffle behind it out to the car, but he managed fine with his pearl-handled cane.

Sheriff Taylor introduced himself as Detective Henry Bernard, but assured us everyone called him Bernie. They didn't cuff us, I think because it was *the* Leslie Watson with me. Bildsten led her to one back door of his car; Bernie pointed me to the other.

"Thanks, Detective Bernie," I said as he lowered me into the back seat.

"No, son. It's just Bernie. Got it?"

"Yes sir, Bernie," I said.

Leslie slid into the middle of the backseat so we were cheek to cheek on the cheap vinyl. Bildsten was behind the wheel and she immediately started flirting with him in the mirror.

"How does a young guy like you get to be a detective?" she asked.

Bernie said, "I'm not as young as I look, ma'am."

"Now that you mention it Bernie, do you work out?" she asked.

There was no point in playing favorites, since we needed them both on our side.

"No, ma'am. This body was acquired the old fashioned way— beer and chips and plenty of couch time."

"What about you, Clint?" she asked.

He didn't seem to mind her familiarity.

"Four days a week. I'd work out more if the job gave me the time, but it just doesn't. I belong to a club out on the east end."

"It shows," she lied. "Did you start in the force right out of high school? You look so young."

"After college," he said. "I'm older than I look."

No kidding.

This sort of thing kept up for the entire ride. By the time we were two blocks away from my house she had them in the palm of her hand; five minutes later we were at the one-five station house. More cops.

Upstairs Bildsten told us that the detective who had caught the case was named Middleton. He said Detective Middleton was known for his bad temper, but he was also widely known to be a lawyer-hater. Bildsten thought that might help us out.

The four of us were sitting around a table in the coffee room when Detective Middleton walked in. He was tall and chiseled, and his black hair was slicked back with too much motor oil. I noticed right off that his nose hairs could use a trim, and he spent most of the time idly playing with them with one hand or the other. After he figured out which one of us was Leslie Watson and which was John Jacobs he was ready to get started.

He said, "Tell me what you did last night."

I looked at Leslie, so she answered, "Well, we started the evening at a party over at Abe and Helen Roth's house. From there we went over to our house. Mr. Spencer was there when we arrived."

"Wait a minute," Middleton said, "Why was he there? He live with the two of you or something?"

"No Detective. Jake is an investigator for Mr. Spencer. He's helping on the Ferguson case."

"An investigator," he said to himself, like he was trying to remember how to spell it as he wrote it down.

Leslie continued, "We sat in the kitchen talking for awhile, but the two of them started talking business, so I excused myself and went out on the back porch."

"Was Mr. Spencer alone?" Middleton asked.

"He told us he was," Leslie said.

"You don't sound like you think he was. Why not?"

"Jake came outside to check on me after awhile, because it was kind of cool last night. We saw shadows of people upstairs in the window."

"How do you know that wasn't Mr. Spencer?" he asked.

Good question.

"There were two heads," she said. "One could have been him, I guess, but they couldn't have both been him."

"Not likely," he agreed. "Then what happened?"

"Well, we assumed Grant knew there were people upstairs, and therefore that he had lied to us. We decided to run down to the pay phone at the gas station and call the police. You know, report an intruder."

"Good idea," he said, scribbling on his little note pad.

"We were heading to my car when two or three shots were fired at us. One hit me, here on the arm," she said, showing him the bandage. "We made it to the car and got the hell out of there. They followed us for a little while, but we lost them and got out of town for the night."

"And where did you go?" he asked.

"A motel about an hour south of here," she said.

The detectives said they needed to huddle and left to do so. Leslie leaned over and kissed me.

She said, "How'd I do?"

"You're sure you're not an actress? You had me believing you."

"I didn't lie. I just muddied the story a little bit here and there. Is that wrong? Is it dishonest?"

"Probably," I said.

"But you still love me," she said, and it was a statement, not a question.

When the detectives returned, Bildsten smiled at Leslie, which I took as a good sign.

Middleton said, "I'm not going to hold the two of you. There were too many holes in Spencer's story. He didn't see who hit him, but assumed it was you because he thought no one else was there. It could have been anyone."

"It wasn't anyone," Leslie said earnestly.

Bildsten pulled out his notebook, looked at it, and said, "Theo McAlister and Maura Ferguson."

Again, he smiled at Leslie.

"No shit?" Middleton said. "Holy jackpot we've got here if you're right."

"We're right," Leslie said. It was her turn to smile.

Middleton assured us the house had been secured and we were free to return there if we so chose. He said he'd have a cruiser check it every fifteen minutes or so to be sure there was no funny business going on. And yes, he actually used those words.

What did Detective Middleton consider to be funny business? Could it be done alone? With a partner? Or did you need a crowd for truly funny business to take place? And was funny business really ever funny?

We took a Silvestri cab from the one-five station house back to my house, which was once again going to be our house. Bildsten took the parting better than I thought he would. He told Leslie to call him if she ran into any trouble, and gave her a card. I think he was hoping I would run into plenty of trouble.

Back home I told Leslie I had to get out of my Ronald Reagan suit and clean up. Ten minutes into my shower she joined me, and it wasn't to help scrub those hard to reach spots on my body, though she did some of that too.

An hour later she was putting on her jeans and one of my sweatshirts, wet blonde hair hanging around her shoulders. I was sitting on the bed, flipping through channels on the TV.

"It's time for the news, Jake," she said.

I punched in her station, because to do otherwise would have been a mistake, even though we were both still in the PCTS. You see, we were almost crossing that line back to a relationship, and any advantage normally gained with PCTS can be discounted once you have reached the relationship stage.

The news wasn't on, as football was running over. The Rams and Broncos were playing an overtime thriller in the middle of an early Colorado snowstorm. I should have been able to enjoy the moment, but all I kept thinking was that Maura Ferguson drives a Bronco. A green one.

I said, "Let's go check Maura's car, see if there's a knife in it." "Was a knife missing?" she asked.

Another good question. No wonder she's in the news business.

I dialed Grant Spencer's phone number. It was Sunday, so someone other than Wanda Gaines answered the office phone. She, of course, was probably doing dirty stuff with Annie's brother in a cheap motel room that I paid for. Grant picked up fairly quickly.

"Thanks, Grant," I said. "Being interrogated is an experience I hadn't yet had the pleasure of. Those lights really are hot, aren't they?"

"Mr. Jacobs, you told me yourself you were a student of the law and wanted to see firsthand all the different parts of the legal process. I was just helping."

"Well, they let us go. It wasn't us that beat your head in, though it sounded like a pretty good idea when my new friend Detective Middleton was telling us your version of what happened."

"You were the only other people there," he said defensively.

"Wrong. Someone was upstairs."

I told him how we saw the shadows, tried to get away, got shot at, and finally did get away.

"So who was upstairs?" he asked.

"Maura and McAlister," I said.

"Mr. Jacobs, I don't doubt that you are committed to the belief that my clients were shooting at you, but I don't think so."

"Sure thing. Your secretary told me you were a wee bit on the overprotective side with your clients. I guess that's a good thing, if I'm ever your client. But it has to be them."

"Why does it have to be them?" he asked.

"Dwight Yoakam's razor," I said, trying my best to remember what the women had been talking about at the motel.

"Dwight Yoakam's razor? What are you talking about?"

"Haven't you ever had a psychology class? The simplest explanation is probably the most likely one."

"It's Occum's Razor, Mr. Jacobs. Occum was English. Yoakum sings country western music. Occum's Razor is the one you want." *Damn him.*

"It has to be Maura and McAlister," I said.

"It wasn't," he said. "They're my clients, so I think I would know."

"Sure, Grant. Say, that brings up another point that needs to be discussed."

"What, Mr. Jacobs?" he asked, the first stages of annoyance creeping into his voice.

"How did you get to my house last night?" I asked.

"I took a taxi," he said.

"You didn't come in the limo?"

"What limo?" he asked.

"Grant, there was a big, black limousine parked in my driveway last night when Leslie and I arrived. You thought you were the only one there. How did you miss the damned limo?"

"There was no limo in your driveway when I arrived in my cab, Mr. Jacobs. It must have come later, but before you."

It was the only rational explanation, wasn't it? Grant hadn't seen it there? It arrived after he did? Maura and McAlister must have sneaked in the house, right? Was it really that easy to get into my house? Was it time for an alarm system? Was Grant telling me the truth? Did lawyers ever really tell the truth?

"Okay, Grant, if that's your story, that's fine with me. We'll run with that one."

"It's the truth, Mr. Jacobs," he said.

"Where did you get Annie's cell phone number?"

"I told you, she called me and gave it to me," he said.

"She says otherwise."

"A female, identifying herself as Annabella Silvestri, called my office and told me to come to your house after one o'clock, if I hadn't heard from her. She gave me that number to call as well. I already told you this."

"Okay, Grant," I said.

"It's the truth. Do I really have to keep saying that?"

"I believe you," I lied, "and that's not really why I called anyway."

"Why did you call?"

"Does the police report say anything about knives missing from the Ferguson kitchen? Did the knife that killed the adulterers come from that house?"

"Yes, the cutlery block on the counter was missing its chef's knife. The police consider that another piece of evidence against Maura. She knew where she needed to go to find a nice big knife, and quickly."

"Thanks, Grant," I said, and I hung up on him before he could say any more.

"It came from her kitchen?" Leslie asked, her hair just about dry.

"It sure did. You coming?"

Waiting for Annie to pick us up I could tell there was no way I would have been able to keep Leslie from coming along on this ride. She was the one with the battlefield wound, after all. It took Annie ten minutes to get to us. Another five minutes and we were half a block down the street from Maura's house.

Yellow crime scene tape presented an obstacle I hadn't really considered, but the dark of the evening sky was on our side. As she pulled the Porsche to a stop, it started raining. By the time we had a plan in mind, it was pouring. Three steps out of the car and I was wondering why I had bothered toweling off after my shower.

The plan was painfully free of details because at least two of us had no idea what we should be doing. Leslie stayed with the car while Annie and I snuck into the garage to get a look at the Bronco. A brick we had brought from my shed took care of a window on the side of the garage, and my hands provided a boost to Annie as she went up and through the opening.

She walked to the back side and unlocked the door for me to walk in. The rain was pounding down on the roof, and it made it hard to hear each other. It also meant it would be hard for anyone else to hear us.

Annie took the brick and was about to bash in a window on the Bronco when I reached out and tried the handle. It opened right away.

"She never locks her car doors," I said with a shrug.

Annie climbed in the back and I took the front. We were both wearing gloves so as not to leave any prints. That was Annie's idea, and it sure sounded like a good one.

I didn't find anything, and was about to give up on her when she said, "What kind of knife are we looking for?"

"Kitchen knife of some kind, with a big, straight-edged blade."

"Like this?" she asked, holding up just such a knife.

Twenty-eight hours left, and we finally caught a break.

CHAPTER TWENTY-SIX

The knife was the kind you might find in most any kitchen in this country. It had a large blade and a wooden handle. Annie did her best not to touch it too much. She had gloves on to keep her prints off, but she didn't want to smudge any prints that might already be on it. She put the knife back under the seat where she had found it and we did our best to make the garage look undisturbed. We swept the broken glass into a corner and hoped no one would notice it.

Back in the Porsche Leslie was giddy with the news. I thought its presence was encouraging, but the knife was not damning in any way. There was no evidence of blood on the knife or anywhere in the car. It's unusual to have a knife in a car, but possible. And why would Maura leave the murder weapon in such an obvious place? Encouraging yes, but our work was far from finished.

"Have you called the police?" Leslie asked when we finished with the details.

"No, we haven't called anyone," I said. "Should we?"

"Dammit, Jake, are you going to keep this from the people that need to know it too? Somewhere it's got to stop, Jake. Somewhere, you have to let people know things like this. The murder weapon is in the backseat of the prime suspects car. That's important information for the police to know."

Annie said, "Don't you think the police already checked her car?"

Leslie was caught off guard by the question.

When she recovered, she said, "Well yes, I guess they would have checked her car."

"And yet the knife is still in there," Annie said. "What do you suppose that means?"

"They missed it?" Leslie guessed.

"That's a possibility, sure. What else?"

"Someone in the police planted it there?" Leslie guessed.

"Not likely," Annie said.

"Someone else put it there?" she guessed again.

"Maybe they did. And if so, why did they put it there? Who put it there?"

"Whoever put it there wants someone to think Maura committed the murders. The knife may or may not be the knife that was used, but someone wants the police to think it is. Right?"

"Do you still think we should call the police?" Annie asked.

"What will it hurt?" Leslie asked. "Shouldn't they be the ones to decide who put it there and whether or not it's the knife that was used? Isn't that there job?"

"Look, if we call the police they'll want to know what we were doing sneaking into that garage, which is part of a crime scene. They'll probably guess we snuck in there to plant that knife. They'll figure we're the ones trying to frame Maura Ferguson."

Leslie looked at Annie and knew she was right. The knife proved nothing, and our telling the authorities only made us look more suspicious.

I said, "What now, then?"

"Call Grant Spencer," Annie said.

"What? Why?" I asked.

"Well, for one thing he was tied up by someone, most likely the same person who put the knife in the car and who killed Sam and Shannon. We still think it's probably Maura's knife and that Maura killed them, but Grant's her lawyer. He'll want to check it out to clear his client."

I thought about it too long, because Leslie took the cell phone out of my hand and dialed Grant's number. Her end of the conversation sounded like this: "Grant, Leslie Watson...Yes, I'm with Jake right now...We stumbled across some information we think you should have...No, we don't think we want to go to the police with it…That's right…There's a knife, under the backseat of Maura Ferguson's Bronco…Her garage…We played a hunch…You'll let us know…You have this number…Thank you, Grant."

And then she hung up.

She said to us, "He's sending over his investigator to check it out. He said he'd tell the police he was playing a hunch and wanted to check Maura's car. He also said he'd have his investigator take a patrol officer with him so the police wouldn't suspect any monkey business."

The three of us were back at my house, sitting around the kitchen table, when the doorbell rang. The start it gave all of us was unnecessary as it turned out to be Donnie and Wanda, back from their afternoon sex romp in the country.

Five people around my kitchen table were a crowd, but we managed. Donnie told us they came back because Wanda told him we may need some help. She was right, but could they provide it?

He said, "In all the months we've been dating, she's never been so insistent about something. I think she kind of likes you, Jake. I figured it was important to her, so here we are."

"*Months*?" I asked. "You've been dating *months*?"

"More or less," he said.

He looked at Wanda and she nodded her agreement.

"And you managed to keep that a secret from me and your sister," I said.

"Grant wouldn't want me dating someone from a family like Donnie's," Wanda said. "It would give him and his firm the wrong reputation. But I wanted to date the man, so it had to be a secret."

"Why didn't you tell me?" Annie asked her brother.

"You never care who I'm dating. I never tell you who they are."

So here we were, all the good guys, huddled around my kitchen table. Four of us seemed smart, and Donnie seemed determined. We set out to lay a trap for Maura Ferguson and Theo McAlister.

Donnie offered himself up as our bait, at least to lure Maura in. Annie said she'd do the same with McAlister. They decided to go to the bar of the Plaza and wait. When the lucky couple showed themselves, the Silvestri kids would move in. Annie said they'd present themselves as swingers, interested in a couple to share the night with.

"Won't Maura recognize you?" I asked. "You were with her at Helen's party."

"I'm the master of disguises, Jake. She'll never suspect a thing."

"She'll definitely recognize Donnie," I said. "She's seen him naked."

Donnie said, "She never asked me anything personal. I could tell her Annie's my wife and she would have no reason to not believe me."

"And you just happen to be in the bar of the hotel she's staying at?" I asked.

"Why not? Lots of rich couples stay there. It's a prime hunting ground for couples who are willing to swap for a night."

"Have you done this before?" I asked.

It sounded like maybe they had. They both just laughed instead of answering. So, had they? Was the mafia using sex as a weapon? Would Maura and Theo be interested? Did we have a better option?

I asked, "What do the rest of us do while you're in the bar getting lucky?"

"Wait upstairs in one of the rooms," Annie said. "Leslie has one, right?"

"Maura's been in there," Leslie said. "We should get a different room so she doesn't suspect."

"I think we can scrape together the money for that from this crowd," Annie joked.

Annie was into her leader role. She had Leslie and I give her as detailed a description of the bar as we could, along with the layout of the lobby, restaurant, and everything else. She sent Wanda to the store for some supplies she said she'd need for her disguise, and she had Donnie call the compound for some manpower. I asked her to have them bring my car home, and she passed that along to Donnie. He assured me they would.

The plan seemed like a good one, though I hadn't tried anything like it before. None of us had, near as I could tell. Annie would pose

201

as Donnie's wife, Stacy, who was from Boston. Annie had gone to school there and had the accent down pretty good.

James, or one of the grunts from the compound, would camp out at the bar, a tiny camera lens in his tie pin. He would be a guy on a business trip, having a drink after a tough day of meetings. The camera would send a picture to a monitor we would have in the hotel room upstairs. We'd know what was going on all the time.

Donnie would approach Maura; say he remembered her from Monday night. If she mentioned anything about the murders, Donnie would say he pays no attention to the news. He'd then introduce them to his wife, Stacy. They'd share a couple drinks and Annie and Donnie would both be as flirtatious as possible.

When Theo finally excused himself to use the restroom, Donnie would broach the subject of swapping with Maura. We all felt like she'd go for it, and that Annie could convince Theo it was a good idea, too.

They would proceed upstairs to our room, where Leslie and I would be waiting. Wanda, it was decided, needed to be somewhere else. Her presence in that room made no sense, and there was the chance Maura would recognize her in the bar.

When Annie finished laying out the plan, I said, "How do we get them downstairs in the first place?"

"You'll call her," Annie said. "You'll tell her you need to talk to the two of them because you may have some information that might mean you need an extension of your deadline. Tell her you want to meet at ten o'clock. Once they show up downstairs, call her cell phone and tell her you can't make it because the police are watching you too closely. When she's done talking to you, Donnie will move in before they leave the bar."

And so the plan was set. We were going in tomorrow night, with a day to put all the parts in place. Annie said her family possessed all the needed technology, as well as plenty of firepower if we wanted some of that. I felt like we had crossed a line and we could no longer go back.

Donnie and Annie as swingers? Would they notice she was older? Would they care? Was Donnie skilled enough at the bedroom arts for Maura to want more? Were we playing with fire by taking ourselves to them? Was there really any choice?

Wanda came back with the disguise kit for Annie. It consisted of a pushup bra, a strapless top and miniskirt, spiked heels, and blonde hair dye. Annie said she already had blue contacts in her purse that she would pop into her brown eyes when needed.

Donnie left to take Wanda to her apartment, saying he'd return in the morning. Annie said that was fine, but that he better not be late. The reinforcements and all our supplies would be here at noon, and Annie wanted us all ready to start then.

As I settled Annie into the guest room I asked, "I'm not going to find you dead on the bathroom floor in the morning, am I?"

She said, "I haven't got anything planned, but maybe I'll stay out of the shower downstairs."

She smiled; I think to let me know everything was going to work out. For a big-time criminal she sure knew how to calm my nerves. Maybe it was battlefield experience or something, but I felt strangely at ease with her in command. I left her alone to color her black hair blonde.

Leslie was wearing a t-shirt and a pair of boxer underwear, both mine, when I finally made it to my bedroom. She was on the bed, sitting on the pillows with her knees tugged up under her chin. I could tell she had something on her mind, so I waited for it.

"Who put the knife in the Bronco, Jake?" she finally said.

"The killer did," I said.

"Ha ha, smart ass. Who's that? I still don't know why Maura would leave the knife in her own car? It doesn't make any sense."

"Maura, or maybe McAlister, did it. Okay? Whoever did it had to get rid of the knife in a hurry. They probably figured they'd go back later and get it, but the police haven't let them near the place."

She said, "Okay, why haven't the police found it then? Annie found it, so it must have been findable."

"Maybe they overlooked the garage. Maybe they haven't gotten to it yet. Maybe whoever was searching the garage wasn't feeling particularly ambitious that day and so they didn't look very hard. Who knows? Maura or Theo did it. That's the knife they did it with.

We'll call them on it tomorrow. Can we just leave it at that for tonight?"

"Okay, Jake," she said.

She relaxed enough to straighten out her legs. She flexed all ten of her painted toes and slid down the bed so her head was on the pillows, hair spread in a halo around her face.

"You still look a little nervous about the whole thing, Leslie," I said, sitting down on the bed beside her.

"Then help me relax," she said, pulling my mouth to hers.

We had finished and drifted off to sleep when the cell phone rang. It took me several seconds to get my bearings, then to find the thing in the dark bedroom. Leslie barely stirred.

Grant Spencer said, "I hope you weren't sleeping," but I knew he hoped I was.

"No, of course not Grant. Who's got time to sleep? What's up?"

"The knife was where you said it would be. I wonder how you knew that?"

"I told you earlier, Annie and I played a hunch and she found it back there," I said.

"And you still don't find it strangely convenient that this known criminal suddenly came into your life? She just happened to find the probable murder weapon, and when you weren't looking. That doesn't arouse any suspicion in you, Mr. Jacobs?"

"I trust her. You're a lawyer, so you obviously trust no one. It's okay; it's an occupational requirement. I understand, really I do. But Annabella Silvestri is a good person, Grant."

"She's the second in command of *the* mafia family in this city, Mr. Jacobs. She's a lot of things—murderer, money launderer, thief— but she is most certainly not a good person."

"I'll pass those feelings along to her, Grant," I said. "Do you want me to send her over to the office right now so you can discuss her professional and personality quirks?"

"Look, you know what I mean. If you trust her, then I guess I'll trust her. Just be cautious with her. Things are never as they seem with the mob."

"Okay, thanks for the advice. So where's the knife now? On your cheese tray?"

"The police officer tagged it and took it in for the detectives. I just spoke with one of them. Apparently the knife has some traces of blood and skin on it, but he couldn't say for sure who that blood and skin came from."

"Last Sunday's roast, maybe?" I asked.

"No need to get snotty, Mr. Jacobs," he said.

He had a thick skin, I'll give him that much. I imagine spending your days with losers of all levels forced you to grow one of those in a hurry. Now if he could just work on that sense of humor.

"When will you know about the blood and skin?" I asked.

"Tomorrow morning," Grant said, "Noon at the latest. They said they'd rush it through, since it could be kind of important to the case."

"You're the master of the understatement," I said. "Thanks, Grant. Thanks for keeping me informed."

I didn't tell him about our plans for Monday night. I figured my new boss just wanted to know the results of my investigations, not the methods I employed to get there.

"There's one other thing," he said.

"What's that?"

"The fingerprints on the knife, at least the one's that could be identified, don't belong to Maura Ferguson or Theo McAlister."

"Not Annabella Silvestri," I pleaded.

"Now you're thinking," he said.

And with only twenty-four hours to go.

CHAPTER TWENTY-SEVEN

Monday morning came, bringing with it a chilly frost. I climbed out of bed onto a cold floor, even through the carpet. I went out into the hall and tapped the thermostat a little to the warm side and went back into my room to warm up the old fashioned way. Leslie was more than happy to oblige.

Later, with Leslie back to sleeping, I wandered over to the window; the same window bullets had been flying out of Saturday night. I looked around a little but knew I wouldn't find anything important. I went across the hall to the room we had first seen shadows in from the backyard. A similar search again revealed nothing. Not one damn red hair. What did she do, vacuum before she left?

Grant had planted his little seed of doubt in my head, and that bastard was starting to take root. He didn't say the prints belonged to Annie, only that she hadn't been ruled out. She had never been booked, and therefore never fingerprinted. Her presence in my life did seem a little random, if I chose to think about it that way. And she did make sure she wasn't with us at some crucial points along the way.

On the flipside of that, she had done nothing to earn my mistrust. She hadn't done anything to earn my trust either, but I tend to give that to someone until they show me they aren't worthy.

The big point in her favor was that she definitely was not the person shooting at us in the Porsche from my bedroom window. She couldn't have been, because she was in the car with us.

Had someone let us get away, so as not to draw suspicion to Annie? Did she hide a twisted mind beneath her soft exterior? Could she be so cold-hearted as to play act as my friend while framing Maura Ferguson, and maybe me, along the way? The bump on her head was real, wasn't it? Not necessarily, when you think about the knife that wasn't really in her back, right? Was Grant right about her?

I knew I didn't want to know the answer to that question, since it might not be the one I wanted to hear. Instead I went downstairs and out into the driveway to fetch the newspaper. As I did, Donnie was pulling up in my car. I didn't wait for him out there because the concrete was a little too cold on my bare feet.

Inside I sat down to a hearty bowl of Cheerios and a big glass of orange juice and tried to forget Grant Spencer's words. The paper didn't have much about the case, just another touching story about pet abuse in the city. Joe, Maura's dead mutt, was now the poster boy for all such pets. I think he'd been mentioned every day for a week.

Donnie joined me after a little bit. He didn't look as tired as I'd expected him to look. Assuming he had gone back to Wanda's apartment, had sex with her all through the night, and got up early enough to get out to the Silvestri compound and fetch my car, he had to be tired. But he didn't look it.

College kids can burn that candle on both ends pretty good. Or, maybe they were to the point in their relationship where they were comfortable just spending the night holding each other. No, I figured, it had to be that candle thing.

"Done with the sports page?" he asked.

He had fixed himself a bowl of Cheerios too, but instead of orange juice he had a forty-four ounce soda from the market down the street.

I handed him the sports and said, "Which team you root for?"

"Depends," he said.

"On what?"

"I root for the teams that are going to make my book the most cash," he said. "This week the Giants fucked me up bad, but I got it back with the Cowboys, the Jets, and, let's see, yeah, the fucking Cardinals. The Cardinals never fucking cover, but people keep betting on them. They usually have big spreads, so it makes sense. But they never fucking cover."

"I'm a Packer fan," I said, not wanting to know so much about his illegal business.

"Bye week," he said, which I already knew. "Speaking of the Packers, I got the books you sent me. Vince Lombardi was quite an Italian. He done us boys proud."

"That he did, Donnie. You read them already?"

"I read one, the one with 'Pride' in the title. I gotta do something while Wanda's sleeping in between. That other one, the 'Daylight' one, I haven't gotten to it yet."

"How is Wanda?" I asked.

"Asleep. She usually requires at least three hours of rest after a dose of the Donnie machine."

He finished off the last scoop of cereal and slurped down the remaining milk like a two-year old would. He picked up his oversized drink and sucked on that as he continued to scan the scores.

The Donnie machine? Who talks about themselves like that? And what in the name of *Beauty and the Beast* was she thinking, hooking up with Mr. Vitalis? Sometimes I really just don't get women, but who does?

"Pro football your only book?" I asked.

"Hell no. College football and basketball, the NBA, baseball, the fucking Olympics; people will bet on anything where there's a score kept or someone wins and someone loses. I take all that action. I'm even taking bets on the elections next month."

"It's illegal here, right?"

"Damn illegal," he said. "And don't tell my sister I told you anything about it. She likes people to get the impression we're not into crime. Who's she trying to kid? Everyone knows our dad is Frank Silvestri. Everyone knows what that means, right?"

"Most people," I said.

"Did you?" he asked.

"I had a hunch, so I did some research," I said.

"Smart move. I'd do the same myself."

"Thanks, Donnie," I said.

"Hey, you still owe me four hundred dollars. I'm not taking any fingers just yet, but you still owe me."

"For what?" I couldn't remember placing any kind of bet, illegal or otherwise.

"You promised me five hundred dollars if I came with you to the lawyer's office. You gave me one, told me I'd get the other four when the redhead said I was the guy with her Monday night. You never gave me the other four."

"Wanda's your girl, right Donnie?"

"Sure is," he said with a certain amount of pride.

"But yet you were willing to spend the night with Maura Ferguson on Monday. Why is that, Donnie?"

"Me and Wanda, we've got what you call an understanding. We've got an open relationship. We don't limit ourselves to just one another, know what I mean?"

"I do, but Wanda seems like a wonderful woman. Why would you want to have that kind of relationship? Aren't you afraid she might find someone she likes better than you and drop you?"

"Well, it was her idea. She said she couldn't pin herself down right now. And come on now—where will she ever find anything as good as this?" He said, both thumbs pointed at his chest.

"So when you were with Maura, you weren't cheating on Wanda. Okay."

"Did she tell you? Did the redhead tell you she was with me?"

"She did indeed, Donnie," I said.

"Not that I need it, but where are my four C-notes?"

I reached into a cookie jar on the counter and pulled out a wad of cash. I found four Franklins and counted them into his palm. You would have thought the guy was flat broke the way he was smiling.

"What's with the smile, Donnie?"

"A fucking cookie jar?" he said. "You serious?"

"For a rainy day. You can never be too careful."

"You've heard of banks, haven't you? Mutual funds? IRAs? A fucking cookie jar. That's hilarious."

Eventually he quit laughing and excused himself to go make some calls. He said he had to talk to the guy who managed the book, see how the numbers ended up. I wished him good luck, but he told me luck had nothing to do with it.

"They're all suckers," he said as he left the room.

Leslie had called in sick somewhere in the middle of the night. They weren't too happy with her, but she assured them they didn't want her to throw up on the air. They agreed and told her to spend the day in bed. I was doing my best to see those orders were followed, but as I moved to the living room and my home theater, she found her way down the stairs.

"Who'd they get to take my chair?" she asked with a yawn. She picked up the remote when I didn't answer her and changed it to her station.

"I just sat down. I don't …"

"Oh shit, not her. Not that bitch. She's after my seat, Jake. I'm telling you, that ugly bitch is after my seat."

She was pointing with the remote at the big screen as she yelled at me. I looked, but I couldn't see anyone I would describe as ugly. I did see an attractive young woman, twenty-five at the oldest, smiling sweetly in my direction.

Maybe she meant ugly on the inside.

"Who is she?" I asked.

"Patty Milton," she said. "She's a fucking bitch."

"And she wants your job?" I asked.

"She wants my fucking job," she agreed.

"Aren't you the highest rated morning news show in the city? Aren't those ratings a direct result of your presence in that chair?"

"Yes," she said.

"She can want your job all she wants. They'll never give it to her," I said.

"Thanks, Jake," she said, "but with all due respect, you know nothing about the politics of television news."

I couldn't argue with that, and didn't want to even if I could. If Leslie weren't my girlfriend I wouldn't care one bit whether I got the morning roundup from her or the fresh young face I saw on the TV. I left her curled up in the recliner, still cursing under her breath at Patty Milton.

Upstairs I knocked on Annie's door, hoping she was awake. I hoped my newfound suspicion of her, courtesy of Grant Spencer, wouldn't show through.

The door swung open and a blonde head stood in front of me. The dye took. I gasped a little, but in a good way. Annie's the kind of woman it would be hard to make homely, though I thought her a better brunette.

"What do you think of the hair?" she asked.

"It looks good, but it's not you. You gonna put it back when this is done?"

"We'll see. It might just work for me, you know."

"Are we still going ahead with the plan?" I asked.

"Full throttle," she said.

Did it look like something was puzzling her? Or was she scheming? Grant would say scheming, wouldn't he? Trust no one, right Mulder?

"You look like a girl who's been doing some thinking," I said.

She waved me out of the hallway and into her room. I trusted her, to hell with Grant Spencer.

She said, "The police arrested Maura Ferguson and no one else. That means they think she acted alone. That means there must be some evidence, other than motive and lack of an alibi that puts her there. And there must not be any evidence of anyone else."

"I guess so, sure."

"We've been working under the assumption that McAlister helped her out, right?"

"Not necessarily. He may just be trying to help her cover it up, get out from under it, like she helped him a few years ago."

She said, "If she killed them, and did it alone, then I have another question."

"Which is?"

"Maura's not a big woman. She's smaller than me, and I'm not that big. How does a woman her size kill a dog and two grown adults with nothing but a chef's knife? The dog would at least give a yelp or something, and the adults would put up some kind of fight for each other. With a gun, no problem—just pop a couple in each of them before they know what's happening. But she used a knife."

"The dog was poisoned," I said. "Grant told me. She probably put something in his water, waited for him to drink it, and then waited for him to die."

"Sick little girl, isn't she? What about the humans then? When she came in with a knife, wouldn't they have just overpowered her?"

"They had just had sex, Annie. They were probably asleep. If she was quiet and quick, she could have done it."

"Do you suppose she just sat outside a window and watched them? Do you think she waited for them to fall asleep?"

"Probably," I said.

"Sick little voyeur, she is."

The details did make the murderer look sick, didn't they? But aren't all murderers sick to a certain degree anyway? I mean, they're killing other people and that's not right, right? So Maura Ferguson was a sick little murderer? A voyeur? Could she have physically done it? Would it really have been that hard if the victims were sleeping? What kind of heartless bitch could kill her own dog? Hadn't she saved that dog from death at the pound?

"I don't think anyone who kills is quite normal, Annie," I said.

I hadn't meant her in particular, but she took it that way. She looked a little hurt.

"I meant what I said before about the family. I'm taking us legit when Daddy's gone," she said.

"I believed you."

"Sometimes things are done for reasons out of your control, you know. Sometimes you have to do something you'd rather not. It's just business."

"I understand," I tried.

"Do you? Do you really? I don't think you do. In my world, if you don't do what you're told, you die. Can you understand that?"

"I've seen the movies," I said.

"Bullshit movies. Most of them aren't that accurate. This business isn't as pretty as the movies make it out to be."

"I figured as much. I'm sorry, Annie. I didn't mean anything personal by what I said. Really, I didn't."

"I'm taking us legit, Jake, when Daddy's gone," she said again. "Legit, Jake."

"I know," I said.

A room was reserved at the Plaza, on the twentieth floor. The reserves from the compound didn't arrive until about three o'clock, but they were loaded with audio-visual equipment and weapons. Eight Italian thugs were sitting around my living room watching *Oprah* and eating pizza that Leslie had ordered. Could this get any stranger?

At four o'clock a cell phone rang. One of the guys grunted three or four syllables into it, then tossed it at Annie.

He said, "It's the nurse, boss."

After a minute on the phone, the color drained from her face. Tears started dripping from the corner of each eye. She thanked the nurse for calling and absently tossed the cell back toward her goons.

"What's up, boss?" asked the guy who had answered.

"Daddy's dead."

CHAPTER TWENTY-EIGHT

Annie said Frank Silvestri had passed quietly. He had finished watching *General Hospital*, something he did every afternoon, and then settled in for a nap. Somewhere in that nap he stopped breathing. There was nothing the nurse could do.

Annie's other brothers had been summoned from their real world jobs. Both were already en route to the compound. Annie told them she had some important family business she couldn't leave at the moment and that she'd be home tomorrow to deal with the details. They didn't ask any questions; just did as they were told.

Next she sent four of the eight guys back out to the country. Eight was too many anyway, she said, and they could use the added security back at the compound. She gave them explicit orders to not talk to anyone, and to be sure the press wasn't allowed anywhere near her father.

She called the nurse back and told her help was on the way. No, she didn't want the ambulance called. What were they going to do for him anyway? Yes, she did want the nurse to call the family mortician; the guy who Annie knew could be trusted to keep it quiet.

She didn't call the accountants and bookkeepers to tell them it was time to start selling, and I didn't expect her to. Instead, she wiped away her tears and focused on Maura Ferguson and Theo McAlister. I wasn't sure it was a healthy thing to do, but she seemed set on the path.

"Annie, we can do this without you," I said.

"Not successfully," she said. "I'll be fine. Don't worry about me."

"But your father just died," I said.

"And he'll still be dead tomorrow, won't he? We have to do this today, or it doesn't get done. Is that what you want?"

"No, but I don't want to be selfish either."

"You're not being selfish. I'm still trying to keep Donnie's name out of this case. I'm doing it for my family as much as for you. Okay?"

And that was it. Leslie and I jumped in my Lexus. I wondered which guy had stopped by Wanda's to pick it up from Donnie, but never got around to asking. Our luggage was packed with the monitor and everything we would need to make it operational. Two of the guys were going to come up to our room and set it up shortly after we had settled in.

Annie took the Porsche. In her hand were directions to Wanda's apartment. In her eyes were the blue contacts. She was wearing the skirt, the heels, the top, and the bra. I barely recognized her, and I knew it was her. She was going to pick up her brother and start pretending he was her husband.

The remaining four goons took the limo. They were heavily armed, and the trunk carried more in reserve. If there was going to be a shootout, my side wasn't going to be the one under-stocked.

Leslie even took a weapon and stuffed it in her purse. Vinnie, I think, assured her the gun was easy to use and she could dispose of it wherever she thought best. He suggested the river, or anywhere deep into the country. He also suggested wiping it clean first, even if she had been wearing gloves. These people had obviously done this before.

Monitors and wires weren't the only things in our suitcases. Vinnie had stuffed two more guns in the zipper pocket, along with several clips of ammunition. I still had the cell Annie had given me the night of the party, and I had her phone's number written on a small sheet of paper in my pocket.

We checked in without incident. The guy working the desk was my friend who had passed a note to Leslie. If he realized she already had her own room, but was checking in with me, he didn't let on.

I slipped him a fifty for his trouble and told him we wanted absolutely no calls to come through. The cells would do. I also told him, under no circumstances, to let anyone know I was even here. He told me it wouldn't be a problem.

In our room, Leslie flipped on the Monday night game while I arranged the equipment as best I could. The Ravens and Titans were playing, two teams neither of us cared much about, but it was better than anything else we could find to watch.

Just as I finished emptying the last of the suitcases there was a knock on the door. I thought about every mafia movie I had ever seen, the good ones and the bad, and half expected a room service cart, rigged to blow. Instead I got Vinnie and Tony, ready to set up the monitoring system.

Tony said, "That's a nice car you've got there. Have I told you that?"

"You mentioned it out at the house. You can have it if I don't survive the night."

"Don't talk that way. No one dies on my watch. You'll be fine."

"Where'd you go the night of the party, Tony?" I asked. This question had never been resolved, and I hadn't seen Tony to ask.

"I went to get something to eat. I always do that. I came back and waited, but you and the boss never came out. I called back to the compound to see what they wanted me to do, and they told me to come home. They figured you had taken the boss with you and that she'd be fine."

"So, you were never anywhere near my house in your limo?" I asked.

"Not until this evening," he said.

Who brought the damn limo then? Had they waited for Tony to leave the party before they made their move? Or had Annie made their move for them when she approached Maura? Limos were pretty easy to get, weren't they? Anyone could have been behind the wheel, right? They just tipped the guy a couple hundred bucks and asked him to look the other way, right? What did they do with him when they got to my house?

216

The guys had things set up in about thirty minutes. Leslie told them the game was a scoreless tie at halftime. They ordered a couple steaks from room service and settled in. The picture on the monitor flickered to life just after their dinners came.

Tony said, "James is in place. The camera is in his tie pin. It's tiny so no one will see it. He'll just have to adjust the camera to wherever the action is. He's pretty good at it, you'll see."

"How do we hear them?" Leslie asked.

"Annie and Donnie are both miked," he said. "You'll hear every word."

About nine o'clock Annie and Donnie showed up. Donnie was dressed in his best K.C. and the Sunshine Band outfit. Annie looked just like she had when she left my house.

Annie's voice came through the speaker, "We're in place. Make your call, Jake."

I picked up my phone and dialed the front desk. I asked for Maura Ferguson and was told she had checked out. I called her home phone, but knew I'd get no answer. Finally, I dialed her cell phone. She answered on the first ring.

"Maura, it's Jake," I said.

"You're cutting this kind of close, aren't you killer? Midnight's coming up in three short hours, and I have a couple detectives who would love to talk to me."

I thought I could find a couple that would like to talk to her too, but I let it go.

I said, "I need to see you. I've found some things out, but we need to talk. Can we do that?"

"We're talking right now, Jake. Keep talking," she said.

Where was she? Was she with McAlister? Did she know where I was? Would she really call the police at midnight if I didn't produce? Did she really think I killed her husband? Why would I do that?

"No, not on the phone. It's too easy for others to hear us," I said.

"Well, haven't we become Mr. Paranoid this week."

"You tend to get that way when you're being framed for a murder you didn't commit," I said.

"Sure thing, killer. Okay, I'll meet you. Where then?"

"The bar of the Plaza. Are you still staying there?"

"Yes," she lied. "It's the best hotel in the city, don't you think? Should I come alone, Mr. Paranoid?"

"No, I won't be alone. Leslie will be with me. Why don't you bring your friend with you?"

"What friend?" she asked.

"Theo McAlister," I said without hesitation.

"Very good for a janitor. I'll bring him. And Jake, not that it matters, but he is just a friend."

"That's your business. Can we meet you in the bar at about ten?" I asked.

"Sure, Jake. Are you coming from your house?"

"Yes, so it'll take us a little while to get there. Start without us if you have to."

She hung up, so I dialed Annie's cell phone. I watched her flip it open and punch the button before I heard her say, "Hello?"

"They'll be there at ten. Everything okay down there?"

"Sure, we're fine. Remember to wait until they sit down and get their drinks before you call her to cancel. They have to have a reason to stay in the bar long enough for us to make our play."

At five minutes before ten o'clock, with the Titans clinging to a three-point lead on the television, Theo McAlister and Maura Ferguson walked into the bar of the Plaza. Theo was wearing tan slacks and a blue sport coat over a gray turtleneck. Maura had on jeans and a leather jacket. They weren't being particularly intimate. Maybe their nerves were getting the better of them, as their big scam was about to come to a head.

They walked out of the field of view for our hidden camera, but James quickly spun on his stool and we caught them taking a table in the corner, their backs to the wall. It was a perfect spot for our little game to take place.

The drinks arrived in a couple minutes and I gave them a couple more to start enjoying them. At five minutes after ten I picked up the phone again and dialed Maura's cell phone. I watched her fumble through her purse for it, and then I heard her say, "Hi."

"It's Jake," I began. "We're not going to be able to get out of the house, Maura. The police are watching me. They think I had something to do with what happened to Grant Spencer the other night."

"What happened to Grant Spencer?" she asked.

Why was she choosing now to play dumb?

"It's not important. What is important is that because of that I'm not going to be able to sneak out of here tonight. I need you to give me an extension until tomorrow night."

"That wasn't the deal, Jake," she said. She gave a thumbs-up sign to McAlister, to which he smiled.

"Come on, Maura. Aren't we friends? Can't you cut me some slack? I need one more day to put together the proof I need. Give me one more day."

"The whole day?" she asked.

"Midnight tomorrow would be great," I said.

I watched her scribble something on a cocktail napkin and slide it over to McAlister. He read it and gave her a nod.

"Okay, Jake, I'll do it for old time sake. I want you to prove me wrong, Jake. Really I do. I don't want to go through my life resenting you for killing my husband."

"Thanks, Maura. Let's say we meet tomorrow night, ten o'clock, in the bar of the Plaza. Okay?"

"Okay. Tomorrow night, ten o'clock. I'll be sitting right where I am now."

She folded the phone and shoved it back in her purse. She said something to McAlister, picked up what was left of her drink and threw it down her throat. Just as they were getting up, Donnie appeared on the screen.

"Remember me?" he asked Maura. "Monday night, at Hud's— do you remember?"

"I do, but I didn't think you would," she said in a rare moment of humility.

"You're a hard woman to forget," Donnie said, sitting down, obligating Theo and Maura to do the same.

Maura said, "I'd introduce you to my friend, but I don't think I ever caught your name. Mine is Lisa Wells."

Liar.

"Donnie Silvestri," he said, thrusting his hand out to Maura. "Is this your husband, Lisa?" He shook McAlister's hand as well.

"No, just a friend. This is Steve Harrison."

Liar, liar.

"Oh, that's good," Donnie said. "I thought for a minute I'd stuck my foot in my mouth when I was talking about Monday night. Hey, my wife's with me. Mind if we join the two of you?"

"Sure, why not. Our plans fell through anyway," Maura said.

"Listen, she doesn't know about Monday night, and I'd prefer we kept it that way, if that's okay with the two of you. I'll tell her you're someone I know from college."

Maura said that was fine, and Theo didn't argue either. Donnie left the picture, to get Annie, and Maura gave Theo a helpless shrug. He didn't look too happy to be stuck at a table with somebody Maura had obviously slept with, but what was he going to do? He stayed put.

Donnie and Annie reentered the picture. Donnie was all smiles, and Annie had the look of someone whose husband had done this to her before. Had she thought about a career in acting?

Donnie introduced his sister as his wife, Stacy. Remember, we lie too. He introduced Theo and Maura to Annie as Steve and Lisa, a friend from school. Small talk ensued and drinks were ordered. Time dragged a little and I was getting more and more nervous, but Donnie and Annie were doing a great job.

The plan fell nicely into place when McAlister said he needed to pee. It came after a twenty-minute stretch where Annie's cleavage was never more than twelve inches from his face. By the looks of him, he had noticed. Donnie leaned over and whispered into Maura's ear, but we could hear every word.

He said, "Listen, Lisa, your friend there, Steve, he seems to have taken an interest in my wife."

Obviously he had. Who wouldn't? Maura tried to dispute Donnie's observation, but Donnie assured her it was okay.

He continued, "Don't sweat it. I'm not going to. I've got a little proposition for you and your friend. Stacy and I, we like to swap. Do you know what swapping is?"

She nodded.

"You enjoyed Monday, didn't you?" he asked.

She nodded again.

"What do you say then? We've already got a room. We were waiting for a nice looking couple to come in. I was happy to see it was you."

Maura leaned over to Donnie's ear and whispered, "I'm in, and I think Steve will be too. Let me ask him."

"Why don't you let Stacy ask him?"

She nodded one more time, and then Donnie nodded at Annie. McAlister came back and sat down and Annie slid over close to him. Annie told him what she had in mind and that his friend had already admitted it sounded like fun. He quickly looked at Maura, knew Annie wasn't lying, and said he'd love to join in.

The drinks were finished and Donnie suggested they head upstairs to their suite. He said it had two bedrooms, if that was how Steve and Lisa wanted to play it, or it had a bed big enough for the four of them, if that sounded better.

When the elevator door slid shut behind them, James snapped off the picture. Vinnie and Tony quickly disassembled the equipment and packed it back into the suitcases. It took less than a minute. Leslie was still watching the game.

"Les, it's time," I said.

She picked up the remote and turned off the game.

She said, "She really is one big fucking slut, isn't she?"

"She's not that big," I said. "And I'm not sure she's a slut."

"Oh come on, Jake. She screwed this guy on Monday. She's probably been screwing McAlister for the last several years. She wanted to be screwing you. She's a slut. And the worst kind, too. One without a conscience."

"Maybe she just has a hard time making up her mind," I said. "Or maybe she's a slut."

Tony said, "She's a slut."

Vinnie was nodding behind him. Three votes to one, and my one wasn't real firm.

At midnight straight up we heard a key slide into the lock of our door.

No time left and nowhere to hide.

CHAPTER TWENTY-NINE

The expression on Maura Ferguson's face was priceless, once she was in the room and realized what had happened to her. I imagine it was similar to the one I had a couple days earlier when I found her in Leslie's room on the fourteenth floor.

"Isn't this an interesting turn of events?" I said to her as they came in.

Tony and Vinnie put themselves in a position to block anyone who thought leaving might be an option. Annie came around behind us, and Donnie went to lurk in the shadows somewhere.

Theo McAlister said, "You're the guy from the party Saturday night, aren't you? You're the guy who thought I was Leslie Watson."

"Jake," Leslie said, "he looks nothing like me."

"Put a fox costume on him, heavily padded, and you try to tell the difference," I said. "He looks much better in a dimly lit room."

"So you're him, right?" McAlister asked again.

"Yes I am, Mr. McAlister. My name is John Jacobs, and this is the Leslie Watson in question." She actually stood up and shook the weasel's hand. "And the girl who's shirt you couldn't look far enough down in the bar just now is Annabella Silvestri. Does that name mean anything to you?"

"Frank's daughter," he said like anyone would know the right answer to that question. "Maura, what's this all about now?"

"Got me, Doc," she said. "It looks like Jake's running the show now."

"Sit down, why don't you?" I said with a wave toward a love seat in front of the couch we were on. "Can I get you something from the bar?"

They both shook their heads slowly. Maura said, "Are you going to tell us what this is all about? Did you figure out who killed my husband and his slut?"

"I thought you were his slut," Leslie said.

"I was married to him," Maura said, a little peeved.

"Technicality," Leslie said.

"I think we did find the killer," I said before a full-fledged catfight broke out. "And thank you for making it so simple."

"Simple?" she said. "How did I make it simple?"

"I think you know, Maura," I said.

She was pleading with her eyes as she said, "Jake, I didn't kill anyone. A week ago you believed that."

"A week ago I didn't know there was a chef's knife in the back of your Bronco, shoved under the seat. A week ago I didn't know you were going to try to frame me for a murder you committed, and try to get my girlfriend to go along with it so you could get some of my money."

"That was Theo's idea," she said, turning on her only ally.

He didn't seem to mind, saying, "Seemed a waste to let the money go to someone you didn't even know. Without a will or heir, no one gets it."

"So just frame me, get the state to kill me with their lethal injection, and get Leslie to give you half the money because it was your idea. Great plan, Theo." I said. "You two seem to get along so well. It's no wonder you covered for him last time Maura, when he was slashing up the flesh and you were just there to tell the court he was with you."

Maura said, "Jake, I didn't kill them."

"But Theo did, at least back then?" I asked.

"I've always assumed he did."

All heads turned to the professor, but he didn't seem to want to talk about it. He couldn't have said anything that would have made any difference anyway. Everyone in the room assumed he had done it, and yet he got off. Why bother saying anything more?

"Why'd you do it, Maura?" I asked.

"I didn't do it," she said again.

She was either telling the truth or acting like a veteran of stage and screen. I went with choice number two.

"How could you kill your own dog? That's just sick. And to just sit and watch the poison work on him; well, that's even sicker."

"What poison?" she asked. Again, she looked like she was telling the truth.

"Joe wasn't stabbed like your husband and his girlfriend were. Joe was poisoned, probably something in the poor mutt's bowl of water. I figure you played with him, got him to run around the yard for a while so he'd be thirsty, and then you sat back and watched the dog die. Am I close?"

"Joe was poisoned?" she said, ignoring my question.

I felt my resolve weaken a little, but continued, "The murder weapon was in your car. Can you explain that?"

"No, but I haven't been near that car in two weeks. The starter's out and Sam hadn't bothered to get it fixed. I told you that at the movie."

Damn.

"I remember," I said. "You were driving a Caddy or something."

"Lincoln Towne Car," she said. "It was a loaner from my sister-in-law; the one who baby sits Brittney. She let me have it for the day, and I let her have my daughter."

Maybe she was telling the truth. I looked around the room for help, but didn't see much coming. This was supposed to be my moment, and here I was pissing it right down my leg.

"What about what you did to Annie at the party Saturday?" I asked. "Why would you do that?"

"Annie was at the party?" she asked.

"Think dark hair, brown eyes, and Richard Nixon," I said.

"No shit? That was her? What do you mean what I did to her, Jake? I flirted with her a little. So what? I had no idea who she was, and even if I would have, I never would have figured she was with you."

"So you're saying you didn't bash her over the head and knock her out?"

"No. I went into the bathroom and when I came out, she was gone. I looked for her some in the house, but she wasn't there. At least I couldn't find her. I figured she chickened out, didn't want to experiment after all."

"And right after you left me in the den," McAlister said to me, "Maura came back. A little patience and we could have avoided some of this unfortunate misunderstanding."

Damn, damn.

"Theo, would you step into the hall with Tony for a second?" Tony stepped forward and let him know that 'yes' was the only allowable response.

When he was gone I said, "Maura, what did you and McAlister do after the party? And I'm going to ask him the same question when he comes back in, so you best tell me the truth. It's easier to remember anyway."

"We came back here, Jake. He walked me to the elevator and left me on it. Where he went from there I don't know. I came up to my room and went to bed."

I nodded at Vinnie who opened the door. Tony led McAlister back to his seat and hovered over him while I asked him the same question.

"We came back to this hotel," he said. "I dropped Maura off at the elevator and went home. I assume she went to her room."

Damn, damn, damn.

"Jake, is it possible these two are telling us the truth?" Leslie asked. "She is a slut, but she sounds like she's being honest. Is that a possibility?"

"We are telling the truth," Maura said before I could answer.

"It's possible," I agreed.

Maura had the look of someone who still had some unresolved issues. Players were changing teams pretty fast, and it was hard to keep track of them without a scorecard. She glanced around the room, searching for the same colored jersey.

She said, "Jake, can't we still be friends?"

I thought about the question for a moment. Did I want to be friends with her after what she had done? After what she thought I had done? After she said Leslie was easy? Hadn't Leslie just said the same thing about Maura? Were they both right? Neither one?

I said, "You said Leslie was easy. Is that something a friend would say about another friend's girlfriend?"

She was trying to figure how I knew that, looked in Annie's direction, and said, "I may have misjudged Leslie. It doesn't mean we can't be friends."

"I don't see how. Friends don't frame friends for murder, Maura. It's a hard thing to look the other way on."

"Jake, I saw your car at my house that Monday. I've been in that car—hell, I'd just dropped you off and saw it in your driveway—don't you think I'd recognize it?"

Tony chimed in from the periphery, "It's a nice car. I just drove it into town tonight, plus I got to drive it the other night. I love that car."

"You drove my car into town *tonight*?"

"I thought you knew that," he said.

"No, I assumed you picked it up from Donnie over at Wanda's apartment," I said.

"Why would I do that? How would it have gotten to Wanda's apartment? Your car's been in our garage since I put it there the other night. No one's touched it. I made sure of that."

So who owned the mystery Lexus? Was it the same one Maura had seen Monday last, in front of her house? Did we finally have ourselves a winner? Did I want to say it out loud?

I didn't have to, because Annie did it for me when she said, "Wanda Gaines drives the same model black Lexus as you do, Jake."

"You're sure?" Leslie asked.

"It's the only answer," Annie said.

"I don't like it," I said, "and I have a hard time believing it."

"Like it or not, you better believe it," she said.

"Are you sure?" Leslie asked again.

"Listen, she's been showing up in a lot of places sort of unexpected, hasn't she?"

"Some, sure," I said.

"She was out at the motel, she was at your house, she was at my house the other night. And she sure did want to help you out, didn't she?"

"Those could all be coincidence," I said.

"Jake, who had access to the boxes of files? Wanda had them sent over, and no one else saw them until you and Leslie looked at the empty pages over at my house. She must have sent you boxes of empty files. Why would she do that?"

"How did she know we were at that motel? How did she know when we were back at my house? How could she track us so easily?"

Annie took a cell phone out of her pocket and held it up in her right hand. With her left, she slid over a panel on the back and popped out a silver disk about the size of a dime. She held it up to us between her thumb and index finger, making sure we all saw it.

"What is that?" Leslie asked.

"It's a sensor that lets people back at the house know where this phone is. If they know where the phone is, then they know where the person with the phone is. It's got a range of a hundred miles or so."

"All your cells have them?" I asked.

"Sure do. We use them to keep track of people who are engaged in any sort of dangerous job."

"How did Wanda get access to the tracking device?" I asked.

I could tell by the look on her face that Annie didn't want to say or hear the answer to that question. She knew what it was, but she didn't want to face it.

"From the same person who was upstairs at your house, Jake," Leslie said. "From the same person who was shooting live bullets into my arm."

Annie said, "Where's Donnie?"

Tony, arms crossed in front of him, said, "He left, Boss. When I stepped into the hall with the old guy, he left."

Wanda Gaines and Donnie Silvestri?
Damn, damn, damn, damn.

CHAPTER THIRTY

A quick phone call to Grant Spencer confirmed that Wanda was the proud owner of a black Lexus, same year and model as mine. He said the blood on the knife was of two types, one matching Sam Ferguson, the other matching Shannon Powell. It was without a doubt the murder weapon. He said there were two hairs stuck to the knife, and neither belonged to the victims.

"Here's a guess for you," I said. "Those hairs are from the head of your secretary."

"You think Wanda killed them?" he asked. "My Wanda?"

"She sure did, Grant. I'll connect the dots for you later, if that's okay with you."

"Why would Wanda kill them?" he asked.

This was a good question, and one I couldn't answer yet. Maybe she'd tell us, if we could find her.

"I don't know, Grant. Here's another question for you. What kind of poison was used to kill the dog?"

"Hydrochloric acid," he said. "A big bowl of it."

"Hydrochloric acid, like you'd find in a chemistry class?"

"Yeah, I guess so. I'm more a man of letters than science, though."

Grant promised to call me if he heard from Wanda. He still was harboring serious doubts about her guilt, but he was the only one who was. Theo McAlister must have been listening to my conversation.

He said, "That acid is common enough in most chemistry labs. An enterprising chemistry student could easily get their hands on some of it."

Annie said, "Donnie's a chemistry major."

He had told me as much the first day I met him. He was on the seven-year plan, he had said. No point in rushing things, he said.

McAlister said, "That kind of acid smells, enough so that the dog probably would have noticed it. The fumes are dangerous enough though to cause serious respiratory distress, especially in a dog, which is smaller than a human. And if he swallowed any of it, well it would just eat up his insides. He'd have been torn apart from the inside."

"Sounds like a great way to go," I said.

"I know Wanda Gaines, too," McAlister said.

"How?" I asked.

"Had her in class a few years back. About the same time Maura was my teaching assistant. I'd have to check my records to be sure, but it wouldn't surprise me if she were in the class Maura assisted in. She wasn't working for Spencer then."

"She did look familiar to me," Maura said, "when I saw her at Grant's office."

"So something happened a few years back that has caused several people to become stabbed to death. What would do that?" I asked.

No one had a good answer. Instead we directed our attention to finding Donnie and Wanda so that they could tell us. They didn't seem to have any trouble finding us, so why should we have trouble finding them? Didn't we possess the same instruments of surveillance as them? Weren't we at least as smart? Weren't we more experienced, what with Annie and the boys on our side?

Vinnie produced a scanner from somewhere and we determined their cell phones weren't anywhere within one hundred miles of us. Or they had been dismantled. My phone, and Annie's, registered nice clear signals. Plenty of good that did us.

Annie took charge and tried to devise a plan. She said there were too many people involved and for all of us to get in on the chase would be dangerous. They'd see us coming and run, or stand their ground and defend it. Either way, we needed to be a smaller group.

"I'm going," she said, "because only I can deal with Donnie."

I thought of Michael Corleone kissing his brother Fredo and telling him he knew it was Fredo who had betrayed Michael, and then ordering his death. Would Annie tell Donnie he had broken her heart?

"She killed my husband," Maura said, "I'm going."

"One of them shot me," Leslie said, taking the third spot.

"What about you, Jake?" Annie asked. "Do you want to come?"

Honestly, I wanted to do anything but go chasing after Wanda and Donnie. Somewhere, though, I found the courage to say yes.

"Four is plenty," Annie said, then to her men, "Arm us."

Theo had plenty of reason to get involved with the chase too, but Annie said we hadn't the room. She told him he could stay behind and man the surveillance equipment. I think I spotted relief in his expression.

No one, not even Annie, had a reasonable guess as to where we might find the young murderers. Taking a drive to her apartment was mentioned and dismissed as too obvious. Laying in wait back at my house was offered, but again dropped. They had no reason to go there. The compound was ruled out for similar reasons.

"Why don't we drive blindly around the city until we see a black Lexus, then force them to stop. We'll see who it is and hope for the best," I said.

"Lacks efficiency," Annie said. "And cover."

Eventually we decided to get in my car and start eliminating possibilities, the first of which was Wanda's apartment. We each had at least two unregistered firearms on our person as we piled into my car. Annie and I took the front seats; Leslie and Maura took the back. McAlister was connected to all of us with earpieces and microphones.

It was almost noon by the time I started the engine and backed out of my spot in the ramp next to the Plaza. As I reached down to shift into drive Annie put her hand on my arm. I looked at it, then her face. Her eyes were staring straight ahead.

"We might be getting lucky," she said.

I followed her gaze to the far end of the ramp. There in the middle of the driveway, engine running, sat a car identical to my own.

"Damn," I said.

"See what I mean?" Maura said. "It looks just like yours."

"A black Lexus in this hotel's ramp isn't really a novelty," Annie said. "It might not be them."

Oh, but it was them. They crawled to within ten feet of our car before they stopped. There in the front seat of the mirror image of my car sat Wanda Gaines and Donnie Silvestri.

Wanda stepped out first. Donnie didn't look like he was too interested in talking to his sister. Neither was showing a gun, but we took no chances.

Annie said, "Leave the motor running. When we get out, you're going to all want a gun in your hand."

"They don't have guns in their hands," Leslie said.

"You'll want a gun in yours," Annie repeated without turning around.

Four doors opened, almost at once, and the four of us stepped onto the concrete, each holding a gun at our side. Wanda noticed and pulled one from her purse. Donnie tried to play it innocent, throwing his hands in the air like he was an unwilling participant.

"Get your hands down, Donnie," his sister said. "I know what you did."

She didn't kiss him, but the message was the same. Donnie was a dead man, one way or another. He did what she said, but tried to make a case for himself.

He said, "I didn't know what she was doing. Not until you were talking upstairs last night. I brought her here for you."

"No you didn't Donnie. Stop lying and take this like a man," Annie said. To Wanda she said, "Where'd you get the acid for the dog?"

Wanda didn't say anything, but she didn't need to. Donnie's face dropped and he knew Annie knew.

He said, "I'm not going to fight you, Annie. I'm not going to shoot at you or your friends. I won't do it."

"They'll shoot at you," she said.

She tossed the gun she was holding toward him. Before he caught it she had another in place, aimed and ready.

"Did I miss something?" Wanda asked. "Wasn't the plan to trap *that* bitch?" She pointed at Maura as she said it.

"Careful who you call a bitch," Maura said. "She just might be somebody's friend."

"After what she put you through, you're still willing to call her your friend?" Wanda said to me.

"I'm forgiving by nature. It comes from being a janitor and cleaning up the messy shit of otherwise perfectly nice people. You tend to forgive them their lack of neatness after a while. But you never forget it."

"How'd you figure it out?" Wanda said.

"Well, Donnie drove your car over to my house yesterday. It just happens to look exactly like my car. Once we realized it wasn't, we made the connection that it was your car Maura saw in front of her house that day. It didn't take too long to finish the maze from there."

"Humor me," she said. "I've never been good at puzzles."

"You called Grant Spencer's office—your office—pretending to be Annie. You told him to get on over to my house if he hadn't heard from you—from Annie—by one o'clock. You gave him the number of the cell I had, told him to call it when he got there."

"Prove it," she said.

"Grant already has the phone records," I bluffed. "Poor guy couldn't even recognize the voice of his own secretary."

"He's more of a talker than a listener," she said.

"I've noticed that," I agreed.

"And that's all you've got?" she asked.

"Well, no. Saturday night Leslie was drunk to the point of unconsciousness, but you got her downstairs to her car. Then you crunched her a good solid pop on the top of her pretty little head. You tossed her in the back of her car and drove it over to Helen's house, where my party was in full swing."

"Why would I do that?" she asked.

"Dearest Donnie was going to meet you there, in the limo, and take you over to my place to wait in ambush. Grant would already be there, since you weren't about to call him before one o'clock, so you could ambush him too."

"But why would I go to the trouble of knocking out Leslie and bringing her with me? Seems kind of risky, doesn't it?"

234

"You were going to use her to bait me," I guessed, "But then you thought Annie might be better bait, since she wasn't schnockered."

"I hit her too?" she asked.

"No, Donnie did. And then he dragged her out to the limo and tossed her into the back seat. You had to test his loyalty to you somehow, so why not have him assault his own sister?"

She didn't argue, so I must have been mostly right, right? She knocked out Leslie? Donnie did the deed on his sister? They brought the limo to my house? Grant knew nothing about it? Was it beginner's luck, or am I really that good?

"You know what your problem is, Jake?" Wanda asked.

"Right now it's you," I answered.

"You've got too many damned girlfriends. I had Maura in check, since you thought she was the murderer. Leslie was drunk and unconscious, so I figured she would be no trouble. And then Annie, too? It's hard to keep track of them all."

"Leslie's my girlfriend," I said. "Maura and Annie are friends. You do know what friends are, don't you?"

Just then an older couple came out from the stairwell in search of their car. Wanda shot a death-glance at them so fast and so hard that they nearly dropped where they stood. They gathered their composure, turned, and scuffled back into the stairwell.

"You have no murder weapon," she said. "Your case is no stronger against me than the case against Maura."

"Grant's investigator found a chef's knife in the back seat of Maura's car. Maura hasn't touched that car in two weeks, since the starter went out. The knife had been wiped, but not enough. There were blood and skin residues belonging to the victims. And there were two hairs from your scheming head. You really need to be more careful about your crime scene clean up," I said.

"That's it?" she said. "It'll never hold up."

"I remember seeing three chef's knives in the sink at your apartment when I was there. I didn't think of it at the time because that place was a mess and your roommate was still moving out. But I got to thinking about it and it made sense. One knife was yours, one was your roommate's, and the third was from Maura's house. You cleaned it off right there in your kitchen sink. Somewhere along the line you slipped it into Maura's car. I'm willing to bet that if we sent someone to your apartment right now they'd find no more than two such knives."

"What about my motive?" she said. "Why would I kill them?"

"You're against breast enhancement surgery and men who like it?" I said. "We were hoping you'd tell us."

The talking wasn't helping ease the tension. At least it wasn't helping ease mine. Annie must have sensed a resolution coming as she moved to a position behind the trunk of a nearby Toyota. Leslie and Maura followed her lead and scattered to the cover of the parked cars. Donnie, too, had found a spot behind a Taurus. Alone in the middle of the driveway, each next to our own black Lexus, Wanda and I continued to stare each other down. I secretly wished I were one of the people who had gone for cover.

"Maura knows. Or she should know. Tell him, Maura," she shouted at the car behind which Maura was crouched.

"I have no idea why you would kill them," she shouted back without getting up. "I didn't even know you knew them."

And then it came to me. In one brilliant white flash of light it all became clear in my mind. She had her motive and I knew what it was. She beat me to it, though.

She said, "Sam Ferguson dated me for two years before you came to school. I loved the man. I thought we were going to get married. Then you came to town."

"You're the girl from the wrong side of the tracks," I said. "Of course you are. This is a jealousy killing. Occum's fucking razor, it's so damn simple."

Wanda looked at me like I was crazy, and I may have been. Sam Ferguson couldn't marry her back then because she lived on the south side of the city, in the same neighborhood as Juan's Salsa Barn. She told me that. She also told me she had gotten out, and made a point of me seeing how well she had done. It was an interesting effect Sam's jilting had on her, but not unique really.

"Funny thing," she said, "Maura's family is probably worse off than mine."

"But they're not from this city," I said, "So they couldn't be from the poor side of town. You got screwed on that deal, Wanda, I'll agree with you there."

"So you see why I had to kill them?" she asked.

"Ah, no. Jealousy hits everyone now and again. I've been jealous of a guy named Lance for four months. But I didn't kill the idiot."

"I thought you'd understand," she said, raising her gun and leveling it at me.

"Cover, Jake," I heard Annie say from behind the Toyota, her voice rich with urgency.

I dove toward a green Volkswagen, and it's lucky I did. The first bullet buried itself in the grill of my car and sent steam rising. Better it than my lungs.

I somersaulted to a kneeling position and tried to regain some orientation. Annie had moved one car closer to the action, and Wanda had disappeared. For thirty long seconds no one said anything.

The silence was broken by Wanda's voice, behind me, saying, "Get up and drop the gun, Jake."

I turned around and saw her holding Maura Ferguson in one arm, the other hand pointing a gun at her red head. Maura's gun was lying at her feet.

I stood and dropped my weapon and put my hands in the air.

CHAPTER THIRTY-ONE

What did Wanda Gaines have in mind? Kidnapping? If so, should I offer myself in exchange for Maura? That's what the English guy did for the young girl in *Last of the Mohicans*, right? Would she want me in that trade? Wouldn't she just as soon kill Maura at this point, since no one else was going to do it for her?

My thoughts were broken by the sound of tires screeching on pavement. I turned in time to see Wanda's Lexus flying in my direction, but more specifically in Wanda's. It was moving too quickly to see who was at the wheel. Whoever was driving had backed up to the far end of the ramp before starting their run. I must have missed that in the commotion. I dove for cover one more time as they sped past me on their way to Wanda and Maura.

Wanda reacted by releasing Maura from her hold and leveling her gun with two hands at the windshield. Maura grabbed her shot at freedom and rolled to a stop one car down from me. Wanda waited longer than I would have before squeezing off six shots in rapid succession.

I think they all hit some part of the car, and probably some of them hit the driver. It veered to the right, heading straight for the restraining wall. They didn't brake, probably because they couldn't. The sound of metal car crashing through metal barrier was frightening, and followed by several silent seconds as the car made its eerie descent to the pavement six levels down, ending with a violent crash and explosion.

No one could have survived that fall and explosion. Maura was still behind the next car over. Leslie was standing, jaw hanging low, behind a blue Nissan. Wanda hadn't moved an inch as the car came at her, and she still hadn't. And Annie was on the run to the hole in the guardrail.

She got there and looked down at the final act of her youngest brother, Donnie. She allowed herself three seconds of looking at it before she turned to where Wanda was standing. Wanda was busy changing the clip in her gun; so I reached out and pulled mine back in.

Annie's gun was still hanging at her side in her right hand, but she didn't look like she intended to use it. Instead she was walking very forcefully toward Wanda Gaines. Wanda was on the wrong end of a mafia death, and she knew it.

The clip was snapped into place and she bolted for my car. She rolled to a stop against the back quarter panel, her back to the car in a squat. She turned in the direction of the ranking mafia person in the city, leveled her gun, and fired.

Annie yelped in pain and fell to the cement. From where I was it looked like she was holding her side, and it looked like her hand was getting more and more red way too quickly.

Wanda jumped into the front seat of my car, behind the wheel. The back door on my side was still open, so I dove through it just as she started to move. I looked up at the seat in front of me and saw the barrel of a gun pointed in my general direction. I grabbed it before she could shoot and yanked it hard as a shot hit the floor of the car.

"You're wrecking my car, you bitch," I yelled.

"I wrecked mine, too," she said. "I play no favorites."

We continued to struggle with the gun in her hand. She was trying to drive at the same time, so I had a small advantage. I twisted hard and snapped her wrist down hard on the back of the seat. The gun came free, and I think the bones in her arm cracked. She cried out, but kept driving.

"Stop trying to play hero, Jake," she said.

"Stop trying to kill everyone, Wanda."

"I can't stop now," she said.

I had to give her that. If she left even one of us standing, she was doomed. She was going to kill us all or go down trying.

In my ear I heard the voice of Theo McAlister, back in the suite, say, "Are you in the car with Wanda Gaines, Jake?"

I didn't want Wanda to know I was talking to someone not in the car with us, so I said to her, "It's just the two of us in this car. You've done enough damage. Let's go somewhere and try to find ourselves a workable solution to your problem."

In my ear McAlister said, "Got it. I've got your cell signal very strong, so if you go somewhere, we'll know where. Police are on the way, by the way. We didn't call 'em, but figured you should know."

What the hell was taking them so long? I was beginning to lose confidence in the city's force. As McAlister stopped talking I listened and heard sirens not more than a couple blocks away. Wanda hadn't said anything about my suggestion, so I tried again.

"Wanda, the police are on the way. You're beat if you stay here. Let's go somewhere and figure this out. There's got to be a better way than killing everyone."

"I'm beat anyway, Jake," she said, which was the truth.

She was idling in roughly the same spot from which Donnie had made his run, facing the same direction. Maura and Leslie were kneeling over the fallen body of Annie, doing what they could. Leslie, it appeared, had a phone in her hand. She must have called the police, and was probably talking them into bringing an ambulance or two as well.

"Did you start going out with Donnie as part of this whole scheme?" I asked, trying to keep her in the same spot until the law arrived.

"Yes," she answered. "I knew who he was and what he could do for me."

"It's not an accident that he was at the bar Maura went to Monday night, is it?"

"These things are rarely ever accidents, Jake. But this one was dumb luck; the only kind Donnie was capable of. I was hoping Maura would go in the house after your little movie date, maybe bloody herself up a little in the process and taint the scene while she was at it. They were already dead by then. The stupid little slut had to go get laid instead. And Donnie's always happy to oblige that sort of thing."

"So it's a coincidence that she went to the bar he was at?"

"Completely. Donnie didn't even know who she was. I tried to keep his level of information as low as possible and still get what I needed."

"And the two of you took such an active interest in our investigation because you wanted to be sure we were convinced of Maura's guilt, right?"

"You're pretty quick for a janitor," she said.

"That hurts me, but I'll let it go," I said. "Did you always have the car, or was that part of the plan?"

"I just told you that accidents are rare, and this wasn't one. I've been keeping tabs on Maura for years, but when I noticed her start to spend time with you, things just fell into place too easily. I went out and bought the car the next day."

"What about the McAlister murders?" I asked. "Your work?"

"Fucking police can't investigate anything around here. There was ample evidence there to convict Maura Winters. More than enough. She would have never become Maura Ferguson. They arrested the wrong guy, and then Grant had to go get him off too. He's such an asshole sometimes."

"So you're not working at that office by accident either?"

"This is the third time, Jake. No accidents. I didn't want him to get another loser acquitted. I knew the time would come and I knew he could be useful. Plus, he pays a girl lots of money to answer his damn phones."

The sirens were close, probably at the bottom of the ramp. She knew it too. She hit the gas and headed straight for Annie's fallen body. Leslie looked up in time and pulled Annie by the ankles behind a car and out of harm's way.

Maura wasn't so lucky. She tried to jump above the level of the hood, but her feet caught the grill. She flipped head over heels, hitting the hood with a terrible thud before bouncing off the car and onto to the driveway.

Wanda raced for the corner switchback, a little too fast. She slid toward the opening Donnie had created, but righted the ship before we joined him down below. She repeated the maneuver all the way down the ramp, finally leaving us looking at a barricade of flashing police lights and the street to freedom behind it.

She stopped to look for an opening, so I said, "Give yourself up, Wanda."

"Why?"

"I forgot to sweep my kitchen. Do you know how embarrassing it would be for the authorities to go into the house of a dead janitor and find an un-swept floor? I've got to get home, and if you try to run that barricade I think they'll take me down with you."

"Get out then," she said. "I don't need you. I'm not even sure why you jumped in here. Why did you?"

"Curiosity with the legal process," I said. "I've never been in a police chase before. And I didn't want you to get away."

"Does it look like I'm going to get away?" she asked.

"No, not a chance."

"Then get out."

So I did. I opened the door and stepped into the afternoon sun; my hands free of any weaponry and pointed to the sky. I didn't want the police to get the wrong idea about me.

Wanda made her move by slicing toward an opening between two local cruisers. I jumped behind a cement pillar as the bullets started flying at the car and beyond, toward me. It reminded me of the end of *Butch Cassidy and the Sundance Kid*, and we know what happened to them. Wanda fared no better.

My car rolled to a stop just under the canopy covering the side entrance to the Plaza. A swarm of police was on it in a minute with someone pulling open the driver's door. They reached in and came back with a shake of their head. All guns were lowered.

Wanda Gaines was dead.

CHAPTER THIRTY-TWO

The police didn't pay much attention to me as I found an elevator and took it back up to the sixth level of the ramp. The door opened and I ran to Leslie. She was leaning against the trunk of an Infiniti, sobbing uncontrollably.

"Oh my God, Jake," she screamed when she saw me. She threw her arms open to hold me and said, "I thought you were dead. I saw the car run the barricade, right through all those bullets. I thought you were dead."

"I'm not. I couldn't do that to you," I said.

"Oh my God, Jake," she said again before kissing me harder than she ever had before. "I love you, Jake."

"I love you, too, Les," I said. "What's the status of these two?"

"Annie's conscious but losing a ton of blood. Maura's breathing, but that's the only good thing I can say. I'm not a medic, so I don't know what hope there is for either of them."

Just then an ambulance rounded the corner and came toward us, lights flashing. The driver got out and realized there were two people needing attention, so he reached inside and called for another wagon. He went to Maura while his partner took Annie.

They worked quickly, and when the second ambulance arrived they had enough information to transport them both. They assured us they would do all they could for both women and said they would be at University Hospital.

Annie pulled through after three hours of surgery. The bullet had hit a kidney, which isn't a good thing, but you can survive with just one. The doctor said the damaged kidney wasn't necessarily lost. It was too early to tell about that, but she'd live.

Maura was in a coma for three days. Other than that, the only damage she suffered was a broken ankle. Her brain was touch and go for a couple days, but the swelling stopped and the pressure relented. The doctor talked about shaving her head, punching a hole in her skull, and placing a shunt to help relieve the pressure. She woke up during the middle of the next night, with Leslie and me at her bedside, and the doctor decided to leave her red hair alone. Her prognosis was for a full recovery.

She's currently trying to return the theaters to the level they had before Sam got his hands on them. She calls me from time to time, as a fan of movies, for advice. I've noticed an improvement, but it's too early to tell.

We don't go to movies together anymore. She's too busy and I just haven't got the heart for it anymore. I take Leslie now, and I never go home frustrated.

Frank Silvestri's funeral was a media event. Annie attended in a wheelchair, one surviving brother on either side. Leslie and I watched from the third row, but skipped the burial. No one asked us what we were doing at the funeral of a mafia don. I guess that's one of those places where association with the mafia can be a good thing. No one bothers you too much.

Donnie was buried two days later. Annie decided to give him a hero's send-off after his courageous efforts in the parking ramp. She never told her brothers the truth about what he had done and said she never would. She said she would never tell anyone the truth about her brother's involvement and made us promise to do the same. She said it was family business and no one else's.

She continued to insist she was going to take her family legit. I check the business section from time to time, but so far I haven't seen it happen. I don't doubt her word. I just wonder how simple it will really be to do.

I sent a brand new black Lexus out to Tony. He seemed to like my car, but it was full of bullet holes now, so I thought a new one was more appropriate. The model held too many memories of the wrong kind for me now, so I bought myself a station wagon instead. I hoped Leslie got the hint.

Theo McAlister keeps showing up on talk radio. He's suddenly become a local expert on just about anything. Wanda's capture, such as it was, allowed the public to finally realize he was innocent, at least of murder. He's a local celebrity now. Leslie even has him on every couple weeks to talk about something. He shows no interest in returning to the classroom anytime soon. I don't know if he still sees Maura. Neither of them mentions it and I don't ask.

Grant Spencer hired himself a new secretary. I stopped by the office one day, just to say hello, and there she was, in Wanda's chair. She didn't want to let me see Grant either, but she relented once she talked to him. He gave me a check for four dollars for my four days of work on his case. He said not to forget to include it on my tax return.

Grant was the person who pulled everything together for the authorities. He talked to the police, presented them with evidence and witnesses, and helped them close six murder cases at once. He returned to the courtroom of Gerry the Merry. It took little effort to convince him it was time to dismiss the case, and the prosecution agreed. I got my bail money back; pretty sure I'd never do that again.

Leslie Watson moved back in, of course. I never made her explain why she had left in the first place. I was just happy she was back. She asked for a week of personal time off from work, but Patty Milton's underhanded smile was too much for her each morning and she returned after just three days. Her show is still number one in town. Patty Milton left for another market just last week.

I talked to Helen Roth at her annual New Year's Eve bash. She couldn't believe all the intrigue that had taken place in her very own back yard. She wondered if the Halloween bash was going to become an annual event of my doing. I told her not to plan on it. Abe's hemorrhoids, by the way, have cleared up without the anticipated surgery. He was sitting comfortably in his den, pipe in hand, reading about cars. She was happy to hear that Leslie and I were back together.

"Jake, darling," she said, "She's the one." I think Helen just might be right.

Leslie's head was nestled against my chest when the phone rang. It was a Saturday, and very early, sometime late in the winter, but not quite spring yet. I managed to get it on the fifth ring.

"You weren't sleeping, were you Mr. Jacobs?" asked Grant on the other end.

"It's what most people do on a Saturday morning, Grant."

"Have you seen the morning paper?"

"No. I'm in bed. My paper boy only brings it as far as my driveway."

"Go get it and look at the front page. You can't miss it."

I told him to hang on the line and stumbled out into the late winter morning to do as I was told. The paper was close to the house, so it wasn't that big of a deal. I folded it open and looked at the front page. He was right; I couldn't miss it.

Back upstairs I said, "Triple murder, right?"

"That's the one."

"And the alleged is a client, I suppose?"

"He is indeed."

"And?" I asked, wanting to go back to bed.

"I'm not paying you a dollar a day to spend it in bed, even if she is smart and beautiful, am I?"

"You want me to investigate?" I asked.

"I want you to investigate," he said.

When I hung up Leslie said to me, "You're going to do it again? You're going to work on another case for him?"

"Looks like I am."

"What the hell, Jake?"

Was it a good idea to get involved in another murder investigation? Was it better than hanging out at the courtroom all day? Did Leslie think so? Hadn't my last investigation ended up with two more dead people than when it started and two seriously injured friends? Was any of that my fault? Would it have turned out worse without me? Did I want to investigate another murder for Grant?

Yes.

What the hell.

LaVergne, TN USA
17 December 2009
167414LV00008B/50/P